# EVERY BROKEN
# TRUST

## ALSO BY LINDA RODRIGUEZ

*Every Last Secret*

### POETRY

*Heart's Migration*

*Skin Hunger*

# EVERY BROKEN
# TRUST

*Linda Rodriguez*

MINOTAUR BOOKS

A THOMAS DUNNE BOOK
NEW YORK

A THOMAS DUNNE BOOK FOR MINOTAUR BOOKS.
An imprint of St. Martin's Publishing Group.

EVERY BROKEN TRUST. Copyright © 2013 by Linda Rodriguez. All rights reserved. Printed in the United States of America. For information, address St. Martin's Press, 175 Fifth Avenue, New York, N.Y. 10010.

www.thomasdunne.books.com
www.minotaurbooks.com

Minotaur books may be purchased for educational, business, or promotional use. For information on bulk purchases, please contact Macmillan Corporate and Premium Sales Department at 1-800-221-7945 extension 5442 or write specialmarkets@macmillan.com.

ISBN 978-1-250-03035-1 (hardcover)
ISBN 978-1-250-03036-8 (e-book)

First Edition: May 2013

10  9  8  7  6  5  4  3  2  1

*To my oldest son, Christopher Niles,*
*without whom I could not have written this*

# ACKNOWLEDGMENTS

I am fortunate to be a member of the Novel Group. Jacqueline Guidry, Deborah Shouse, and Jane Wood are constantly there for help, support, and celebration. The Latino Writers Collective is my writing *familia* and dear to my heart. My fellow bloggers at Writers Who Kill and The Stiletto Gang are always a help and support. Julia Spencer-Fleming has been incredibly generous to me in so many ways and introduced me to my other wonderful friends at Jungle Red Writers.

For valuable technical assistance, I would like to thank Harry Hylander, retired after many years with the campus police force of the University of Missouri–Kansas City, and Chato Villalobos of the Kansas City, Missouri, Police Department. What I have right is their doing. Any mistakes I have made are my own.

I have made changes in the structure of the federal courthouse in Kansas City, Missouri, for the sake of my story, but the rest of Kansas City is as depicted.

I have a gifted editor, Toni Plummer, a wonderful publicist, Sarah Melnyk, and a fantastic agent, Ellen Geiger, and I am grateful for all of them.

I am also grateful for my tremendously supportive family, Crystal Christian, Jason Christian, Niles Rodriguez, Denise Brown, Joseph Rodriguez, Gustavo Adolfo Aybar, Erika Noguera, Becquér Francisco Aybar, Sam Segraves, Becky Ross, and Patrick and Andrew Ross. Most of all, I thank my husband, Ben Furnish, my partner in everything.

# EVERY BROKEN
# TRUST

# CHAPTER 1

"This won't work!" I slammed the door to Forgotten Arts behind me, shutting out stifling late-August heat. Ignoring the bell swinging on red handspun, I glared at Karen Wise, who was hosting a party at my house because her farm was too far from town. She promised I just had to make my house available and show up. I'm not a party-giving woman. Now, I was hosting a welcome party for the new dean of Chouteau University's law school.

Karen looked up from spinning the fluffy mass of gray wool into yarn, stopped the wheel, and wound a strand of wool over a peg, taking her time as I fumed. Normally, I enjoyed the spinning wheels and looms around us. I bought colorful yarn and fondled fiber from sheep, goats, and alpacas. This Thursday, I wanted to throw things.

"Lunchtime, Skeet," Karen announced in her usual mild tones.

"How many more did you invite to this 'little' party?" I tried not to grind my teeth. "You're out of control."

Smiling, Karen strolled over to the wall, plucked a filmy lace shawl from a peg, and threw it over her sundress. "Look in the mirror for the out-of-control person."

I huffed. "You're not sticking to our agreement."

Just before leaving my office at Chouteau University, I received more RSVPs for Sunday evening. I'd ask her to stop inviting people, reminding her she promised just a few. Then, more RSVPs would roll in, leaving me livid, Karen calm and cool.

She stepped to my side, taking my arm with a smile. I looked down at her dark, serene face. Years as a therapist had taught her to keep her countenance under control. I resented the heck out of it. "They'll be waiting. You really don't want to see Annette when she's had to wait for lunch."

I sputtered in exasperation. Karen laughed, tugging me toward the door. By the time we walked in blistering sun and thick air across the town square to the Herbal Coffee Shop, I was resigned. Sunday night would be a disaster, my house packed with people I didn't know. The university carillon played its on-the-hour measure of Bach, sounding like a dirge.

"Sometimes," I muttered.

"Perhaps," she said. "But not now. Mel was Jake's best friend. Many of these people were his friends. You'll do it for Jake."

I'd do this miserable party. For her late husband's sake—and Karen's.

Entering the Herbal's air-conditioning was a relief. The cooler air filled with scents of mint, lemon balm, and angelica drained the last of my anger. Dolores Ramirez, the owner, and her college-student waitresses bustled back and forth between kitchen and tables, carrying plates of food, herbal iced tea, and fresh lemonade. Enough to calm any temper.

Maybe I was just irritated by Missouri's late-summer heat. Maybe I'd hide out from the party in the kitchen, playing video games with my fourteen-year-old ward.

"Over here. We already ordered." Annette Stanek waved us

to the corner table she and Miryam Rainbow shared. Annette, a tall, heavy redhead, looked elegant next to Miryam, a blond former model.

Once settled in, I ordered curried chicken salad, and Karen ordered herbed walnut-quinoa salad. Annette and Miryam had already been served the special, Asian peanut slaw.

A scrawny old guy with a red-veined face called, "Karen." He trudged over from the doorway, calling her again.

Karen muttered, "What's he doing here?"

"Who?" I asked.

Karen faced me. "Leonard Klamath. I wouldn't know him, if I hadn't run into him at a fund-raiser. Amazing the damage alcohol causes."

The man looked thirty years older than he had four years earlier when Jake died. This man could be that Leonard's father.

He shuffled to the table. "I want to talk, Karen. Been thinking about this."

"Leonard, sit down. Can we pull up another chair?" Karen placed her hand on his arm, looking into his worn face with concern.

I stood automatically, pulling an empty chair from the next table. "Here you go." I pushed it from behind to help him into it. He looked disturbed. I wondered what happened to the man I used to know.

"Skeet? What are you doing here?" He peered into my face, frowning.

"She lives here now. I finally talked her into it." Karen sounded and looked self-satisfied.

Leonard examined my face as if not sure I was really Marquitta "Skeet" Bannion. "Do you commute?"

"No, I left KCPD. I'm chief of Chouteau University's police

department." My voice held a little defensive stiffness. I made a good decision for my life, but most folks I knew as a homicide detective and administrator with KCPD saw my move as a step or three downward.

"You still a cop?" Leonard struggled to his feet again.

"Always. You know me."

He nodded. "What else could you be? Big Charlie Bannion's daughter."

I cringed. That's what I'd fled—always being Big Charlie Bannion's daughter, living in his shadow, tied to his name and his mistakes. Here in Brewster, no one knew Charlie. I could be myself, unshadowed.

Karen tugged at his sleeve. "Sit back down. You don't look well. You want to talk to me. What is it?"

He brushed off her hand. "Changed my mind. We can talk Sunday. Can't we?"

Karen looked puzzled. "Yes, but . . . If you want privacy, we can go to my shop."

Leonard shook his head, looking at me rather than Karen. Frightened. He wasn't when he arrived. Just determined.

"No. Gotta go back. See you Sunday." He exited faster than he'd entered.

"Why did he change his mind?" Karen mused.

"Looked like he was scared of Skeet." Annette gave me a long look. "Did you do something to him?"

I threw up my hands. "Not that I know of. We got along fine when he worked with Jake."

"Of course you did." Karen shrugged. "I'll find out Sunday night."

"Leonard's coming to this party, too?" I tried to keep bitterness out of my voice.

"Are you two still fussing over that?" Miryam took a big bite of salad.

Annette gave me a disgusted look. "No one would guess you're best friends. All over a party."

"We've made up," Karen said. "It's all good."

I tried to look like it was all good. "Change the subject."

"I know." Miryam bounced with delight. "Annette told me about this new mystery she read with a woman detective who's a sniper in the army."

I smiled. "They don't allow women snipers in any of the services."

Karen's laugh was deep. "Maybe she's a sniper in the Israeli army? Women do everything there."

"They let women go into danger over there?" Miryam asked.

"We let them here," Annette said. "Look at Skeet. Women police officers go into danger every day. It can be as dangerous on a city's streets as any war zone."

The waitress brought Karen's lunch and mine to the table. Behind her stood Reverend Matt Lawson, waiting to get to his own table. He smiled, nodded as our eyes met, then moved on as his path opened.

"There's someone who could tell you about women in the military." I indicated Reverend Matt with my head. I'd grown up with folks who believed pointing a finger directed power. Rude and dangerous.

"He was a chaplain, wasn't he?" Miryam watched Reverend Matt join his wife, Helen. "I've never figured out why such a handsome man married such a plain woman."

We all looked at Matt with his thick auburn hair going slightly white at the temples and his clean-cut features with soft, full lips. Next to him sat Helen, ex-nun, graying dishwater-blond hair hanging limp to her shoulders, prominent nose, the rest of her features faded. Yet as she spoke, passion behind her words animated her face, making her look more alive than anyone in the room.

"It's not all about looks." Karen frowned. "Helen has lots of charisma."

"Before he became a minister, Matt was a Ranger in Somalia and Bosnia," I added.

"*Black Hawk Down*?" Miryam's voice rose. "They should have had him in the movie. He's better-looking than any of the actors. Except Orlando Bloom."

Karen made a disgusted sound. "When will you learn life's more than appearance?"

"How'd you hear this?" Annette stiffened. "I'm on the First Methodist council and didn't know."

"River running early in the morning. We're not always out on the same days, but often enough we stop to compare battle stories. He downplays what he did overseas. I Googled him. He was given medals. I don't think he likes what he did as a Ranger. Modest man."

"I can see why he wouldn't want to publicize any killing he had to do as a soldier," Annette said.

"If it was like the movie, he had to do a lot of killing," Miryam said in a cheerful voice and took another bite of slaw.

I smiled at Annette. "He'd agree with you that city streets are as dangerous as a war zone."

"Don't you miss the excitement of the streets?" Annette lifted her chin, examining me.

"Gran always said, 'Happy's lots better than exciting.' Now that I'm older, I agree." I took a bite of chicken salad.

"Still, your days here aren't full of action like when you

tracked down murderers in Kansas City," Annette said wist-fully.

"What about when she tracked down that murderer here last spring?" Miryam turned to me with an excited smile. "Maybe we'll start having them all the time, like the city."

I shuddered. "I can do without that."

"Miryam, someone has to die for a murder." Karen raised an eyebrow. "Maybe it should be you. Think of the excitement as you breathe your last."

Annette laughed. Miryam stuck out her tongue.

I choked back laughter. "No, thanks."

"Surely you miss the adrenaline from the streets!" Annette pointed her fork at me.

I shook my head. "That life was as boring as anything here and much more stressful. Even working Homicide, which I do miss, was nothing like your mystery novels."

Annette stabbed her salad. "What's the good of having a real police detective as a friend if she's as boring as I am?"

"She'll find the killer if someone murders you," Miryam said with satisfaction.

Karen and I laughed. Annette pinched her mouth in exaspera-tion.

"I promise to track down and imprison your murderer." I laid my hand over my heart.

Karen shuddered. "Someone's walking on my grave."

I sat back as we continued to joke with one another. In Kansas City, I had few women friends. Since I worked mostly with men, my friends wound up being male cops. Here, Karen made me part of this group. My decision to relocate was paying off.

A short time with friends swept away my irritation. Still, the party hung over me like a distant threat.

At day's end, I headed for my Crown Vic, fitted out with radios for city and campus police systems and a twelve-gauge shotgun. Not exactly a family car. Still, I was picking up my ward, Brian Jameson, from after-school tutoring. Thunder growled in the west. I stopped halfway to the car to see if a storm would finally bring us needed rain, but the air was thick and heavy, no promise of rain in its burned scent. In the distance, I heard a train, Brewster's daily background music. Lightning flickered way across the Missouri River. I got in the car, throwing my briefcase in back with a frustrated sigh. Another false promise.

When I pulled up at the entrance to Ormond, Brian darted out of the air-conditioned building into the car, slinging book bag and flute case into the back.

"Watch that!" I ducked his backpack. "How was class?"

"We're getting into real cool stuff. Pentatonic scale used in tribal folk music." Brian leaned back against the seat. "It doesn't look like much. So short. Professor Garton says it shows what you do, even with simple materials, makes art—not the materials themselves."

"Sounds good." I tried to sound interested.

Garton taught the university's music students. He tutored Brian because he thought Bri, a gifted flautist and promising composer, could get a scholarship to Juilliard. He told me working with Brian made up for the dull students he had to teach. I'd have been one of those students, but Brian always came from class excited.

He chatted about his day as I drove College Hill Road's narrow twists. Where it ran into Girlville (name given before the college turned coed), I turned left to the town square with its courthouse surrounded by beds of purple coneflowers and black-eyed Susans. In the old days, I wouldn't have known the flowers. My new life had turned me into a gardener, dog owner, and—well, *mother* might be too strong a word.

Once parked, we walked past shops as a train rumbled through town. We waved at Bob and Kathy Lynch on their B and B porch and hurried past, trying to get to Pyewacket's before the wait became too long. I cooked at home more now that Brian lived with me. Simple food, pleasing to a fourteen-year-old. When I didn't want to hassle with it, we went to Pyewacket's.

Inside the restaurant, Pal Owens put names on a waiting list, long gray ponytail cascading down his back. Pal always wore tie-dyed T-shirts and bellbottom jeans with Birkenstocks. His wife, Sandi, supervising the kitchen and wait staff, wore the same.

The Owens kept themselves and the décor of Pyewacket's locked in the sixties. The food, however, was twenty-first-century. Basil-tomato tartlets with lemon balm bread. Broccoli-potato torte with chives. A nice change from my cooking.

"Brian, Skeet, how's it shaking?" Pal asked.

"How long's the wait?" I looked at the crowd without much hope.

He ran his eye down the list. "Thirty minutes. Jumping to-night, babe."

I sighed. "Put us down."

"Sure thing." He scribbled my name and greeted the couple behind us.

I stepped back, and Joe Louzon's daughter Julie waved us to a place next to them. Waving back, Brian headed over.

Eleven-year-old Julie had her golden brown hair skinned back from her round face in a ponytail with several long strands hanging down, escaped from the elastic. Her mother had left her and Joe when Julie was a toddler, but Julie always seemed happy, no hidden shadows. Now, shadows appeared in that little face from her ordeal earlier in the year. Brian's face and even mine held shadows from the same incident. Karen was helping us all make it through the shadows.

"How's your day been, Skeet?" Joe said.

I shrugged. "Karen's inviting crowds to a party at my house that I don't want to give. The faculty senate wants me to stop building the desperately needed parking structure and give the money to them for European junkets. The half-hour wait to get in here's just frosting on the cake."

"We should be called next," Julie said in an enthusiastic voice. "You can eat with us. I'll tell Pal."

She darted away on her errand of mercy, ponytail bobbing at waist level through the crowd. I took a deep breath of air filled with rosemary, garlic, and sizzling meats and began to relax.

"You know Julie," Joe apologized. "She'd love to eat with you. She never stops to think you might not feel the same."

Brian laughed. I smiled at Joe. "It's okay. Company for dinner sounds good, doesn't it, Bri?"

Brian nodded. "It'll feel more like a family."

I stiffened. Wasn't I giving him a real family experience? I wasn't much good at family stuff, never had been. But I was trying to do my best for him.

"I always wanted a sister," Brian went on. "When we're all together, it feels like a TV family."

"I feel the same way, Brian." Joe smiled at him, not looking at me. He wanted a relationship but didn't pressure. One of many things I appreciated about him.

Julie dodged back through the crowd. "Pal says no prob." She giggled. "I love his old slang. Groovy. It's so fun coming here. Like walking into a sitcom."

I nodded. "I come for the food, but the hippie thing's amusing. Even if it's before my time."

"Louzon, party of four," Pal called out, and we walked over. "Way to go, man. You and Brian have the foxiest chicks here tonight, Joe."

As we followed the waitress, Julie giggled. "Foxy chicks. Way to go, man."

I winked at her. "Don't make fun of your dad's time period. You shouldn't hurt his ancient feelings."

Julie giggled. Brian grinned. Joe assumed a look of pain. "That was my older brothers' time. I was a toddler."

Laughing, we settled into our booth, Brian sliding in next to me, with Joe and Julie across from us. I felt the day's tension melt away. Once the waitress left with our order, Joe told a funny story about breaking up a fight between Art Williamson and Bea Roberts. Bea and other upscale shop owners had been trying to get Art's working-class bar off the square for years. Their verbal brawls were legendary.

Our food arrived. I started on salmon-lentil salad. Brian munched a steakburger with onion strings, and Julie nibbled chicken fricassee with mashed-potato cakes while Joe ate orange-steak kabobs on rice pilaf. A waitress led four people in and seated them across the room.

"There's the source of all my troubles." I tipped my chin toward the group and realized I'd avoided pointing my finger again.

"Who?" Joe asked.

I looked at the lone woman in the group. The first time I'd seen her in person. I'd heard way too much about her. I nodded in her husband's direction. "George 'Mel' Melvin, former U.S. attorney for Western Missouri. Failed candidate for Missouri attorney general. New dean of the law school. The reason Karen's

11

stuffing my house with people Sunday night. I wish to heck he'd stayed in Kansas City."

"Which one is he?" Brian asked.

"The stocky one with the wife who looks better than any model. She can afford to. She's richer than anyone, except the tall guy." With a sigh, I turned to slather butter on my lemon balm bread.

"Who is she? Who's the tall guy?" asked Joe. "And that long-haired tough guy?" Intently, he checked them out, small-town police chief pondering new residents and the troubles they might bring.

"The tall guy's Walker Lynch. Millionaire. Still lives in Kansas City, last I heard. He and Mel are tied politically. I don't know the dark bad boy. Bodyguard, maybe."

Joe nodded. "He's got the look."

"The woman's Liz Richar. Stovall banking, real estate," I said. "MidAmerica United and L. J. Stovall Properties. Her mother was Stovall's only kid. She married Gard Horner. Horner Petroleum. Not as rich as Stovall but up there. Whole family's dead and little Lizzie's everyone's heir. Never met her. Just seen her on the news. She's involved in politics."

Julie stared at the quartet. "She's beautiful!"

"Skeet's better-looking," Brian tossed in loyally.

I grinned. "It's okay. I'm nowhere near her class. I know it."

"Some of us prefer our women more natural, don't we?" Joe smiled at him.

Brian nodded. "She looks plastic."

"This guy Lynch? What's the scoop?" Joe asked.

"Big philanthropist. That's how I know him. He supports causes I worked for. Met him at events and on boards. Shelters for the homeless, runaways, domestic violence. He gives tons of money. The kind of rich person I'd want to be."

Joe nodded. "A good guy."

"How are they a problem for you, Skeet?" Julie asked.

Brian jumped in before I could answer. "Karen's giving the new dean a party. At our house, 'cause she's out in the boonies. Skeet said yes."

"Not knowing the 'few people' she mentioned would balloon."

"You could have said no." Brian's face was stern.

I shook my head. "I couldn't really."

"Why not?" Julie asked.

I stared at Mel again. "Karen's husband, Jake, worked for Mel. They were friends."

Joe looked at me. "The dead husband?"

I nodded. "She says Jake would have given the party." I shrugged. "I don't think Karen likes Mel much since he dumped his first wife to marry Liz. But she's sure Jake would want this, so . . ."

Joe quirked an eyebrow at me. "As Brian mentioned, you could have said no."

I looked away. "Jake and Karen sort of adopted me when I first came up from Oklahoma to the academy. My dad wasn't happy about it. I was all alone. They were my support system." I looked back at him. "Jake would have given Mel a big party to introduce him to folks in his new town. I couldn't say no."

Brian tapped my shoulder. "So quit fighting with Karen about it. After Sunday, it's over."

"The hostess with the mostest," Joe muttered.

"She's supposed to handle all the work. I'll hold her to that, no matter how many hundreds of people she invites to my house." I put a melodramatic frown on my face and folded my arms in front of me, doing my best bad-gangster impression.

They laughed. I joined in. We ate the delicious food, talking and laughing. As I savored the mix of flavors in my salad, the cloud of dread over the party moved out of my mind.

The kids ordered dessert. Joe and I decided on coffee. As Julie ate her orange pound cake à la mode and Brian dug into his hot fudge sundae, I settled back into my seat next to Brian, feeling content, unwilling to move.

Walker Lynch and his shadow moved into my view, stopping at our booth. "Skeet! Are you in Brewster now?"

"Walker." I nodded. "More than a year."

"Is it your house we're going to Sunday night? I heard Karen's party was at someone else's house." Walker took in Joe and the kids, and one of his eyebrows rose slightly.

"Karen's your hostess. I'm not the Martha Stewart type myself."

He chuckled. "I wouldn't have thought so. But then Martha's not a decorated homicide detective."

The hard-muscled guy with black hair, mustache, and goatee leaned forward to inspect me closely.

I smiled. "Walker Lynch, this is Joe Louzon, Brewster's chief of police, and his daughter, Julie. This is my ward, Brian Jameson."

Walker's brows lifted again at Brian's introduction. "You, a family woman? That's unexpected."

"Skeet's a great family woman," Brian said sullenly.

Joe's jaw tensed. "Skeet does a terrific job as a parent. In a few more months, Brian's adoption will be final. She'll be his mother."

Walker held up his hands in defense. "I meant nothing negative. It's simply not a role I'd ever seen Skeet in. It surprised me."

I laughed softly. "It surprised me, too, but I try to do my best.

Brian's forgiving of my errors." I smiled at Brian. "We landed together by accident, but we do pretty well."

He reached for my hand under the table and squeezed it. "We make a great family."

"One of the best I've seen," Joe added.

Walker laughed and pulled the dangerous-looking guy farther forward by the arm. "I don't think you've met my associate Terry Heldrich."

I extended my hand to shake his. "No, I haven't."

Terry took my hand in a firm grip and stared into my face. His high cheekbones and straight slash of nose separating large, dark eyes could have belonged to any of my uncles or relatives down in Oklahoma. He was more alert than anyone I'd ever seen, almost canine in his awareness, like a highly trained guard dog hearing higher frequencies and smelling scents that passed the rest of us by.

"What do you do in Walker's company?" I asked, making conversation with someone who seemed to expect attack.

"Terry's my chief of operations," Walker replied as Terry shook my hand and gave me his measuring stare. "Every man of theory needs someone practical to get things done." Walker gave another chuckle. "Terry's that guy. He makes my dreams work in the real world."

Terry let my hand go and switched his assessing gaze to Joe as they introduced themselves and shook hands. He looked like a wolf preparing to attack while Joe reminded me of a family pet facing a threat to that family. I could almost see the hackles rise on both of them.

"How did you two find each other?" I asked Walker, trying to break the tension.

To my surprise, Terry answered, dropping Joe's hand to face me. "Walker recruited me. He knew my previous . . . employer."

His voice was softer than I expected from that muscular body. He had no accent, but the clear way he fully enunciated every word, along with his bone structure and slightly darker skin like mine, made me wonder if he wasn't from one of the tribes.

Walker laughed, slapping him lightly on the back. "Terry really is my right-hand guy. We'll let you go back to dinner. I look forward to the chance to talk Sunday night."

The two men strolled out as Joe and I watched. Once, Terry turned and looked back at us before following his boss.

"That one's serious trouble." Joe spoke softly as Brian and Julie started a joking conversation behind us. "Recruited him from the SEALs or special forces."

"Higher status than a bodyguard." I stared after them. "I thought you two would come to blows or at least growls."

Joe laughed sheepishly. "He gets my threat response going, that's for sure. I wouldn't want to face him in a dark alley."

"How about the party Sunday night? He's with Walker, so Karen's probably invited him." My jaw tightened. "She's invited everybody else."

Joe stared at the doorway through which they'd left. "Makes you wonder what kinds of things Walker needs that freak for."

"Walker's a good guy. Special forces uses strategists, too. Maybe that's what Walker pays him for." I set my hand on Joe's shoulder. He turned with a smile. We sat back and let the kids finish their desserts.

Now my worries about the party included the need to keep Joe and Terry apart. Also, Joe had me wondering what kind of operations Walker needed Terry for—intimidation, protection . . . I didn't want to take that any further.

# CHAPTER 2

Sunday dawned hot and humid. The air grew hotter and soggier as the day wore into evening. Karen and I snapped at each other across my kitchen island full of trays of green-chili-smothered pork with corn tortillas, roasted root vegetables, and bowls of dips—black-bean-corn, zucchini relish, and orange-peanut. Guests were due any minute.

"A normal person has wineglasses." Karen huffed out her breath, straightening her shoulders. Her emerald dress brought out her café au lait skin. She'd taken her silver hair out of its braid and coiled it at the back of her head, making her look like an Egyptian queen instead of a short, round Italian-African-American retired psychologist.

"I don't drink by myself. I don't give parties. Why would I have wineglasses?" I glared down at her, taking advantage of my height.

"Will you two stop?" Brian shoved his way past us into the kitchen, carrying a musty-smelling box. "I found these in the basement." He set his box on the counter by the sink. "We just have to wash them."

"Where— Those must be part of the stuff from my aunts I've

lugged all over. Are you sure they're not broken? They ought to be by now." Karen's frown said I sounded too hopeful. I tousled Brian's hair. "Good thinking. I'll wash, you dry."

Karen opened the box. "They're perfect. Brian, will you wash them quickly while Skeet and I welcome guests?"

Brian pushed me toward the door. "I'll wash them. Go on. You agreed to do this."

I had no choice but to walk out and welcome people to my house, which didn't look like my simple, comfortable home anymore. Karen had put so many fancy decorator touches around that I hardly recognized it, smelling perfumy and fake from the scented candles and potpourri bowls. My collie, Lady, sat out in the fenced backyard for the duration. My cat, Wilma Mankiller, with the survival skills of a street fighter, hid in some out-of-the-way corner. I wanted to join them.

"Smile," Karen whispered as the doorbell chimed. "Be a grown-up, Skeet."

I forced a smile to my face. The first one through the door, however, was Vice Chancellor Jeremy Coulter. That wiped the smile off.

"Marquitta! Good to see you." I stiffened as Jeremy hugged me. "How's Brian?"

Jeremy was a smooth-tongued snake, but he'd pulled Brian out of a hellish foster home when I couldn't because I was in the hospital. Then, he and his wealthy wife used their connections to help me gain custody with the long-term goal of adoption. I owed Jeremy big-time. I hated that as much as he loved it.

"He's great," I said with all the false warmth I could manage. "He's in the kitchen. I'll get him. He'll want to see you." Brian didn't know what I did about Jeremy. He only knew the Coulters had helped him, and he was a grateful, loyal kid.

"Nonsense! I'll go later. I don't want to take you from your guests." Jeremy's eyes twinkled.

I managed a smile. He tugged me out of the path of Bob and Kathy Lynch as they hurried over to Karen. The guest of honor and his wife arrived next. I'd never cared for Mel when I was with KCPD—too political. I wasn't thrilled at his invasion of the sanctuary I'd found in Brewster and Chouteau University. Remembering how much Jake liked his boss, I resolved to behave like an adult. As Jeremy chuckled at my discomfort, I moved forward to greet Mel and his wife with a warm smile. Reverend Starkey Rayber of the local AME church walked in with Helen and Reverend Matt Lawson right before Miryam and Annette crowded through the door. I left Mel's welcome to Karen.

"Skeet, you look lovely." Starkey reached out to give me a hug.

"Glad to see you, Reverend Starkey. I assume Lucette's working." My hug was sincere. Starkey, Karen's pastor, was one of my favorites.

"Or she'd be here to keep me in line." He laughed. Starkey patted my shoulder and moved on into the living room.

"I never thought I'd see you give a party." Reverend Matt smiled and winked at me. "We've both come a long way."

"Hush, Matt. Starkey's right, Skeet. That red tunic really sets off your dark eyes and hair. The place looks lovely, too. I've got some ceramic pieces that would go great in your living room. Come by the shop later in the week. I'll set them back for you." Helen gave me a hug, then examined my face. "You're not happy. Can I help?"

"It's nothing," Annette said. "She'll be fine."

I nodded. "Scoot on in and grab something to eat and drink."

Helen examined my face. "This is really not your kind of thing."

I gave her a grateful look. "Having you here makes it better."

Matt looked at me seriously. "If you need—"

"Thanks. Really." I tried to brighten my tone. "It's a party. Go celebrate and meet the guest of honor."

He kept a concerned gaze on my face until Helen pulled him into the living room.

"Look a little less down." Annette pointed a long scarlet nail at me. "Or everyone coming through the door will wonder whose funeral it is."

"Skeet's not looking that unhappy. Those two are sensitives. Probably why they went into ministry." Miryam put on a wise look totally at odds with her deliberately sexy appearance and the rainbow necklace of crystals that drew attention to her black dress's deep décolletage.

The doorbell rang again. Annette and Miryam headed for the drinks table as more guests arrived. For a while, I smiled at people pouring into my house, shook hands, and passed the guests off to Karen. She handled the crowd as if she was born to it, hugging, air-kissing. I wished I could be more like her.

Realizing I stood with my back to the door, I turned to come face-to-face with Walker Lynch and Terry Heldrich. Again, Terry's alertness told me he'd spent a lot of time in dangerous surroundings and survived. He caught me watching him and smiled, lighting his face with handsome appeal that surprised me. I turned to Walker. Along with Mel's rich new wife, he'd underwritten Mel's campaign for attorney general. Not a good investment for either of them.

"Terrific to run into you the other day. It's been far too long." Walker took my hand and held it rather than shaking it.

I hadn't made up my mind yet about Walker. Bright, good-looking in a tall, nerdish way—movie star playing a scholar. Loaded with charm. Sometimes I really liked him. Sometimes the charm felt like a game. Tonight, he was affable.

"I'm surprised you came from the city for this. What's up your sleeve for Brewster?" I took my hand back from him.

"I'm staying with Mel and Liz for the next week. Political strategizing." He looked as if he'd just told a huge joke.

"Oh, no, Skeet!" Mel's voice came from behind me. "You don't get out of giving me a hug that easily." Turning me to face him, he began to squeeze me, smashing my breasts into his chest. Unable to breathe, I tried to pull away. "One of the incentives Chouteau had to offer, Walker. My favorite girls right here—Skeet and Karen. It's like old times, isn't it, Skeet?"

I couldn't answer. It was all I could do to take in air dripping with his cologne.

"Mel, you have to let her take a breath if you want her to say anything." Liz pulled him away from me.

The edge to her voice puzzled me. Was this wealthy, model-perfect woman jealous? Word on the street said she'd taken him from his first wife to finance his run for attorney general and eventually governor. Now she was stuck with a stocky guy twice her age, probably not going anywhere politically. With her looks and money, why didn't she run for office herself?

Walker laughed at Liz's remark. Mel loosened his grip. I sucked in a deep breath, noticing Liz's elegant, hard-edged face soften when she turned from Mel to Walker. Terry's smile widened into a boyish grin at my embarrassment.

"Good to see you, Mel," I wheezed.

"Been too long. But that's over. We're colleagues again." Mel's ruddy face broke into a big, sincere smile.

I mentally kicked myself for never liking the man. I wasn't as big a person as Karen or Jake. "Yeah, Mel." I gestured to the living room past Karen, still greeting everyone with aplomb. "Why don't you move into the air-conditioning? Get a drink? Karen wants to introduce folks to you."

Grinning at me, Walker took Mel's arm. "She's right, as usual. That's the reason for all this—to meet people from your new town." He pulled Mel into the room. Liz followed, eyes locked on Walker. Terry trailed behind, checking out the room.

Wondering if Mel would find himself replaced soon, I closed the door against the Indian-summer blast furnace outside. The first rush of guests had stopped. I'd missed greeting some because so many came at the same time, but Karen had taken care of things. Now, she introduced Mel to Brewster's mayor and some local businessmen.

Bob and Kathy Lynch caught Walker and introduced themselves, ignoring Terry. "We're Lynches, too." Kathy gave a hearty laugh.

"Kathy by marriage," Bob added. "Are you from the Pennsylvania Lynches? Or the Southern Lynches?"

Walker's face tightened, eyes flashing around, seeking rescue.

"We made a study of Lynches in this country." Kathy laughed again. "You wouldn't believe. They're all descended from one ancestor. It's fascinating how the family's spread."

"Where are your people from?" Bob asked.

Walker looked uncomfortable. Bob wasn't sensitive to others' feelings. Did Walker need rescue?

Terry said, "Mel and Liz are waiting to introduce you to the mayor."

Walker gave Bob and Kathy a sheepish grin. "I've gone off track. Excuse us." Before Bob or Kathy could speak, Walker and Terry hurried into the living room.

"Goodness!" Kathy watched them press through the crowd.

"Guess we're not good enough." Bob looked as if he'd like to punch someone.

Kathy's expression turned thoughtful. "Maybe he thought we wanted something. He's wealthy. Probably people hit him up a lot."

22

Bob's face reddened. Kathy put her hand on his arm. "Forget it. Enjoy the party. Later we'll find out about his family." They strolled into the living room, heads unnaturally high.

Could I sneak off to the kitchen to hang out with Brian? The doorbell put an end to that fantasy. I opened the door to a wall of humid heat and groaned. Randy Thorsson was DA for Deacon County before recently becoming Missouri state senator. His incompetence and politicking as DA was a hindrance repeatedly. Now, he had more power but less impact on my work. The state's trouble was my luck.

"Good to see you." Randy wore his made-for-TV smile. Before the senate race, Randy'd hired an image consultant, lost fifty pounds, traded snaggled teeth for an Osmond smile, and began wearing elevator shoes and a toupee. It looked good on TV.

"I hardly get to see you since I spend so much time in Jeff City." His chest lifted with pride at his words.

"I'm glad you came." I could be political, too. We shook hands.

"Mel's my colleague and friend. I'd never miss this." His eyes were on the room behind me, calculating rank and status. Same old Randy.

Suddenly, his face brightened, eyes shining like a kid's at Christmas. "Great to see you. I'll greet the guest of honor." Pushing me out of the way, he headed not toward Mel but straight for Liz and Walker on the other side of the room. Which of them caused that excitement in his face?

I started to sneak off to hide in the kitchen with Brian. The doorbell pealed. I gave up, doomed to remain at this party.

After two hours, my head throbbed from the roar of voices and pounding electronic music. Someone had brought that. I was a blues and jazz person.

Some guests drank a lot. Leonard Klamath looked worse

than he had on Thursday. He drove from Kansas City to the party, an aging caricature of himself.

The air-conditioning couldn't keep up with the heat generated by all the bodies. The green-chili-pork and black-bean-corn salsa I'd eaten burned a hole in my stomach. I saw a vacant chair and decided to sit the party out.

Helen Lawson approached, glass of wine in her hand. "Great party!"

"Thanks. It's really Karen's." Sometimes I tried to imagine Helen, a nun before she married, in a nun's habit. It never worked. Probably why she left.

She looked around the crowded living and dining rooms. "Quite a cross section of town here, plus imports from the city."

"Didn't you two live in KC?"

"Yes. Matt taught at St. Paul's School of Theology. I ran an urban mission for refugees. Kansas City resettles hundreds that the government's granted asylum. We're the Midwest's Ellis Island." Her face brightened as she discussed her former job. "Several agencies collaborate and coordinate services. Translation. Cultural education. Job training. Those were my areas."

"I knew KC had immigrants from places you wouldn't expect." I nodded. "Didn't know they were refugees. Were you based in the Northeast?"

She nodded. "People with so much love and faith. So many desperate needs." Her gaze fell. "So many unscrupulous people exploiting them."

"Your work surely helped." Obviously, it was a painful memory.

Passion faded from her face. "I couldn't handle the stress. That's why we came here. My store's fair-trade merchandise lets me help in a tiny way without putting me . . ." She looked ashamed. "It's not enough, but it's all I can do."

24

"Everyone has a tipping point. Especially cops and social workers." I wanted to take that haunted look from her face. "The wise recognize that point and step back before doing real harm. It's the smart thing. I've seen damage resulting from people trying to keep on. It's not pretty."

She emptied her wineglass and held it up. "You're right. Think I'll get some more. Want some?"

"I'm fine. Thanks." As she walked off, I wondered if she self-medicated with alcohol. Wouldn't be the first time someone who'd burned out had taken that route. I hoped not, though. I liked her. Had I ever seen her drunk? I didn't think so. Just an unfortunate topic cropping up.

Annette wandered over. "You're not having fun, Skeet. It's a great party."

I nodded, instantly regretting it. The head throbbing grew with movement. "Where's Miryam? Haven't seen our high priestess since she arrived."

She laughed. "She's in her other guise. Femme fatale." She pointed with her margarita toward Miryam in the center of a circle of men, looking like the Hollywood star she'd always wanted to be in that black dress that clung to her curves and showed some thigh through its side slit.

Annette turned back to me. "Why should she have all the fun? Get up. We'll go over and show those guys a couple of real women."

"No, thanks. Headache." I motioned for her to go without me. After a second's thought, she did. Soon, the circle of men had a double center, short blonde and tall redhead.

Walker began cutting out Miryam's other admirers to get her alone. Miryam clearly was not happy at that. I wondered if I should rescue her, but Annette sleekly gathered Walker's arm, shepherding him toward the drinks table, chattering all the while.

Terry turned up at my side. I'd wondered what happened to Walker's enigmatic shadow.

"Sitting this one out?" He smiled slightly, his senses still engaged with everything around us, not really with me.

"Seemed a good idea. Are you enjoying yourself?"

He shrugged. "I'm not a party person. At least, not like this."

"What kind do you like?" Probably one of the drink-and-dope brawls with strippers so many soldiers loved.

"A few people. Friends. Sitting relaxed. Talking." A new smile involved his whole face appealingly.

In the background, Joe stared at us with a frown. I smiled to show I didn't feel threatened. Though part of me knew this was a dangerous man.

"I don't know if that's a party, but it sounds lots nicer." I looked around.

"I hope I didn't hurt your feelings. I guess this is your party."

I held up both hands in reassurance. "It's Karen's, not mine. Say what you want."

"Brave woman, offering that to a man you don't really know." He laughed. "I researched you after we met. You're quite special."

I blinked in surprise. "Why would you look me up?" I couldn't decide if it was flattering or creepy.

He spread out long-fingered hands in explanation. "Walker called you a decorated homicide detective. Not many women you can say that about. You studied at the FBI."

I closed my eyes. He would find that. "Just a course on profiling psychopaths and serial killers that they gave for homicide cops around the country."

His eyebrows lifted, and his eyes held a bit of twinkle to warm them. "Not many women at that course, I'll wager."

It hadn't been easy. But the male instructor never allowed any

26

overt harassment. That helped. "There were two of us. The other woman had to leave halfway through. Her kid had an accident."

He nodded. "See. Unusual woman."

"If I did it again, I might be called home. I have a kid now." I thought about that a second. Brian might make a difference in my career. I congratulated myself for taking this less demanding job.

He laughed. "It's not the same. He's just a kid you take care of."

I wondered. I couldn't call myself a real mother. Mothers had instincts and knowledge I was missing. "He's a lot more than that to me. But you're right. It can't be the same. I can't replace the mother he lost."

He leaned in closer, studying me. I wasn't sure I liked it. His intense gaze felt dangerous. Nothing to trifle with. "I like you, Skeet. I don't usually like women except to bed them. They get too emotional. They always want to pretty up reality. You don't."

I glared at him. "What am I supposed to say to that? Thanks for telling me I'm not a normal woman?"

He laughed again, a warm, resonant sound. "Normal is highly overrated. I don't see you as less than most women. You've much more going for you. That interests me." He pulled back, sensing I was still upset at what he'd said. "You needn't be like them. You're better as you are."

He gave me a smile that made promises I didn't want and walked away, as if he were walking unarmed through a jungle, alert to any hint of attack.

Who was he? Where was he from? What did he really do for Walker?

Leonard's argument with two law professors grew louder by the minute. I saw Helen stare at him. On the other side of the room, her husband watched Leonard with concern also. Did I need to deal with him?

Karen took his arm, speaking in calm tones, doing her therapist shtick. No need to worry. Helen moved in her direction to help. She'd probably done counseling as a nun. He couldn't be in two better sets of hands.

"Someone's had too much." Joe sat on the arm of my chair.

I smiled at him. "Jake's death hit Leonard hard. He retired. Took up Olympic drinking."

"He worked for Melvin, too?"

"He and Jake were two of three assistant U.S. attorneys under Mel."

"Is the third one here?"

"No. He left for a judgeship in Illinois before Jake died. Mel replaced all three of them after Jake's death." I remembered the late-night call. Jake fell down flights of marble stairs in the federal courthouse while working late. I slammed the doors on that memory.

Joe nodded, pointing at Leonard. Karen and Helen led him into the dining room. "This one already had more than a few when he showed up."

I nodded. Joe had noticed and kept an eye on Leonard. Good cop.

"You think you're so smart!" Leonard yelled. He pulled his arm from Karen, turning his back on Helen. "Hell, you don't know anything. You don't even know about Jake."

Helen jerked as if startled. Her eyes grew huge.

"What don't I know about Jake? What are you saying, Leonard?" Karen asked.

Everyone turned and stared. Reverend Matt started forward. Mel forced his way through the crowd.

"Stuff you don't know. About Jake." Leonard's words rang out angrily.

Helen began edging away, as Karen tried to soothe Leonard.

"You'd drink, too. If you knew the truth." Leonard threw his head back and chugged his drink, dropping the glass to the floor, where it shattered.

"What do you mean? What don't I know?" Karen looked puzzled. Helen rushed off toward her husband.

"What the hell are you doing?" Mel grabbed the shorter man by the shoulders. Leonard fought hard. I got up to go make the drunk leave my house.

"Let me alone!" Leonard yelled at Mel, twisting out of the stronger man's grasp.

"You're drunk. Upsetting Karen with crazy talk. You need to go home." Mel tried to grip him again. With the wiliness of the drunk, Leonard dodged his hands.

I reached them and grabbed Leonard from behind by his arms, pulling on his shoulders. "Let's take this outside. You're upsetting Karen. You don't want to do that."

Leonard twisted his head back, then seemed to shrink inside his clothes. "No, Skeet. Don't want to. Not Karen. Karen's good. Didn't deserve . . ."

I moved him to the door, half choking on the alcohol smell that brought back bad times with my dad. Karen walked with us, eyes fixed on his face. I looked back to see Joe with Mel, trying to calm him. Helen hid behind her husband, peeking out.

When I looked back to move Leonard along, he'd leaned forward to whisper to Karen. Her brown face turned pale.

I jerked him away. "Come on. Karen, don't pay attention to him. He's drunk. He'll call tomorrow and apologize. Won't you, Leonard?"

He nodded. "Sure. Tell Karen I'm sorry." Each word was a belch of booze breath.

Opening the door, I ushered him onto the porch. "Give me your car keys. I'll call you a cab."

"That's good, Skeet." He dropped into an old wicker chair as if he couldn't have stayed upright any longer. I stood with my hand out. After a few seconds, he pulled out his car keys and dropped them in my hand. Then he crumpled back into the chair.

"Wait right here until the cab comes." I knew from experience with my father that he could get a new surge of energy any minute.

He nodded and closed his eyes with a wince. The sun had set, the air cooler now but still warm and sticky. In the distance, a train whistled. Leonard opened his eyes at the sound, stared as if expecting the cab any second. I turned to find Karen in the doorway, glaring at him.

"Come on. Let's take care of the guests." I pushed her back inside and closed the door behind us. "I'll call a cab."

Inside, the party had returned to normal with the distraction gone. Conversation buzzed. Music roared. Brian and Helen knelt on the floor cleaning up the broken glass with paper towels and a trash bag. People stayed clear of the door area where we stood.

"He can sit out there and rot," Karen muttered.

"I doubt he even knows what he said." I faced her. "There's nothing about Jake you don't know. Leonard's a drunk. You've dealt with them before. He said the most hurtful thing he could think of. Drunks do that."

She nodded. Looking at the closed door, she avoided my eyes. Karen never let what people said bother her. A skill I'd often wished for. What had Leonard whispered to her? More than what I'd heard, to bother her so much.

I gave her a hug. "Get back in the swing with everyone. I'll go to the kitchen and call Tony's cab. He'll be glad of a paid trip to the city."

She shook her head as if coming out of a daze. "I can't face all these people right now. I'll call Tony. It'll give me a chance to catch my breath."

I sighed. "Okay. But don't stay in the kitchen all night. You don't know what disaster I might cook up."

She forced a smile. "I have faith in you." She slipped through the crowd toward the kitchen.

"Beautifully handled, Marquitta. You haven't lost your touch." Jeremy offered me a margarita. Though I'd been drinking club soda all night, I took it. I had no energy for a verbal skirmish.

Jeremy clicked his glass against mine. "I love to watch you work. You're such a professional, even when you're off the clock."

I rolled my eyes. "If that were true, you wouldn't be in Brewster any longer."

His hearty tenor laugh had a musical ring. "You can't help it if occasionally you're outmatched. I was right, though. You cleaned up that mess of murder and blackmail without breaking a sweat."

"Just a nicked femoral artery," I muttered.

"That's my girl. The exact letter of the truth. I can always count on you."

"Jeremy, give it a rest." I took a swig of my drink. Too much tequila.

I looked around. Brian had taken his bag of broken glass to the kitchen. Everyone else had gone back to their conversations. Watching them, I let out a breath I hadn't known I was holding.

"Looks as if everything's stable," I muttered.

Jeremy laughed. "Always trying to control life. Even at a party."

"Go torment someone else for a while." I was too tired to put any fire into the words.

He winked at me and walked off, still laughing. I remembered liking and respecting him. There's nothing worse than learning someone's a crook and not being able to prove it.

Joe found me in a bleak mood. "Where's Karen?"

"Calling a cab for Leonard. Pulling herself together. But she's taking too long." I sipped my margarita. The bittersweet mixture warmed its way down my throat. I looked around for some place to leave it. After seeing the damage booze did to my father and the fights my then-husband picked when drunk, I'd never been a drinker. Alcohol was too dangerous for me to mess with. I never wanted to end up like my old man. "I should never have agreed to this party."

Joe smiled. "It's actually a good party, Skeet. Drunks can happen anywhere. He's gone. Everything's smooth again."

I had to smile. Joe's not a handsome devil like my ex, but something's so likable about his face that he always makes me smile.

My cell phone began to vibrate against my leg. I pulled it out of my pocket and answered.

"Skeet!" I was shocked to hear Karen, her voice quavery with fear. She was supposed to be in the kitchen.

"You've got to come to the Caves, the parking lot. It's— Unh!" Karen groaned. Her phone sounded as if it had hit the ground.

"What's going on? Karen! What do you mean, the Caves?"

I could hear the tinny echo of my voice, her phone feeding it back to mine.

"What is it?" Joe asked, as I started running toward the kitchen. He fell in behind me. Brian sat at the kitchen table, eating a mini cherry-chocolate cheesecake.

"Did Karen come in and use the phone?" I could still hear the strange frightened sound of her voice.

"No." He swallowed and grinned at me. "She walked through on her way out the back door."

Jeremy poked his head in the kitchen door. "Is something wrong, Skeet? I saw you and Joe running."

"Jeremy, I've got to go to campus. Can you handle things here for me?" Further into his debt, but I had no choice.

He nodded. "Go on. We'll deal with everyone here, won't we, Brian?"

"I'm with you," said Joe.

"Thanks. Glad of the backup."

We ran out to my car and headed the few blocks to the Chouteau University Underground Storage and Business Center. What had happened to Karen? Why did she lie to me and leave her party to go to the campus? What had Leonard whispered to her? And what trouble had it drawn her into?

My cop sense buzzed in the back of my skull. My best friend and surrogate mother was in real trouble. I couldn't bear it if anything happened to her. From the sounds of that phone call, something had. Something bad.

The Caves were spooky. When I first became Chouteau University's chief of campus police, I went on a tour of the big underground facility only a few minutes from my house. Coming from the Kansas City Police Department, all I could see was what a horribly convenient place for crime it was. A whole business/industrial complex with parking underground to take advantage of the controlled temperature and humidity in the limestone caves beneath much of the campus. Even the campus library had only one floor aboveground and three below, with an entrance into the main underground parking lot. Still, in the year I'd been at Chouteau, nothing beyond normal undergraduate mischief had ever occurred in the Caves. Until now.

I headed from the night outside through the entrance into the main parking lot. Claustrophobic, I always felt tense the minute I moved underground, even with twenty-two-foot-high ceilings carved out of the rock of the hill on which the college sat. The air always smelled funny, thinner in here than out in the surface world. The mercury-vapor lamps illuminated the area with yellow-tinged light and left plenty of shadowed nooks and corners.

"Over there!" Joe pointed to two mounds in the space between rows of parking slots. I indicated the radio with my head. He called in the request for ambulance and backup.

I pulled up, blocking the space between the rows, and remembered that neither of us had our handguns. "Grab the shotgun," I called as I jumped out and ran to the two bodies, lying on the chilly stone ground. I knew the first was Karen from the long silver hair, shining in the shadows, and knelt, checking for life with a shaky hand. She breathed with difficulty, pulse thready. Blood smeared the back of her head.

"How is she?" Joe knelt beside the other body, gun in hand, checking vitals on Leonard.

"Unconscious. Weak pulse. Bashed over the head with something."

"Probably the gun that killed Klamath." Joe stood and looked around, searching for gun or gunman. I stayed on the ground with Karen, trying to pour strength and life into her with my hands the way my gran can do.

No atheists in foxholes, they say. Guess I believed in the traditional healing of my people in my own version of a foxhole. If stubborn desperation had any power, Karen would not die before the ambulance arrived. I worried that the ambulance, placed under the jurisdiction of the sheriff's office a year earlier in a political move, would be as slow to arrive as usual. "If that ambulance is delayed again, I'm going to beat the sheriff to death with my bare hands."

Joe nodded at my muttering but kept his eyes searching the

perimeter while he stood guard with the shotgun from my car. We didn't know if the killer was still here or had fled. A train rattled through town on the tracks that ran past the college, hooting its whistle over and over.

"Whoever it was knew what he was doing," Joe said. "Two shots precisely placed so either would have killed him."

Karen's breathing grew steadier and stronger. In the distance, sirens wailed. Karen would live. Leonard hadn't.

What was either of them doing in the Caves? Was Leonard followed to Brewster to be killed? Was all this connected to Leonard's drunken scene at the party? Must be. I didn't buy coincidence. Someone wanted to shut him up. What did he know that made murder worthwhile? And Karen? Why did she lie to me and sneak off to the Caves?

The sirens shut off abruptly as a campus cop car and the ambulance rolled into the Caves right behind each other. It was time to stand up and be the chief. Time to stand up and deal with violent death the way I'd done so many times. But inside me was the little girl who'd felt betrayed by her mother and found a substitute— only to find herself betrayed again. What in hell was going on with Karen?

# CHAPTER 3

The chemical-scented chill of the hospital air hit me with a pleasant shock as I entered the ER waiting room. As I crossed the threshold, Joe paced the foyer between outer and inner doors, talking on his cell phone. He'd gone back to the party, closed it down, and brought Brian to the hospital while I supervised the crime scene.

As I passed him on my way through the inner doors, he said, "Gotta go now, princess. Skeet's here. I love you, too. Get to sleep now. Let me talk to Mrs. Nieman."

Brian sat facing me in an aqua vinyl chair with one of his handheld video games, looking rumpled and tired. He shared the game with a girl who switched her attention between it and her cell phone. She looked several years older with red, purple, and green tattoos running down both arms—dragons, witches, and gargoyles—short, spiked hair, burgundy with metallic blue streaks. She had a stud in her nose, a ring in her eyebrow, and enough makeup for an aging Hollywood star.

Instantly, I wanted Brian away from her. I'd dealt with too many lost children of the streets in Kansas City. Vulnerable, damaged, going down fast because of abuse or neglect suffered, too often they took others with them. I didn't want this girl dragging Brian down.

He frowned at the game before looking up in surprise at me standing over him. "Skeet!" Tossing the game to the girl, he stood and threw his arms around me. "You're okay!"

I patted his shoulder. "Of course. Didn't Joe tell you that?"

"He did, but Brian's been certain that very evil dudes have been having their bad, bad way with you." The girl never took her eyes off her phone as she spoke, but I had the feeling she watched me in some way. "I told him you were probably enjoying the ravishing and bodice-ripping, but he just fretted more. Kids!"

"This is Angie," Brian said, releasing me. "Her mom's in the emergency room, too. We've been waiting together."

The girl looked up with sad, scared eyes that switched immediately to an attitude of scorn. "Yeah. Angie." She threw her head back, adding, "Daughter of asshole Mel and druggie Denise."

I felt my eyebrows rise. "Angie Melvin? I haven't seen you since you were little. I never would have recognized you."

"I recognized you, Supercop. Still as drab as ever." She snapped a photo of Brian and me with her phone before turning back to Brian's video game dismissively. I guessed my red silk tunic wasn't as fashionable as I'd hoped.

"How's Karen?" I asked Brian. "Have they let you see her yet?"

"She was still unconscious the last time they came out, but her vital signs are all strong now," Joe said, coming up on my left side. "Everything okay at the scene?"

I nodded. "Gil and Trish are finishing. I had to call him back from his first date with Dolores. Hope he doesn't hate me for it. Sid thinks it was a big-caliber gun."

Sid Ambrose was our part-time county coroner. Gil and Trish were my investigators, Lieutenant Gilbert Mendez and Officer Trish Cassell. Trish had just finished investigator training in Kansas City. I wanted her tagging Gil to get some real experience.

I gave Joe a tired smile. "Thanks for getting Brian. Was that Julie on the phone?"

Joe returned his genuine nice-guy smile. "Yeah. She's at Mrs. Nieman's, but she has trouble going to sleep if I'm not there."

"I don't blame her. She's been through a lot. Why don't you head out and take her home so you can both get some sleep? Brian and I can take it from here." I looked at Brian and then back at Joe. "I really appreciate your help."

"Without you and Brian, I wouldn't have a little girl to go home to. Any time you need me, I'm there. Count on it." Joe's face grew sober at the six-month-old memory of his daughter's ordeal.

Angie tore her eyes from the video game. "Really? Did you save some wittle girl's life, Brian?" She held up her phone to snap his photo and then held it like a microphone to record his answer.

Brian blushed brightly. "It was really Skeet. I was just there." He didn't like to talk about having blasted a killer's gun arm as he was about to finish off Julie and me.

"Go on home." I gave Joe's solid shoulder a little push. "This could take a while. I should send Bri with you."

"I'm not leaving till we know Karen's okay," Brian said.

"I know when I'm not wanted," Joe said. "If you need anything, call me."

I waved him toward the door. "Get out of here."

"Brian, let me know if you guys need something. I know how stubborn Skeet is." Joe gave me a stern look.

Brian nodded, his face serious. "I will. Don't worry."

As Joe left, I sank onto one of the hard plastic chairs.

"Touching concern for your welfare." The words dripped scorn from Angie's bloodred lips. She checked something on her phone.

Brian sat back down between us. "Joe's a good friend."

"Obviously, if you went all heroic and saved his kid's life." She lifted her shoulders in a slight shrug. "Downside of being a hero. Unwanted friendships."

Brian blushed again. "It's not like that."

Angie forced an unpleasant laugh. "So you say, big boy."

I recognized the attitude. I hadn't dyed my hair or tattooed my arms when my parents divorced, but I'd poured scorn on my mother who divorced my dad and took me to a whole different place to live, away from my beloved father, Big Charlie Bannion.

"Angie, why are you here?" I asked her bluntly. Her eyes filled with hurt and fear again before the sullen mask covered them.

"She brought in her mom who'd overdosed on prescription medicine." Bri's tone was low and tactful. "She found her outside her dad's new house collapsed in her car and drove her here."

Angie whipped her head down to the video game again and began to play intently.

I'd heard rumors about Denise Melvin's downward spiral after Mel divorced her for Liz Richar. Mel had all the connections and power in the legal community and committed her for drug abuse and attempted suicide, taking everything, even her kid. A nasty situation. Another reason I wasn't happy he'd invaded my peaceful little town.

Angie didn't look as if she'd welcome vapid comments about her mother getting better. She probably knew too well that, no matter the outcome of this trip to the hospital, her mother would get worse. Her attitude was fine with me because I sucked at consoling or making encouraging comments.

"Skeet," Brian offered tentatively. "There's a message from your mom on the answering machine at the house. I don't know for sure when it came in tonight."

My head jerked back. "What does she say?"

"She wants you to call her. Said it's important."

"Did she say anything was wrong with Gran?" If she didn't mention Gran, it couldn't be bad news about Gran's health.

Gran might seem ageless and immortal, but deep inside I knew she was old and someday I'd get a message about a fall or an illness, the beginning of the end. She was old enough to be my dad's mother, and he was recovering from a major stroke. Still, it didn't sound like today would be that day, and I was grateful. I couldn't handle any more than I already had on my plate.

"She just wanted you to call her." Brian looked so tired. Poor kid. This had been one hell of a year for him.

"If she didn't mention Gran, whatever it is can wait." I reached out to tousle his hair, dropped my hand awkwardly instead. I doubted he'd appreciate it in front of Angie.

Fortunately, Lucette Rayber, head emergency room nurse, came out and beckoned. Brian followed me. Angie darted a hopeful look at the nurse, then turned her eyes back to her phone, holding it awkwardly as if inspecting something on its side. I realized she was filming us as we walked to the emergency room door. When all this was over, I'd have to talk with her about not filming people without their permission.

"Skeet, Karen's conscious. Came to about fifteen minutes ago, but Doc's been running tests. She keeps calling for you. Now, he says you can come in." Lucette's hoarse, gravelly voice was the best music I'd ever heard.

Brian tagged behind me as I followed Lucette through the

double doors that closed securely behind us. The faint astringent smell of the waiting room air concentrated into a definite mix of medicinal odors.

Lucette was my height and greyhound-lean. She walked rapidly, leaning forward as if driving uphill against the wind. I had to push myself beyond my normal pace to keep up with her. Her husband always said she was racing the devil and winning. Since Starkey Rayber pastored the local AME church, presumably he knew something about the devil's sporting events.

Karen looked older than I'd ever seen her, lying on the emergency room bed, normally olive skin drained to a pale, yellowish cream and long hair tangled and bloody with a chunk missing for the bandage at the back of her head.

"Skeet! Finally!" Karen reached out her hand, and I grasped it.

"You definitely scared me." Leaning down, I hugged her awkwardly, trying to be gentle. "What happened? Why'd you leave the party for the Caves? Were you following Leonard?"

Moving up next to me, Brian took Karen's other hand and stroked it. She smiled. Returning her gaze to my face, she said, "Someone killed Jake. Leonard knows who killed him. That's what he whispered to me back at the house. He said to meet him at the Caves, so he could tell me everything."

"So you lied and left through the kitchen to go to the Caves?" I tried to keep the sudden hurt out of my voice. It ended up flat and artificial-sounding.

"I'm sorry." She didn't look sorry, though. She looked determined and stubborn, a new look for Karen the therapist. Stubborn was what I usually did. "I was stunned after he said that. I couldn't think. I just went."

She pulled free of my grasp and waved her hand, disconnected IV needle still in it, as if wiping away any consideration of the frantic worry she'd put me through.

"Leonard was drunk." My voice sounded closer to normal, I was glad to hear.

Lucette moved me and began to remove the IV in Karen's hand.

I shook my head, trying to clear the childish sense of betrayal. "Never mind. What happened when you got there? Did you see who killed Leonard?"

"Leonard's dead?" Karen cried. "How will I learn the truth about Jake now?"

I looked at Lucette in confusion.

"Short-term memory loss. Not unusual with a head injury. She might eventually remember. She might never." Lucette spoke without looking at me. She slid out the IV needle and slapped down a cotton ball and surgical tape. "Nothing to be concerned about. Par for the course." She looked up, shrugging her thin shoulders. "Doc says she can go home if there's someone to check on her every hour the rest of the night."

"Ignacio can do that."

"I'll do——" Karen and I started to speak at the same time, but she finished her sentence ahead of me. I gave her a questioning look. Ignacio was her Chilean shepherd, a silent man, good with sheep and goats, but I wasn't sure how great he'd be at taking care of Karen. "Ignacio?"

"He's good at that kind of thing. Absolutely reliable. When the sheep or goats are lambing or kidding, he checks on them every hour and sometimes more frequently. He can sleep in the house in the guest room instead of his trailer. That'll make it easier." Karen pulled herself up to a sitting position.

"Let me get the release and instructions from Doc. I'll be right back." Lucette darted out of the room with her racer's walk.

"Skeet, you've got to help me find out who killed Jake," Karen said, scooting to the edge of the bed and swinging her legs over to dangle, trying to reach the floor.

I stepped forward and grabbed her hand to support her as she got to her feet. "We don't know Jake was killed. Leonard was drunk. You and I both know drunks will say anything."

She fixed me with an intent stare. "And Leonard's dead now, you tell me. Killed right after saying that. He was speaking the truth."

I bit my lip to keep from saying the wrong thing. "Why wouldn't he say something at the time Jake died? Why wait until now? Who would kill Jake? A sweetheart of a man like that!"

Karen teetered a little as she let go of my hands and found her balance. "I don't know." She looked as if she might start to cry. Carefully, she stepped into her sandals. She looked back up at me with a set face, angry in a way I'd never seen before. "But I'll find out. You'll help me find out. They'll pay for killing the love of my life."

That look stayed with me throughout the process of signing her out of the hospital and getting her in a wheelchair out to my car. This Karen was new, different from the one I'd known for years. I had a feeling this Karen could be dangerous.

I dropped Brian off at home on the way to Karen's farm. I used Lady and Wilma as an excuse to send him in to bed. Someone had to feed them and let Lady back in the house. Brian loved my animals. I thought they were why he chose me to take care of him when his parents were killed. They'd be good company for him after this night that had to be bringing back as many bad memories for him as it did for me.

By that time, Karen dozed, half reclining in the backseat for the silent drive to her farm. Since the night air had finally cooled, I turned off the air conditioner and rolled down my windows, enjoying the smell of drying grasses.

Driving in the country at night soothes me. I learned that after the divorce when my mother moved us back to Tahlequah, Oklahoma, to live with Gran. Before I could drive, Gran took me driving in the hills outside of town whenever my arguments with my mom grew too heated and bitter. Once I had my license, I did it for myself.

I can only imagine how scary it must have been for Gran and Coreen to let a new teen driver take the car or pickup and head out into the night hills. To give them credit, they let me go, and now I can drive under any conditions. If you can drive those winding, switchback mountain roads at night, avoiding the deer, bobcats, and black bears that pop out of the woods crowding the narrow roads, you can drive anywhere.

When we arrived at Karen's farm, I noticed a light in Ignacio's trailer to the side of Karen's big, old farmhouse. At the sound of the car on the long gravel driveway, the light grew larger. Ignacio opened the trailer door, pouring out light onto the wooden porch in front. I was glad to see he was alert and watchful.

"Just honk," Karen murmured, pulling herself to an upright position with a slight moan. "He'll know we want him. He'll have to dress first."

I tapped the horn lightly. "Let's get you inside and into bed before you fall down."

"Patience, Skeet." Karen had said that to me so many times before that I felt tears sting at my eyelids.

By the time we struggled through the back door and I seated Karen in the lavender-scented kitchen, Ignacio joined us, wearing clean blue jeans, rolled at the bottom, and a T-shirt rooting for the University of California–Santa Cruz Banana Slugs, his hair slicked back with water. I wondered about the T-shirt.

"Karen! You've been hurt. What happened?" He started toward her, hand outstretched, but stopped himself mid-gesture. It was the most I'd ever heard him say.

Karen waved her bandaged hand airily. "Ignacio, I'm going to ask for your help tonight. I want you to sleep in the house with me and wake me every hour all night long."

Ignacio's dark face took on a tinge of red as confusion and embarrassment spread across his Incan features.

"She's got a head wound, needs to be checked on all night long," I explained.

"Like the pregnant sheep," Karen said with a little laugh. "You can sleep in the guest room so you won't have to trudge back and forth."

The flush under his skin faded. "I see. Should you be home?"

"The doctor released me." Karen smiled. "I just got hit on the head. You know how hardheaded I am."

Ignacio's face suddenly bloomed in a smile that left his eyes shining and changed his entire appearance. He nodded gravely. "Yes, I do."

Karen sniffed. "You're not supposed to agree with me."

His smile retreated to just the corners of his mouth. "*Pero* it was true, what you said, señora." A strong theatrical Spanish accent crept into his words, though I realized he'd spoken with only a hint of an accent before.

"Oh, please. Don't you start *that*." Karen looked like she was trying to laugh but couldn't.

"Do you want another pain pill before you go to bed?" I still held the bottle of meds and hospital instructions for her care.

"No. Too dazed and dizzy as it is." She tried to frown. "You have to find Jake's murderer."

I shook my head. "I have to find the person who killed Leonard and attacked you. If you're right, there'll be a connection. I haven't got the time, personnel, or authority to investigate an accidental death in Kansas City four years ago."

"Then tell Dan Wheelwright to investigate it if you won't." She glared at me fiercely.

I sighed. "You know it doesn't work that way. It wasn't our squad that investigated. It was Banville's. Dan can't open it, even if he thought there was a connection."

Karen frowned, wincing at the pain it caused. "But we know now it wasn't an accident."

"Do we? That stuff Leonard spouted probably came from the alcohol fumes in his brain, and someone he crossed when he was with the feds followed him to Brewster and the Caves. His murder looks very professional."

"That's pretty far-fetched." Karen looked scornful.

I wondered what had happened to the calm, controlled woman I'd known for so long. Then I remembered those days right after Jake died. She was going through all that pain again. She hadn't really healed, just papered over her grief. Leonard's words brought it back to life.

"So's the idea someone murdered Jake without arousing suspicion," I replied as calmly as I could, "and then murdered Leonard for just mentioning there was something about Jake you didn't know. Someone at the party cold-blooded and skilled enough to kill him in that professional way. No one else heard him tell you Jake was killed."

She stared at me in horror. "He did say that. Don't you believe me?"

I spread my hands, palms downward, in a motion I used when confronting volatile characters on the streets of the city. "I believe you. But I was closest to both of you, and I didn't hear it. No one else could have. I'll have to look for facts and follow them."

"Fact, Leonard told me Jake was killed. Fact, right after that—immediately!—he was murdered." Her face was flushed. "You surely don't buy the coincidence of that just happening right after he told me of Jake's murder."

"Okay. Follow this all the way to the end and see where it leads, Karen." I tried to make my voice as smooth and calm as I could. "Someone at the party tonight would have had to kill Leonard. Someone who knew Jake at the time he died."

Karen looked hesitant, then nodded. "Mel, Randy, Liz, you, me, Walker. Who else?"

I shrugged. "That's it. Now which of those people not only murdered Jake so cleverly the police were fooled but also shot Leonard with the accuracy of an assassin? Which of your friends did this?"

Karen stared at me, then looked away. Her eyes searched the room, seeking an answer. "Maybe someone else knew Jake back then."

"It's Brewster, Karen. Not a lot of options. Sid Ambrose knew him well, but Sid wasn't at the party. Judge Magda and the other judges probably met him at some time. Other than Randy, no one in the DA's office. They were all hired straight out of law school after Jake's death. Who else?"

"It had to be someone at the party."

Ignacio had scooted his chair closer to Karen's sometime during the conversation without my noticing. He held himself back from actually touching her but hovered protectively over her.

"I think we can agree that neither you nor I killed Jake." I gave Karen a small smile.

"Of course. His death just about killed both of us." She closed her eyes for a second, shuddering at the memory.

I didn't want to stay there among those memories. "Do you see what I'm up against here?" I reached over to set my palm gently on her shoulder for a second. "Neither of these scenarios is likely, but they're all I have. So I have to pursue both. Facts are all that will help me right now."

Ignacio reached out toward Karen but stopped with his hand in the air, dropping it back into his lap. "You must let yourself heal. Perhaps then your memory of the murderer will return."

Karen slumped for a moment, then straightened and stared, eyes wide in surprise. "Someone there must have called someone else to kill Leonard."

I looked at her. "Called someone who was conveniently waiting in Brewster?"

Her lips tightened as she glared at me. "As easy as the convenient ex-con who followed him here and to the Caves."

"Okay. I'll give you that. Equally as unlikely. Leonard had been drinking himself to death and losing control. Whoever the murderer was may have realized that seeing you would bring forth his remorse over Jake and a confession."

Karen's face grew animated. "They'd come prepared to deal with that."

"Only why not kill him ahead of time in KC if he's been getting to be that much of a danger?" I tried to keep my voice as gentle as possible.

"Perhaps they only worried about what he might do once he met you again." Ignacio looked from her face to mine. "Perhaps he has not been a problem, but they knew he was drinking so much, and they were not sure how he would react to seeing Karen again."

We both nodded. She gave him a grateful smile and seemed to relax, as if she felt someone was on her side. I hated that she saw me as someone who wasn't.

"But you see how complicated it gets?" I ran my hands through my hair in frustration.

Karen's jaw tightened. "It's got to be Mel."

I looked at her in surprise. I hadn't thought she'd be willing to admit one of her friends might be involved.

"Mel? You think Jake's best friend killed him?" I could see Mel betraying someone—I'd never really liked him—but as I remembered the case, Mel hadn't been in the federal courthouse that night to knock Jake down all those marble stairs.

"Of course not, but he knew who did it. He must have." Karen's face was flushed again. "Maybe he was afraid that if he told what he knew, Jake's killer would kill him, too. Maybe they told him to call if Leonard opened his mouth about Jake."

Ignacio gave me a questioning, almost skeptical look. I found myself rethinking my previous assessment of him. He seemed a far cry from the illiterate, non-English-speaking migrant worker I'd originally assumed he was.

"Go question Mel," Karen directed. "Make him tell you the truth. Make him tell you who killed Jake."

I sighed. "That's what I'll do tomorrow. Question everyone. I'll ask Mel lots of questions, believe me, but I can't go after him with a rubber hose."

"You must rest and heal, Karen," Ignacio said. "Then you will remember the killer's face."

She shook her head slowly and carefully, all animation gone from her face, now wrinkled with pain and fatigue. "I may never remember."

"Enough. Let's get you to bed." I stood, and Ignacio followed suit.

Karen got to her feet, and I stepped up beside her to let her lean on me. At the stairs, Ignacio offered to carry her up, to her distress. We helped her climb the stairs and make it down the hall to her room.

Ignacio waited as I maneuvered her over to the armchair next to the bed. "If you need me, I'm here," he said quietly and pulled the door closed.

"Karen, I'm worried that whoever killed Leonard may believe you can identify him," I said as I helped her into the chair. I walked over to the dresser. "Which drawer for your nightgowns?"

"The second. But I can't identify anyone."

I pulled open the drawer, getting another puff of her beloved lavender. The white nightgowns folded into neat stacks still showed their high Victorian necks with lace and ruffles.

"The killer's not going to know that." I took out the top nightgown.

Karen nodded slowly and stiffly. "I'll be fine. If he'd wanted to kill me, I'd be dead."

"I worry about you out here at night." I shook the folds from the nightgown and brought it to Karen, who'd begun to undo her dress.

"I'm not alone," she said, her voice muffled by the dress going over her head. "Ignacio's here, too. You saw how quick he was to check us out tonight."

She handed me the dress to drape it over the back of a nearby rocking chair. "We've got to find out who killed Jake and bring that murderer to justice. I should have known he wouldn't get dizzy and fall down marble stairs he'd gone up and down every day for years."

I walked over to turn down the bed. "You had every reason to believe Jake fell during one of his dizzy spells. We tried to get him to the doctor for weeks. I'm still not sure that isn't exactly what happened." I folded Karen's handwoven red-and-white over-shot coverlet at the foot of the bed. "I'm sure Ignacio's reliable, but he won't be up to dealing with whoever shot Leonard."

"Why not?" Karen's voice was muffled again.

Turning down the sheet and blanket, I fluffed up the pillow. "Because the killer knew exactly where to put shots to kill. That's not as easy as you might think. You have to be trained to do that."

I turned back to find her standing in the nightgown with her long hair streaming over her back. Only the bandage looked out of place. She held tightly to the back of the chair.

"I think Nacio's enough protection," she said. "If this person's such a pro, he meant to leave me alive."

"Just rest and heal your body." I helped her climb into bed.

"You have to find Jake's killer." Karen pushed back my hands as I spread the covers over her. "Skeet, listen to me!"

"Okay, okay." I placated her as if she were a fussy child. "It's my turn to check on Charlie tomorrow. I'll talk to Homicide in Kansas City and get what I can on Jake's case."

I turned off the overhead light, leaving on the bedside lamp so she could turn it off when she was ready. She looked small and old. I knew she wasn't really old. Karen was just sixty and the most energetic, active person I knew, but tonight, injured, in the big walnut bed with her silver hair streaming over the pillow, she looked old, fragile, and infinitely precious to me. I'd almost lost her.

"Good night, Skeet," she said with a dopey smile. "Don't forget your promise."

I stepped out into the hall, closing the door gently behind me. Ignacio stood in the shadows. I turned to him and motioned toward the stairs with my head.

We made our way down the stairs and through the dining room in silence. Once back in Karen's cheerful kitchen, I sat at the table with a sigh. Ignacio still stood, so I kicked another chair a little ways out from the table. "Sit down. We need to talk."

He pulled out the chair, turning it around to sit on like a horse and lean his chest against the back. "You're worried about Karen's safety."

Nodding, I set my elbow on the table, leaning the side of my face into my palm, suddenly unbelievably weary. "The killer may come after her."

Ignacio said nothing but raised his thick eyebrows.

"She needs to be watched tonight as she told you earlier, but she needs to be watched over, too. Do you understand? I can try to take care of that in town, but out here . . ." My voice trailed off. I really had no right to ask this man hired to take care of sheep and goats to risk his life for his boss.

"Don't worry. I'll protect her." Ignacio's quiet voice held an understated strength. "Karen's a good person. No one has a right to harm her."

This next was going to be delicate. "The other thing's her obsession with Jake being murdered. She's determined to find the killer. We've got to stop that, if we can, before she gets hurt again."

Ignacio stared at me. "Karen won't be stopped if she believes this. She's not the kind of woman who would let her husband's death go unavenged."

I stared at him. He certainly wasn't who I'd assumed he was. "She doesn't need to be doing any avenging. She needs to recuperate from this attack, get on with her life, and let me catch this killer."

He flashed a smaller version of the earlier smile. "She will never listen to you or me about this. I'll watch and keep her safe while she's at the farm. Better if we keep her here until you catch this killer."

"Yes. Try. Please. I don't want her hurt again."

The smile disappeared from his mouth, and his lips tightened into a stern line. "No. Karen must not be hurt again."

I let myself out after giving him her pain meds and the emergency room instruction sheet, which he read and understood quite well.

Chilean shepherds were famous in the Western states for their skill with sheep. Often, generation after generation from the same family would make the trek to the same Wyoming or Montana ranch where they lived under terrible conditions, nothing like the nice trailer Karen had for Ignacio. Missouri sheep breeders had learned of their skills and started hiring Chilean shepherds recently, but Missouri didn't have the tradition with them that the Western states did. From all I'd heard, mostly these shepherds were illiterate and spoke little English. I wondered where Karen had found Ignacio.

More pressing issues soon took over my mind. Tomorrow was my day to check in on my father, who was recuperating from a major stroke. My ex-husband and I alternated days. *Awkward* wasn't even close to the word for that, but my dad considered Sam the son he'd never had and Sam loved Big Charlie Bannion, so it worked somehow. I'd promised Karen I'd get the case information from Dan Wheelwright, my old Homicide boss. I would also ask Dan for info on anything questionable with Leonard's old cases, though. There was no doubt that Leonard had been murdered.

If Leonard was murdered because of what he said about Jake at the party, someone at the party must have killed him. Karen certainly believed this. The Karen I'd known for years who was smart, reasonable, in control of herself all the time, had vanished. I didn't recognize this version of her. I wanted my old Karen back. I was apprehensive about this new Karen. There was no telling what this woman might do.

# CHAPTER 4

The next morning after little sleep, I rose earlier than usual for my morning run. I left the smell of hot pavement to race alongside the Missouri River next to the wildlife sanctuary in the brightening darkness. The silence, except for the river's hushed rippling, helped calm the whirr of questions, fears, and thoughts in my head. As the earliest birds called into the dark and answered each other, I became a body racing through the still air beside the constantly moving river, breathing in the fresh scent of running water.

I came often to run or sit beside the river when troubled. "We Cherokee always take our illnesses and troubles to water," Gran said. "That's why we settle near rivers and creeks. When harmony and peace are disturbed, we go to water to be restored." Once again, it worked. By the time I reached my Crown Vic, my mind had stilled from the night's squirrel cage.

A great flapping sounded from the top of one of the old oak trees by the parking lot. I watched a red-tailed hawk take wing and fly out over the river, spiraling higher into the morning sky until it soared back over me, seeming to hang immobile for a second in the brightening air. A hawk sighting always made me feel better. It was a good sign.

I headed over to the Herbal for the best breakfast in town and my first hit of caffeine before facing the chancellor and Jeremy. Interim Chancellor Willett never made a serious move without his vice chancellor of community development to steer his course. I'd need sustenance to withstand the chancellor's irrational demands and Jeremy's smooth diplomacy, which would put me even more in his debt. Getting there ahead of the usual breakfast crowd would also give me time to think about Leonard's murder now that my head had cleared, to start teasing out the tangled mess and undoing knots.

The morning air warmed as the sun rose, bringing scents of lemon balm, peppermint, and the licorice smell of anise and fennel from the big barrels of herbs that Dolores grew in front of her herb and coffee shop. I knew before the morning was half spent the air would be swimming with humidity and heat. Dawn's pastel light was still creeping over the town, but it would turn hot yellow and brassy in an hour or two.

Listening to the poignant whistle of a train in the distance, I entered the coffee shop. As the bell above the door rang, I inhaled and smiled. The Herbal always smelled like heaven or something about that good.

Dolores waved at me as she passed through the swinging doors to the kitchen. A group of kayakers from Muddy Bottoms River Outfitters fueled up for a float trip. I turned to head for my usual spot to find Annette already there with Miryam.

"How's Karen?" Annette asked as I slid into the booth next to her.

Miryam's sleepy eyes popped open. "Will she be all right? That killer didn't hurt her too badly, did he?" she asked in her breathy voice.

"He can't have." Annette's voice was flat and even. "Doc would never let her go home if she was in bad shape." She shook her head, sleek pageboy flipping from side to side. "Think, Miryam."

"I think all the time. I'm a deep thinker." Miryam's mouth made a little irritated moue. "I spend my days meditating on deep metaphysical and philosophical questions while all you do is worry about budgets and which of your faculty members is gunning for you today. So who's the thinker?"

Annette laughed uneasily. "I can't even deny that. I'm no artist any longer. Just a bureaucrat. But I still think more than you do. I can figure out the killer in most of my mysteries halfway through. You only read celebrity magazines."

"And *Cosmo* and *Vogue*. Don't forget that. They have interviews and articles. I read tons of metaphysical texts that you'd never be able to understand." Miryam yawned daintily with a satisfied smile. "Now, Skeet, tell us everything. Who hurt Karen? Why? What's going on? What are we going to do about it?"

"We're going to help Skeet catch the murderer who hurt Karen, of course. What did you think we'd do?"

I suppressed a groan. Most of the time, I appreciated their idiosyncratic personalities, but not when I had something major to investigate. Karen was usually the one who kept them out of trouble. Given her new obsession with finding Jake's hypothetical murderer, however, I didn't want her anywhere around them.

Dolores showed up to take our orders and save the day. I asked for scrambled eggs, biscuit, banana, and coffee while the others wanted omelets and tea. It's a shame I'm so hooked on coffee since I'm told Dolores's herbal teas are masterpieces, but I'm a plain old black-coffee woman.

"You haven't told us how Karen is?" Miryam leaned across the table as Dolores left for the kitchen. "Who got killed?"

"Karen will be fine. I suppose one of the EMTs is Annette's neighbor's nephew and the dispatcher a cousin of one of your regular customers." With my first murder here, I'd learned the hard way that information about crimes and crime scenes traveled the whole town in minutes on some wild gossip network.

"Is she at your house?" Annette asked as Dolores brought out cups and a pot of strong black Colombian, my drug of choice. I inhaled that rich, acrid smell as she poured it. "Did you leave her alone? Does the murderer know she saw him?"

"Of course. He's the one who beat her up, right?" Miryam shook her head at Annette. "He knows she saw him. He left her for dead."

I held up my hand to stop the flood of wild speculation. "First of all, Karen wasn't beaten up. She was hit once on the head. She's safe at her farm with her shepherd sitting guard over her. Could we please not escalate this into the fantasy realms? I haven't had enough coffee yet to deal with that." I picked up my cup and scalded my throat with hot coffee.

Annette smiled sheepishly. "I guess we do get a little carried away."

"Speak for yourself." Miryam pulled herself up against her chair back with a prim expression, suddenly playing a different role.

I learned when I first met Miryam, who'd failed as an actress in Hollywood before returning to her home state, that she always played different roles—her own life a performance. I still didn't know which role was the real Miryam.

I nodded and gulped more coffee, despite its heat. I was going to need a lot more. "Karen doesn't remember seeing the murderer. Doc says she never will." I'd use the town-gossip grapevine to get misinformation to the murderer's ears and buy time. "The blow to the head."

Both women nodded their heads, one sleek and coppery-red, the other fluffy with blond curls and waves. "Amnesia," said Miryam eagerly.

Other customers had entered as we talked. I gave my friends a stern look. "Could we be a little more discreet?" That would make them think the amnesia was a key secret. If that got out, it might help keep Karen a little safer.

Annette leaned forward conspiratorially. Her voice dropped to a husky whisper. "Who was killed?"

"A lawyer from Kansas City. Former prosecutor. Probably some criminal he sent to prison tracked him down." If a rumor must float around town, this was the least likely to interfere in my investigation.

Both women nodded with knowing looks. Dolores brought our orders. I asked for more coffee. I often worried that my need for coffee was a sign of Big Charlie Bannion's addictive personality coming out in me, that I was a coffee drunk. It could be worse. I could be a real drunk like my old man. If coffee kept me from that, I'd take it.

The Herbal was filling up. Trim, petite Dolores moved quietly and expertly around the room, taking and delivering orders. She showed up like magic to refill my almost empty coffee cup and left.

"Any clues?" Annette asked.

I sighed. "No, and I have to finish eating so I can meet with the chancellor about all this." I filled my mouth with scrambled eggs and made a big show of chewing. Both of them turned to their own plates. Silence settled on our table for a few minutes.

I was about to finish and make my good-byes when the bell over the door jangled again. We all turned to watch Walker and Terry enter. Walker waved to me. Terry touched his hat with a nod my way. I waved back as they headed to the other side of the room.

"What are that man and his henchman doing in Brewster?" Miryam asked, shivering slightly. "He was at your party. What brought the shark to these calm waters?"

Annette laughed. "Are you going poetical on us? Using similes all of a sudden."

"That was a metaphor, Annette. Similes use *like*. I'm not totally ignorant, you know." Suddenly, Miryam played a different role, inwardly laughing at Annette. I had a feeling I might be seeing the true Miryam.

"What is it about Mr. Rich and Handsome that prompted your nasty metaphor, then?" Annette asked, affronted. "How do you know him anyway?"

Miryam shrugged. "When I modeled in Kansas City, I was engaged to a dear old guy who had business dealings with Walker. We'd run into him socially. Whenever we did, Harold warned me to keep my distance. He hired an investigator to research Walker Lynch and Terry Heldrich. Terry's an ex-mercenary. What does an honest businessman need with a mercenary?"

I could practically feel my ears open wider. Someone with that background could have placed those precise shots in Leonard.

Annette shrugged. "Lots of wealthy people hire bodyguards. Your old man was probably jealous. That's why he warned you away from Walker."

"Harold wasn't jealous. He had no reason to be. I'd agreed to marry him. He learned something about Walker that left him nervous. When I asked what he'd found out, he wouldn't tell me, said he was protecting me. He said people who learned too much about Walker invariably had serious trouble, and he didn't want that for me." Miryam's forehead creased. "He was right. Shortly after that, he died unexpectedly."

"What happened to him?" Annette leaned forward in fascination. I found myself mirroring her. "Murdered? Maybe Walker's the killer in Skeet's murder."

Miryam looked distressed at the memory. I had to restrain an impulse to give her a hug. "They said it was his heart. He was supposed to have another five to seven years before things got bad enough for surgery, but his heart just gave up. The doctor said he wasn't really surprised. Then why did he tell Harold to wait for the surgery?" She shook her head slowly. "Telling the rich guy what he wanted to hear. There's a lot of that."

I sat back. Solving this murder wouldn't be that easy. When I began to look into it, I'd find that a number of people involved had been in the military or had arms training.

"I'm going to have one of Dolores's scrumptious muffins," Annette said. She looked at her watch. "We got here early to catch you. We have plenty of time for an extra treat. Will you join me?"

Miryam shook her head. "You know I don't eat sugar. It's a dangerous toxin."

I looked at my watch and jumped from my seat, slapping down bills to pay my check. "I'll be late if I don't hurry. Try to stay out of trouble, okay?"

On my way out, I looked over at Terry as he sat with Walker, bronze skin surrounded by black hair falling past his chin under a large gray fedora. Lean and muscular, a tattoo showing under the edge of his T-shirt sleeve. Nothing soft-looking about him.

Before I finished, I knew my memory would be full of bits and pieces of information about everyone involved, much of it disreputable. Almost everyone had something to hide.

Fortunately, nothing in downtown Brewster is far from Chouteau University, which broods over the town square from its hill next door and orbits Old Central, a nineteenth-century stone castle built on the top of that hill. I parked in my slot behind Old Central.

With the sun heating up the air and grass by the minute, I hurried across the quad, empty at the early hour because classes hadn't started yet. In a few weeks, this same quad would be bursting with young people.

Just inside the glass doors of New Admin, Jeremy Coulter waited. "Marquitta, let's talk before we go in there, so we both know what we want to say."

I kept moving. "Talk while we walk. I don't want to be late. There's nothing to plan. I'll tell him the truth. He'll yell at me. I'll tell him more truth. He'll threaten to fire me. If I'm lucky, he will, and I can go back to KCPD where no one blames me if a crime is committed. They just expect me to solve it."

"That's exactly what I want to avoid. Will this be like last time when you wouldn't tell the chancellor or me anything?" Though a tall man, he hustled to keep up with me.

"Nothing seems to suggest you or anyone at the university is involved, unless it's Mel." I stopped at the elevator to wait for it to arrive. "But who knows? You may be involved, for all I know. I suspect I don't know the half of what you're involved in."

"No, Marquitta, you know all of it. You're the one person in the world who knows all my secrets. And you're still my friend. I call that loyalty." He smiled at me. I wanted to shove his gleaming white teeth down his throat. Fortunately, at that moment, a loud ding signaled the approach of the elevator.

"I'm in your debt because of Brian. I can't prove what I know about you, or you'd face charges. I'm definitely not your friend." I charged ahead through the opening elevator doors. He rushed in behind me.

"But you won't keep me blacked out of this investigation. That means I can keep the chancellor under control." In the close quarters of the elevator, I noticed Jeremy's expensive cologne. I avoided looking at him as we clicked up through the floors and stopped with another ding on the sixth. Jeremy trailed behind me as I led the way to the chancellor's suite. He sounded suspiciously like he was chuckling behind my back.

The outer office where the chancellor's secretary and executive assistant worked sat empty, and we walked straight into the chancellor's office. I expected to find the mayor, who also headed the board of trustees, with him, but Willett waited alone for us, as enraged as he was six months earlier when I explained that the editor of the student newspaper had been killed. We weren't making much progress, I was afraid.

"Jeremy, thank you for coming. Chief Bannion, what the hell is going on now?" The chancellor came out from behind his desk.

"Marquitta assures me this is not like the last one." Jeremy smiled and used his smoothest, most calming voice. "The man came from Kansas City. It's just bad luck he was killed on our property. There's no reason to believe anyone at the university had anything to do with this."

"Except possibly Dean Melvin of the Law School," I added. Jeremy frowned. "He knew the victim. They were friends and worked together in the U.S. attorney's office for years."

Willett's face grew pink. "Are you telling me my new law dean is under suspicion in a murder?"

"That's where we look for suspects—among people who knew the victim, worked with the victim, or were friends or family of the victim. Melvin qualifies on all counts."

The chancellor's face swelled and reddened. "Are you serious? Mel Melvin's a war hero who almost became our state attorney general. He was the U.S. attorney and may quite possibly be our governor someday."

"Not if he killed Leonard Klamath, I hope."

Jeremy shook his head wildly at me behind Willett's back. "I think what Marquitta's trying to say is that it's important for the university's reputation and for Dean Melvin's career that she not seem to be granting him favors. That she visibly investigate him as thoroughly as any other suspects. Caesar's wife and all that, sir."

Willett's face subsided slightly back toward its normal state. I was glad he wasn't going to stroke on us while I was there.

"And because he's the only one on campus who possibly could be involved," Jeremy continued, "Marquitta will be able to share her progress in the investigation with us more than she could last time." Jeremy's words were slightly hurried, rushing to prevent another explosion from either side.

Jeremy's words calmed Willett. "You'll keep me informed through Jeremy?"

I nodded. "No problem with that this time. No vice chancellors involved. At least not to my knowledge."

Jeremy rolled his eyes.

"How will you handle the media?" Willett asked.

I relaxed a little. "Like before. Frank Booth can handle the media with the help of Jeremy's staff. My investigators are witnessing the autopsy right now and should be back soon with information. The county crime techs are working on evidence found at the scene of the crime. We have a good, solid investigation under way."

At the words *county crime techs,* Willett opened his mouth as if to yell, so I spoke right over him. He relaxed. Must have remembered what I told him last time. If we didn't use county crime scene techs, I'd have to bring in KCPD's techs. Maybe this meeting wouldn't be so bad, after all.

"We'll try to keep a lid on the media," Jeremy reassured him.

"No press conferences this time." Willett blanched as if reliving the disastrous press conference he'd pressured me into during the last murder investigation.

"I wouldn't recommend it," I agreed. Jeremy frowned and shook his head at me. "Let Jeremy's people find the right way to word what we absolutely have to tell them and give it to Frank to get it across to them. We'll work as quietly and as quickly as we can. You can have a press conference when we have the killer behind bars."

Willett opened his mouth as if to make a demand but closed it without saying anything. Since he was actually being halfway reasonable, I decided to toss him a bone.

"I don't see anything remotely like campus involvement. That could change, of course. Melvin has a long history with this man. But at this stage, it doesn't look as if anyone else at the university could be involved."

"Thank God!" Willett squared his shoulders again and threw back his thick white mane. "Get this solved and out of our hair, Bannion. It's the last thing we need right now."

Murder was always the last thing anyone needed, but I refrained from telling him that.

# CHAPTER 5

I hit my office ahead of all but the night shift in for shift change. My secretary, Mary Boudreaux, was bewildered to find me already there when she arrived. "What's going on, Skeet?"

I explained about the murder and the early Monday-morning meeting with the chancellor. Halfway through my tale, my second-in-command, Captain Frank Booth, joined us.

Frank's not an investigator; he's an administrator, which was why I'd been hired for the job he thought he should have had. We've had our ups and downs, Frank and I, but when blood's on the ground, we're both good cops. We make it work.

"You do know we never had a murder before you came, don't you?" Frank asked.

I nodded. "It looks like they hired me just in time, doesn't it?"

He rolled his eyes and slurped some more coffee while Mary smothered a laugh.

By the time I was coming to the end of the night's story, Gil Mendez and Trish Cassell came in from the coroner's office. Until recently, Gil had been my only investigator. I'd sent Trish and another officer for investigative training in Kansas City, and she was just back and eager to get her hands dirty in a real case. I'm not sure witnessing the autopsy our retired part-time coroner did on Leonard was exactly the way she'd expected to begin.

"Good timing," I said as they walked in. "Fill us in on what Sid had to say at the autopsy."

Mary scurried out to her desk and closed the door behind her. Gil took out his notebook. "Shot with a .357-caliber gun twice. Either shot would have killed him, but the shot from the front was probably the first. Shooter was maybe three feet away from the victim."

"It's slack time before the semester begins, and it was a Sunday night, but maybe someone heard that shot reverberating in the Caves." I was thinking out loud and caught myself. "Go ahead, Gil."

"Not much more. Victim was intoxicated at time of death. Signs of severe cirrhosis of the liver from chronic alcoholism. Sid's sending the usual samples to Regional Crime Lab for tox screens but doesn't expect to find much more." Gil closed his notebook.

"Not much more is about right." I caught myself and tried to smooth the frustration from my voice. "Nothing much from the autopsy. There won't be much from the crime scene, either, I'll bet. All stone. The Caves were a perfect place to kill him and leave no trace. A pro couldn't have planned this better. Yet it was a spur-of-the-moment choice of the victim to go there. No one could have planned for Leonard blowing his silence at this party out here near the campus during the dead intersession time. It's all coincidence, but it all worked for the killer."

"If he was a drunk while he was assistant U.S. attorney, he might have been dirty." Frank leaned forward, pulling his chair a little closer to my desk in his enthusiasm. "This could be a professional hit. A pro learns what's going on in the target's life and plans around it."

I nodded and gestured for Gil and Trish to take seats. "The only problem with that theory is it makes Leonard's blowup at the party into just a coincidence. One coincidence too many on top of these others."

I stood and stretched my lower back. "I'll get a list of everyone Leonard put in prison and all the cases he worked because I don't believe in ignoring anything. But I'm starting to think he was knocked off because of what he said while drunk last night."

I walked over to my big whiteboard with cork strip above, pulled off everything pinned up on it, and started erasing the parking structure figures and timeline.

"What you told us he said out loud wasn't much. 'You don't even know about Jake.'" Frank shook his head.

"Put it together with what he told Karen privately about Jake being murdered, and it's way too much if someone involved in Jake's death heard. Did someone there follow and kill him or call someone else to come in and kill him?"

"Unlikely. The murder happened so soon after he opened his drunk mouth." Gil looked as if he'd rather not have said that.

I nodded. "It had to be someone at the party who followed him. Unless whoever it was planned to kill him on the road back, say, and had someone waiting nearby to follow him. Planned or impromptu, it was tricky, and all the damn breaks went their way."

I turned to the whiteboard and started a list of names down the side. Mel Melvin, Liz Richar, Randy Thorsson, Walker Lynch, Terry Heldrich. I looked at Frank. "Some high-powered names here. If the media find out any of these people are possible suspects, your job's going to get very difficult."

Frank grimaced. "Let's try to keep it all under wraps."

I looked over at Trish and explained. "These are the people at the party who knew Leonard from his time with Jake and Mel. I'll write all the questions as we think of them or encounter them. We'll tie them to one or more of the names on the side. As we investigate, we'll clear first one, then another, until—we hope— only the murderer will be left."

Inhaling the smell of the markers for a second, I took another look, then slowly added my own name, Karen's, and Sid's. When I turned back, three pairs of eyes questioned me. "The three of us knew Leonard back then also."

"That's right," said Gil. "When Sid was in the Kansas City ME's office."

I nodded. "Back when Sid was off the wagon, he and Leonard were institutional drunks together. Now, Sid wasn't at the party, Karen couldn't have pistol-whipped herself, and I was with Joe Louzon at the time of the murder in plain sight of half the town, but we did know him then. That may connect up somehow."

"Glad to see you've got a solid alibi," Frank said with a little smile. "After last spring, I wouldn't want to be the one who had to take you in."

Gil grinned at Trish and me. "I'm with Frank. If it comes time to take down Skeet, you'll have to do it, Trish. I value my undamaged body too much to go up against her." Trish laughed and blushed immediately.

I rolled my eyes. "Isn't it fortunate we don't have to worry about that?"

I started writing questions on the board. Who left the party early? Where did the gun come from? What did Leonard know? Was Jake murdered? If so, who killed him and why? Why not kill Karen, too?

"On that last one, Chief, could it be the killer didn't have time? You can see someone coming up that road quite a while before they get there." Trish's tone was hesitant.

"Good point. So he knocks out Karen and flees. How'd he escape?" I wrote that on the board.

"Depends on whether he was on foot or in a car." Gil bit on his pen as he stared at the board, then pointed. "Leonard walked to the Caves, and Karen followed on foot. The killer could have followed Leonard, not knowing Karen was behind him. He could have slipped out the entrance and on up the hill in the dark."

"So who'd he see coming? Karen was hit while on the phone to me. It wasn't my car he saw coming up that road." I wrote "Whose car?" on the board.

We spent another hour, asking one another these questions and others. I drew a schematic with times around the murder point. Lines connected names to Leonard. I had printed my list of questions on one side and then drew lines to the names on the other side that were involved with each question. As Frank, Gil, and Trish brought up new questions, the whiteboard looked like someone had drawn a map on it. I felt my brain clicking on in this case. But I knew this was just the beginning.

Later in the morning after calling my old boss at KCPD Homicide and asking for copies of Jake's files, I was ready to leave when I got a call from my ex-husband, Sam Musco.

"Skeet, don't forget the new nurse's aide is going to start with Charlie today. She'll stay until you get there, so she can meet and talk to you." Sam's low, husky voice sounded less honeyed than usual.

"Yeah. I need to get there a little early. Thanks for reminding me. It's a little crazy here. I'm not sure I'd have remembered." I felt my lips tighten. "I don't want to start on the wrong foot with her."

"Let's wait for Charlie to do that. It shouldn't take long." Sam sounded worn-out.

"I hope to God he doesn't drive this one away." I closed my eyes. "We'll run out of people and places to work with him."

"Cheer up. I have a feeling he'll like this one. Heard you caught a corpse up there again? Klamath from the U.S. attorney's office?" Sam was still with KCPD. He too often listened to my department's frequency on scanner.

I leaned my head back against my desk chair. "At least it wasn't in my house. He was at that damn party Karen made me give Mel."

Sam chuckled. That brought him right into the room with me, golden-brown hair falling into flirtatious eyes and the little twist at the corners of his mouth. "Giving parties for the almost attorney general. You sure have moved on beyond me. I'd love to have seen that. I'll bet you were pouting in the corner all night long."

"I don't pout. You know that. I just get pissed off sometimes."

"Sometimes?" He chuckled again. Then his voice turned serious. "Listen, if this case gets going heavy, and you need to switch times with Charlie, just let me know. I can probably do it if I've got a little notice."

I closed my eyes. "Thanks. I'll try not to take you up on that. You have your own life."

"Hell, Charlie's the closest thing to a dad I've ever had. We're in this together." The fact that we were no longer married and the divorce had never been what he wanted hung between us for a long silence after that.

"I'll get there early tonight. I'll try not to have to take you up on your offer. But I appreciate it, Sam."

"You watch yourself." His voice paused for a second. "I've got a vested interest in your survival. I don't want to have to take over Charlie's care one hundred percent."

I laughed softly. "I'm always careful. You know that."

I knew he was thinking about the last murder I'd investigated. I'd been shot three times in that one and only survived because of my Kevlar vest and a good surgeon. I am careful, though. I'm no cowboy. Don't have to impress anyone.

Sometimes, though, you can be levelheaded, and circumstances force you to put yourself on the line. I hoped to avoid those kinds of circumstances this time around.


The Brewster Wildlife Sanctuary extended in a long triangle between the original town site and the river. For decades, town boosters and businessmen cursed old Dolph Brewster for leaving that strip of land in trust, preventing the town from accessing riverfront land for industrial development.

Now, outdoor enthusiasts who spent money in town were drawn by the wildlife sanctuary. As a buffer, it'd saved the heart of the town from massive damage in at least five major twentieth-century floods. Dolph didn't look like such a dummy today.

The Wickbrook subdivision, newest and most expensive in town, caused a storm of protest when the developer laid it out across the north side of the wildlife sanctuary. The developer knew he could sell custom home lots with a wilderness view for a premium, and the town government wanted the tax revenues and jobs the project would bring. What I thought most reprehensible was the ugliness of houses in that project, huge eyesores against a backdrop of natural beauty.

I parked in front of a house that could have been designed by the architect of all the awful buildings of the 1960s. Who on earth paid a fortune for a beautiful wild view to plop a concrete warehouse on it? I would have thought Liz, at least, would have better taste than that.

Trudging from the street to the front door left perspiration dripping down my back and bits of hair stuck to my sweaty cheeks. From this distance the sound of trains, constant soundtrack to life in Brewster, faded. Wickbrook was truly sheltered.

Angie Melvin opened the front door, frowning, in an electric-blue bikini that matched part of her hair. Brian stood in the room behind her. What was he doing here? I now knew she wasn't a street kid as I'd first assumed, but she was older and troubled—no doubt about that. I didn't like having Brian around her.

"Angie, I've come to speak with your parents."

She shrugged and let me in. "The only parent you'll find here is good old asshat Mel. Denise is still in the hospital in a chemically induced stupor. Liz is no relation to me. Or probably to anyone else, for that matter." She turned her back and started to walk away. "My best guess," she called over her shoulder, "is that she's an alien construct found on the moon and brought back to escape and masquerade as a human being."

I dropped a stern look over my face to cover my impulse to laugh. "Please let your father know I'm here." I glanced over at Brian. "What are you doing here, Bri?"

"Angie called to remind me she still had my Nintendo DS, so I walked over to pick it up." He smiled and looked at Angie. "I didn't realize how wilted I'd be when I got here. Angie's been pouring liquids back into me."

"It was stupid to be out in this heat, walking." She frowned at him. "You could have given yourself heatstroke or something. You need to learn to use that stuff taking up space in your skull, dude."

I smiled at both of them. "She's right. It's way too hot right now to go walking. I'll give you a ride back. When I finish talking to Mel and Liz."

Angie moved toward a hallway and shouted. "Mel! You got a visitor. Mel! Get a move on! It's the KGB." She turned to Brian. "Come on. I'll get you another lemonade."

Brian looked at me. "Skeet, you want one?" I nodded. "Angie makes this killer lemonade with fresh lemon juice."

Angie's face flushed under the heavy makeup. "Mom—Denise taught me how when I was little." She gestured Brian to follow her, and they left through the dining room end of the great room.

I watched them disappear around a corner, hoping they'd bring the lemonade soon.

"Skeet!" Mel erupted from the hallway with Walker and Terry right behind him. "How's Karen? What happened last night?"

Behind the men, Liz appeared at a slower pace. Her golden-girl skin, white sundress, and sandals turned her into a model of all the perfect, airbrushed summer that money could buy. Mel sweated in a knit polo shirt and Bermuda shorts, as if his middle-class body's radio hadn't received the same messages of perfection and cool that his wife's had. Walker was on Liz's wavelength, though. Something out of *Gatsby* for the twenty-first century.

Terry wore camo cutoffs and an army-olive T-shirt with worn deck shoes on bare feet. He wasn't just on the wrong station. He didn't even have a radio. Yet, with his hyperalertness, strong body, and confidence, he was the most attractive of them all.

"God, it's hot!" Mel complained as he drew nearer, even though the air-conditioning in his concrete mansion was frigid.

"Sit down, sit down. Liz, we need something to drink. Where's Maria? What do you want, Skeet? A beer? Glass of wine? Walker? Terry? Your usual?"

"Maria's doing the grocery shopping." Liz stood with an expression of distaste, watching us all seat ourselves on the expensive leather furniture. I took a chair, as did Walker, while Mel flopped on the couch and patted the spot next to him for Liz. Terry sank gracefully to the floor next to my chair and sat with his legs crossed like a yogi, looking up at me from under surprisingly long lashes. I looked away when I realized I'd noticed.

Angie and Brian appeared, carrying three glasses of lemonade. Brian brought one of them to me, and I thanked them both.

"Angie, go bring your father and Terry chilled beers and pour Walker and me glasses of that Riesling in the refrigerator. You can use one of the serving trays to bring them in." Liz turned her back on the girl as soon as she'd given the order and sat next to Mel.

Angie's face turned crimson under the makeup. She glared at Liz, then whipped around and left the room, pulling Brian behind her by his shirtsleeve. Neither Mel nor Liz noticed Angie's fury, but I didn't think she'd bring any drinks.

"Tell me—" began Mel, wiping his broad face on the short sleeve of his shirt.

I spoke right over him. "Walker, you knew Leonard Klamath well, didn't you?"

Walker hesitated. "I hadn't seen him in years. I was appalled at the deterioration. I wouldn't say I knew him well. Certainly knew him socially and professionally, but at a distance."

"Terry, did you know him also?"

Terry shook his head. "We were introduced once. Saw him at events with Walker. We never really spoke. I'll not be much help to you, I suspect." Again, I sensed American English was not his first language.

He smiled up at me, eyes full of secrets. I looked away.

Liz fixed her eye on an unwanted insect, me. "I barely knew the nasty drunk."

"Liz! Leonard was my friend, a darned good prosecutor." Mel turned to me. "What's going on? We heard Karen was attacked and Leonard killed."

"What was Jake working on when he died?" I fired right back.

Mel pulled back in surprise. "Jake? He died four years ago."

I nodded. "It's possibly connected. What was Jake's project when he died?"

"Because of the crazy stuff Leonard spouted last night? Fumes from his pickled brain." Mel frowned.

Liz pouted. "I thought he was your friend, a darned good prosecutor."

"Better than that damn Randy Thorsson." Mel's face reddened in mottled patches. "Idiot!"

I did a double take. Mel jealous of Randy? Walker hid a grin. Terry lounged against my chair.

Liz smiled coldly. "I've told you, Mel. I've no interest in the man. I can't help it if he hangs around."

So! It was Liz Randy ran after at the party.

"His tongue hanging out like a hound after a bitch in heat." Mel's mottling grew worse. Liz's cold smile enlarged. "Another man's wife. No shame, no sense. Leaving messages on our home phone."

"I don't dispute what you say," Liz said. She smoothed her magazine-perfect hair. "He's amusing when I'm bored."

I choked. Randy? Amusing? I could detect a hint of mirth on Terry's face. Walker laughed outright.

Mel's eyes bulged. "When you're bored with me?"

Poor Mel—dull as he was, he stood head and shoulders above Randy. Not to mention his actual competence as an attorney.

Liz glanced at me, as if to say, *Do you see what I put up with?* "When I'm bored with business talk."

"The only business I talk is politics," Mel said fiercely. "You'd rather talk politics than eat or sleep."

She shrugged, a beautiful motion, a movie star shrug, expressing indifference, contempt, total arrogance in one graceful movement.

"It's not always about you, what you say or do." She stood up. "At a party where men talk business, I'll be bored. Randy's chatter amuses me. You're not the center of the world." She examined him as if he were an exotic animal, shrugging in that remarkable way again. "You're not, in fact, the center of anything."

Turning, she sauntered back down the hall, her steps gliding as smoothly as any model's on a runway. Mel stared after her. Maybe he'd just figured out what he'd married. Maybe he still hadn't. Either way, lust or love, he needed her money behind him and her perfect image beside him if he wanted this political career. Because Mel without Liz was just Mel and never enough in the world of major politics.

I tapped his shoulder. "Back to my question. What was Jake working on when he fell down all those steps in the courthouse late at night?"

"He'd worked late for months." Mel turned to me in anger. "You know better than to pay attention to anything a drunk says."

I shrugged, just an ordinary shrug, not a whole dramatic conversation like Liz's.

Standing, Walker gave me a questioning look, asking to be excused. When I nodded, he left. Terry glided to his feet. I'm pretty fit, but I couldn't have done that. He fixed his eyes on my face for a second. Finally, he padded after Walker like a big cat that's not quite tame.

I turned back to Mel. "I have to pay attention if Leonard's murdered right after saying something. What was Jake working on?"

He took a deep breath. "Jake had started the human trafficking task force for western Missouri."

I vaguely recalled Jake mentioning this. Caught up in marital and new-administrator problems of my own, had I not paid enough attention?

Mel licked his full lips. I'd been right about no drinks coming. "It was his baby. He fought for it. Got the funding, much of it from Walker's foundation. Got other agencies to cooperate. He'd worked on it for months, just getting it started. Nothing was going on with it yet. It was just getting off the ground."

He leaned toward me. "It was too early. Nothing there led to his death. Which was accidental."

"Human trafficking? Sex trade?" I didn't want that hitting Brewster. We were too close to KC to avoid the crime overflow, but organized stuff usually stayed in the city.

"The part that always gets the press, sure. The real story of human trafficking is forced labor. All kinds. Essentially slavery. According to Jake, lots in Missouri."

A border state, Missouri was torn apart before and during the Civil War over slavery. Hell, KC was deliberately burned to the ground, the reason no buildings predating the war were left. How could slavery happen here again?

"Is that task force still operating?"

Mel nodded. "We've actually had good prosecutions. More than anywhere else in the country. Most came after I left the office and started my campaign, but the task force started under me, thanks to Jake. Most of the work for those prosecutions was done under me. Not as much as Jake had hoped, of course. A couple of sensational sex schemes. Two small forced-labor setups. Penny-ante compared to the big operations Jake wanted to go after. Trafficking's hard as hell to prove. Jake was on the right track, though."

I scribbled in my notebook. "Did Leonard work on this with Jake?"

He shook his head. "Jake consulted us, but it was his project. I moved Leonard in charge of it when Jake died. Leonard wanted to retire. Jake's death shook him. I asked him to stay until I got a replacement. In a few months I brought in a guy I'd worked with as assistant U.S. attorney in Virginia."

He watched me write. When I stopped and looked up again, he leaned toward me. "What is all this? I don't care what Leonard said, even if he was killed right afterward. Jake's death was accidental."

I sighed. "Could be. But it's all reopened now with Leonard's murder." I sat back and gulped some of Angie's lemonade. Brian was right. It cooled my whole body as it slid down my throat. Mel licked his lips. "So Walker funded this task force on human trafficking?"

Mel nodded, looking weary and much older. "His foundation. The folks who get trafficked are people he helps—runaways, homeless, immigrants. If you want bodies for forced labor, that's where you go."

I chewed lightly on the tip of my pen, considering all the charity functions where I'd seen Walker.

"Once Jake got that foundation funding, the government turned some extra money loose. Other agencies wanted to cooperate." Mel shook his head, a sad look on his broad face. "If Jake hadn't died, he'd have been able to parlay that task force into a U.S. attorney position somewhere. Maybe even Kansas City when I retired."

He wiped his face on his shirtsleeve again. "It was a damn shame he fell down those stairs."

I closed my eyes. More than a shame. A devastation. From what I'd seen last night, Karen still hadn't recovered from it. I began to fear she might never do so.

We both stared ahead, lost in separate thoughts for a second. Mel had aged a decade while we talked.

"So Walker knew Jake in more than just a social way?"

Mel shook his head like a dog coming out of the rain. "Sure. Jake convinced him of the need for his task force."

I needed to question Walker more thoroughly. I checked my watch. It would have to wait. "Will Walker be staying with you for another day?"

Mel smiled, coming to life again. "He and Terry are staying with us for another week."

My eyebrows lifted. A long visit for someone within easy commuting distance.

"We're strategizing for the next election. I'm going for Missouri attorney general again. This time, I'll win. You have to start way early, raising money."

I drank the last of the lemonade with regret that there wasn't more. "I want to talk with Walker in more detail. He made it sound as if he didn't know Jake."

Mel's face closed. "I don't think you'll get much. Jake and Walker had some kind of falling-out before Jake died. He didn't want much to do with Walker all of a sudden. Walker didn't know what he did to bother Jake. He tried to get me to find out so he could fix it. He liked Jake."

Everyone liked Jake. For just a second, the grief I'd felt at the loss of that sweet man, who showed me how a good father acted, rose up and almost overwhelmed me. I pushed it back down with a fear that, like Karen, I hadn't come to grips with my grief.

"Jake wouldn't tell me," Mel continued. "He said there was nothing." He shook his head. "But you could see he didn't like the guy anymore."

"That's not . . . That wasn't like Jake." I stared at Mel. "He was a pussycat. Jake liked everyone." I thought, *Jake even liked you.*

Leaning forward with elbows on bare knees, Mel supported his chin on his left palm. "I never could figure it out. Walker's such a great guy. Neither's the type to disagree or get their feelings bent out of shape." He gazed at something distant in space or time. "Jake wasn't feeling well. He had those dizzy spells. When we tried to get him to the doctor, he snapped at Leonard and me. Even Linda—you remember? The secretary? Toward the end, he hardly spoke to Leonard, avoided him as much as he could. Jake was never like that."

I sighed. "He was a little irritated when Karen and I tried to get him checked for the dizziness." Karen told me she thought Jake was afraid he had cancer. Denial, she said one afternoon in a teary phone call just one or two days before Jake died. Ironically, the autopsy showed hypertension was the cause of the dizziness. Simple high blood pressure.

"Before he died, Jake stopped having anything to do with Walker and Leonard?" I tried to get the questioning back on track.

"He wasn't Jake," Mel repeated.

Silence fell. I watched Mel, his attention increasingly drawn to the hallway down which Liz had vanished. I had everything I was going to get from him now.

"Was there anyone Leonard had pissed off while with the U.S. attorney's office? Someone with a grudge. Probably in prison until recently."

Mel looked at me, face brightening. "That's the right trail to follow. A recently released con."

"Who?" I was tired of everyone wanting this to be some anonymous ex-con. Unlike movie and TV villains, most guys just out of prison didn't go gunning for the prosecutor or judge who put them away. Not for the cops involved, either. Maybe witnesses or victims but not folks protected by the system.

Mel shrugged. "Could be any of them. I can't remember all Leonard's cases. No idea who's just out."

Of course. Just John Angry-Criminal Doe. "I have a meeting this afternoon with KCPD. They'll have that info for me." I tucked my notebook into my pocket. "Thanks. I'll run Brian home before I head out to the city."

Mel held up his hands quickly. "Let him stay. Angie hasn't had a chance to make new friends yet since school just started. She and Brian are in the same class, you know."

I stared at him in surprise. "I thought she was older than Bri. He's a year young for his grade because he started school early. I thought Angie was older than the rest of his classmates."

He shook his head. "She's only fifteen. She was held back because she missed too many classes last year. Angie's a smart kid. She started school a year early like Brian did, but if she's running around trying to find and take care of her idiot mom and missing school, she's not going to have the chance to do well." He shook his head, face mottled with anger again.

"I didn't know." I'd figured Angie for at least seventeen. The smart part, yes. A very bright kid who was angry, sad, and hurt.

He stared toward the dining room where Angie had disappeared with Brian. "I know what Denise spread around town about me. How I drove her to a breakdown. But she endangered our daughter. That's why I fought for Angie's custody."

"I didn't really know anything about it." I thought he'd rather hear that than, *Yes, Denise trashed your name all over the city.*

He stood, aiming a distressed glance in the direction Liz had gone. "Liz isn't thrilled with a fifteen-year-old stepdaughter who hates her guts living here. It's not easy for me, either." He looked back at me, and his jaw firmed. "But Denise is going down the skids. I won't let her take Angie."

For the first time, I could see what Jake saw in him. The man was willing to risk his reputation to protect his kid.

His face softened again. "Brian's a nice normal friend for her, instead of the crumbs Denise hung with. Let him stay to talk and play computer games. We'll feed him and deliver him home tonight. What time will you be back?"

I wasn't thrilled about Angie as Brian's playmate, but he'd lost most of his friends because of what he went through earlier in the year. This might be good for both of them.

"I should be home by nine P.M. You can take him back earlier, if you want. He has a key, and Lady will keep him safe." I breathed a sigh of gratitude. Last winter I was afraid—for good reason—to leave Brian alone with anyone who wasn't an armed police officer. Thank heavens that nightmare was over. "Let me make sure he's okay with this. I don't want him feeling abandoned." Brian had been through too much. No way would I leave him with someone for even an afternoon without checking with him.

Mel nodded. "Angie!" he bellowed.

After a minute, both kids came trailing into the great room.

"You roared?" Angie replied with her head tilted quizzically on her shoulders.

I stood. "Bri, Mel's invited you to stay with Angie while I go to KC to meet with Dan Wheelwright and Charlie and Sam. He'll take you home later. Okay?"

Brian made a small grimace. "I hate to go to Charlie's."

Angie's face leaped out of its deadpan mask into that of an excited teen girl before lapsing back. "Whatever. Go ahead and stay. Keep the grown-ups out of my hair."

Brian didn't like my dad. Much of the time, I didn't like my dad, though I loved him. Brian also didn't like my ex. The expectations Sam and Charlie had for me and the things they said to me pissed him off. Smart kid. I got pissed off, too, but grown-ups had to deal with them anyway.

"We can catch up on our homework together for tomorrow." His face lit up when Angie agreed. Brian really liked Angie—as just a friend, I hoped. I'd have to learn to like her myself.

"That's your idea of a good time with an older woman?" Angie's voice was as scornful as if she were thirty. "You have so much to learn."

I'd have laughed if I wasn't worried what Angie might teach my good kid.

Mel's face brightened at the mention of schoolwork. "Good. Get your homework done. Catch up after last night at the hospital with—"

"Settled." Angie whisked Brian out of the room.

Mel watched her, sighing. "Denise comes out here to OD in the front yard, so Angie can drive her to the ER without a license. What kind of mother does that to her kid?"

I didn't know what to say. I used to resent my own mother, but she'd never done anything like that. The older I got, the less I could justify that resentment. I pushed that thought away.

Mel sighed. "Okay. That's settled." He turned back to me.

"This move to Brewster is what Angie needs. Quiet town. Decent friends. The stability I want her to have."

I smiled. Mel echoed my own thoughts. After all Brian had gone through, I'd do anything to give him stability and security. "Brewster's a good spot for that. Give her some time."

He walked me to the door. "She wanted to be a U.S. attorney like me, you know. Had her career all planned out. Harvard Law School. Now, I pray I can get her through high school."

"It'll all work out. Tell Walker I'll be out tomorrow to talk with him."

He nodded, his eyes narrowed with concern.

Walking into the force field of heat, I gave a prayer of thanks to the god of air-conditioning once I was in my car.

Jake had been building a task force to go after modern-day slavery. Quite a motive for murder. What if Jake learned more than anyone now knew, even on the task force? What if he kept it to himself because it was dangerous? That was Jake. Take all the danger upon himself. That danger only lay quiescent after his death. It had reared its head again to destroy Leonard.

Who would be next? Karen? Not if I could help it.

# CHAPTER 6

I checked with the office on my way out of town. Gil and Trish were tracking down the guests at the party with no connection to Leonard, seeing if they noticed anyone's early departure and if they could pin down where the key players were when Karen called.

It's fifteen minutes to downtown Kansas City from downtown Brewster, ten minutes longer than it should be. There's constant construction around Riverside, slowing the trip. Without Dolph's buffer of wild land, Riverside floods regularly. The Corps of Engineers builds more and more structures to protect it from flooding.

Just before reaching Riverside, I passed a spot where last spring's flood took out a guardrail, pulling a car into the river's maw. The Corps was active there, building a levee between river and highway embankment. They never replaced the guardrail with anything but construction cones and orange-striped wooden barricades. They were only halfway up to the highway with the levee. They wouldn't replace that guardrail until it was done. At night or when the weather was bad, only orange cones, flimsy barricades, and drivers' expertise kept cars from flying into the river, an accident waiting to happen. Since I could do nothing about it, I tried not to think about it and headed into the city.

My old Homicide partners were meeting me at Los Alamos, a hole-in-the-wall Mexican market and café southwest of downtown on the Westside, the old Mexican neighborhood going back to the 1890s. Now, it was turning into an extension of the trendy Crossroads Art District. Gentrification. Next door to Los Alamos a hip new restaurant/bar recently opened. Across the street, the Bluebird Café had been one of the earliest to see the opportunities of this poor neighborhood on the edge of the now expensive Crossroads—low rents and real estate prices, eccentric, colorful businesses and homes.

Los Alamos stubbornly stuck to its corner, continuing to serve the best breakfast burritos in town and a delicious assortment of authentic Mexican meals for lunch and dinner to its working-class customers amid its shelves of groceries and household goods. I greeted the rows of rusty metal mariachi sculptures at its entrance with pleasure. Los Alamos, still around and still the same.

Inside, beyond the shelves of fresh corn and flour tortillas, bottled *frescas*, and canned soups, I dodged past the corner beer fridge and caught up with my old partners as they finished turning in orders for carne asada and chile relleno.

Dan Wheelwright still looked like he did when I first joined his squad. Back then, I thought he reminded me of RAF pilots in World War II movies. He still did. He was barely taller than me, but his big hug almost pulled me off my feet.

"Good to see you, Skeet."

Hoag Masters overshadowed us, dwarfing both Dan and me. "What kind of trouble'd you bring us this time, girl? You better have some bright socks on to make it up to me."

I pulled up my slacks leg and posed like a pinup girl, flashing him with red, orange, and pink striped hand-knit socks. "They call this Crazy Candy."

Dan laughed. Hoag stared. "Hoo, girl! Those are some wild socks. Remember the time old Major Pantoune caught you with those rainbow socks. I thought he'd throw the book at you. You're lucky you're fine-looking 'cause a man or ugly chick would still be working off punishment."

"What I remember is Dan threatening to make me teach you to knit." I held up imaginary knitting needles in my hands.

"Just wanted him to do as good a job with his cases as you did with yours. You said knitting helped you think. I figured Hoag could use all the help with thinking that he could get. It's foreign to his nature, you know." Dan grinned as Hoag shot him the bird. Some might think Hoag was just big muscle, but Dan and I knew he was as sharp as they come.

We laughed at the memories. We'd been through years of cases and stress together. We'd been a hell of a team.

I turned to Conchita and put in my order for pozole with corn tortillas and a cup of their good Mexican coffee with cinnamon, then headed over to the booth. Hoag took up one side, and Dan scooted over to make room for me on the other.

Dan pointed to a box of files sitting on the floor beside the booth.

"Leonard's cases?" I sighed. How would I ever get through all that? Delegate some to officers and Mary when they weren't busy elsewhere. I knew in my gut all that work would be wasted. Jake's death was behind this. No matter how much I wanted Dan to tell me otherwise.

Dan shook the box. "I asked around. None of Klamath's cons threatened to come hunting him afterward. Mostly white-collar. It's going to be the folks you had up there that night."

I nodded. "Then it had to be Jake's death was really murder."

"I don't know about that." Dan pointed to a file on the table in front of him. "I've been over his file like a mouse looking for crumbs. They didn't just call it a day. Jake was a favorite. No one was going to skimp on his death."

I nodded. "But that has to be it. Leonard comes to a town he's hardly ever been in, gets drunk, and says Jake was killed. Immediately after that, he's murdered by someone professional. What's that sound like to you?"

"Hell of a coincidence if it's some ex-con out to get him," said Hoag. "How'd he know where to go? How'd he know about your cave-thing? Hell, I didn't know about that! We got some of those here, but who knew that college had one?"

"He could have followed Klamath to Brewster and then to the Caves." Dan rubbed his hand over his mouth and lower face. "Sure makes for one hell of a coincidence—and I hate coincidences."

"You see where I am. Stuck." I grabbed Jake's file and read over it.

Jake died in one of the most secure buildings in the city, the federal courthouse. Security scans with armed federal marshals just to get into the lobby. Then everyone had to sign in and out before going to the elevators or stairs. It was late, everyone but janitorial staff and night marshals signed out and gone home. No one was in the building who wasn't supposed to be.

Because of the building's emptiness, he lay dead at the foot of the upper two flights of stairs for at least an hour. No drugs or toxins in his body. No one drugged him and threw him down the stairs.

I looked up at Dan. "No sign of struggle or force, according to the autopsy report. How could they tell? He'd tumbled down two long flights of hard marble stairs with all kinds of bruises, cuts, and scrapes. How'd they know they were caused by the fall and not by struggling against someone?"

Dan shook his head. "There weren't any inconsistent with the fall?"

"Hell, someone could knock him out and toss him down the stairs." I frowned at the report in my hand. Not to consider the possibility that some of those injuries could have resulted from an attack seemed sloppy.

Dan spread his hands. "Who? The only people in the building were two janitors and two marshals. Vetted by the feds. No connections of any kind to Jake."

I sniffed. "Wouldn't be the first time someone with a security clearance was turned. That's happened again and again."

Dan closed his eyes for a second and shook his head slightly. "I know. I know. I don't like it. But it sure looks like everyone's clean."

"Can I have a copy of this autopsy report? I want to talk with Sid Ambrose about it." I handed it back to him.

"Sid didn't do that autopsy." Dan shoved the paper back to me.

"But he knew the guy who did. He can read between the lines of these things." MEs were like cops—some at the top of their game and some just jumping through hoops without real thought.

Dan pointed to the file. "I copied the whole Jake file. That's yours. Leonard's cases came from the feds. We have to pass on hefty copy fees they charged. Hoag and I looked through them quick and dirty. Nothing there to connect with Klamath's murder."

Hoag nodded. "Klamath handled mostly white-collar cases. They don't risk themselves once they get out. Too busy digging up the money they squirreled away. Getting on with their lives."

I closed my eyes in frustration. Everything seemed determined to prove Karen right. I didn't want that. I worried how far she'd go in her obsession if I had to say, *Yes, Jake was murdered.*

I realized I'd left Dan and Hoag just sitting there after they had gone out of their way to help me. "Guys, I really appreciate it. I'm just stupid with worry about Karen right now."

"Taking it hard, huh?" Hoag asked softly.

I laughed harshly. "Kind of nutty, actually. She's decided that not only was Jake murdered but Mel's involved, and I should make him confess."

Hoag whistled. "All her old grief brought back hard."

Dan shook his head. "If she's right, it'll really piss me off. Jake was a strong ally. I hate lawyers, especially prosecutors. The only thing worse is defense attorneys." He made a spitting sound. "To think our guys didn't cover this right for Jake pisses me off big-time."

Hoag nodded grimly. "Makes me sick."

It made me sick, too. "Will you guys do me a favor when you have time?"

Dan raised his eyebrows. "What more do you want?"

"Sure, doll." Hoag ignored Dan's glare. "What you want us to do?"

"Get me any info you can on the janitors and guards in the courthouse that night. I've a feeling no one seriously looked into their connections. I think they just got a pass." I knew I was asking a lot.

Dan shook his head. Hoag smiled and said, "You got it, babe."

"I don't know why we bend ourselves into pretzels for you." Dan was still shaking his head.

"Because I love you two oafs," I said with a laugh.

He rolled his eyes. Hoag roared with laughter. "You got him, girl. You got him good."

Finally, Dan joined in the laughter.

Conchita brought over Dan's carne asada and Hoag's huge

chile relleno. She hurried right back with my pozole and tortillas and more coffee for all of us. We set aside the talk of murder and death to eat, joke, and remember good times.

At the end, I took Jake's file and headed out to the parking lot, Hoag behind me lugging the box of case files, while Dan bought fresh tortillas for his wife. As I walked back with Hoag to say good-bye, a couple exiting the trendy Bluebird Café across the street caught my eye—Liz Richar and Randy Thorsson.

Beautiful and rich, why was she drawn to unattractive losers? She must have thought she had a better chance of being First Lady with Randy than with Mel.

I turned my back, kissed my two guys good-bye, and headed to my father's, wishing I'd never left Homicide. Trying to please my unpleasable father, who wanted me to be a big administrator. Then I thought of Brian and my pets, my friends and coworkers in Brewster. If I'd stayed in Homicide, they wouldn't be in my life. So I turned my back on the good old days and concentrated on the present again.

More than ever, the roots of this crime led to Kansas City. Now I'd have Kansas City help in tracking the criminals down. The best help KC had to offer. Something to hold out to Karen to keep her out of the case. And out of danger.

I made the trip to my dad's house without the usual dread, mind preoccupied with the puzzles of Jake's and Leonard's deaths. They were like those black-and-white drawings that seem to be one thing when you look at them one way and then something different when you look at them another way. I didn't see how to make sense out of the two cases, but I was determined to do so.

I pulled up in front of Charlie's house earlier than planned and saw a blue SUV parked in the driveway instead of Charlie's "classic" Mustang loaded with rust or Sam's silver Malibu. The new nurse's aide was still around.

I was almost out of the car when a roiling stomach and tight breathing reminded me I was about to spend time with my father, a task I'd avoided for as long as I could. Until he was beaten savagely and had a major stroke trying to get back in my good graces.

I took a deep breath, reminding myself this wasn't the old Charlie—at least, not completely. This Charlie wanted my company and tried hard not to insult or hurt me, even if he failed often. Charlie was trying to heal the harm he'd dealt our relationship with years of drunken rages, outrageous demands, and demeaning insults. We were delicately forging a new relationship in the midst of his often painful rehabilitation from the damage done by the stroke and beating.

Once my breathing steadied and my stomach settled, I headed for the front door, which opened as I stepped onto the rickety front porch. A robust bleached blonde in pink print hospital scrubs stepped out. She looked my age and wore dangly crystal earrings.

"You must be the daughter. I'm Marie Doerr. Your Home Health Agency sent me." She looked me over with frank curiosity.

I held out my hand. "Yes, I'm Skeet."

"I've talked with your husband, and he explained the problems Charlie's had with his nurses. I think we'll do fine." She gave a firm nod to underline her words.

I smiled cheerfully. "Sam's no longer my husband. We've been divorced for years. Sam and Charlie are very close, though."

She frowned and looked warily at me. "I hope this won't mean conflicting orders. That's one thing I can't—"

"Sam and I see eye to eye on Charlie's care." I'd make sure any differences we had were settled before she heard of them.

She looked at me with open skepticism. "I don't see eye to eye on anything with my ex. Don't know anyone who does."

I used my firmest voice. "Sam and I do when it comes to Charlie's care." And pretty much nothing else.

She gave me a guarded look and stepped back, pulling the door open. We walked into the house in silence. I scolded myself for getting off on the wrong foot with this woman who was going to play an important role in my life. If she stayed. None of the other three had. Charlie'd driven them all away, and I couldn't fault them for leaving. I had left. Run all the way to Brewster and only come back when he was sick and hurt. Because he was my father. He was no kin of theirs, as Gran would have said.

"Skeet!" Charlie sat in a sagging wing chair with a rolling table pulled up in front. A partially eaten cheeseburger in a fast food wrapper sat on the table. Charlie was not allowed hamburgers or cheese of any kind. They were killers for anyone with his arteries. The doctors' orders clearly stated what he could and couldn't have to eat and drink.

As I drew closer, I could see the wrapper more clearly. "Charlie, what are you doing with that?"

"He wanted one so bad. Just one cheeseburger won't do him any harm." Marie bustled up to the table, grabbed the wrapper, and headed for the trash can.

I followed, intending to explain why even one cheeseburger could be a major problem for Charlie, who was not only post-stroke but also had severe coronary artery disease. But before I could start, I saw the six-pack carton in the trash, topped with two empty bottles.

I turned to face her, breathing deeply and trying to count to ten. "Charlie isn't supposed to have alcohol. It states that clearly in the doctors' orders."

She shrugged. Her voice took on a petulant, whiny tone. "A little won't hurt him. Just one. It can be relaxing and therapeutic."

I tried to speak in reasonable tones. "My father is a recovering alcoholic. Or he was until you came today. Now he'll have to start all over." My voice had begun to slide upward in volume and pitch. "You can't buy him beer and bring it here. I see he's had more than just one."

"I only had one. Marie had one with me to keep me company." Charlie looked down at the floor. "Hell, it was just one beer. I'll go back on the wagon."

I took in a deep breath and tried to calm myself. After a few seconds, I walked back toward the chair where Charlie sat. "Okay. But no more of this now."

He pushed the table away and to the side and tried to stand by himself. This was still one of the most difficult things for him, to rise from a seated position without help.

"Use the cane," I said. "That's what it's for. To help you with your weak side."

Marie hurried over and helped him out of the chair with little murmurs and pats. The cane sat untouched against the wall.

I wanted to yell at them both but said softly and reasonably, "You have to get comfortable with using the cane and getting up on your own. Without leaning on someone else. That's the only way your muscles will strengthen again." This was an ongoing argument.

He looked at me, eyes as fierce as ever, hair all white and straggly now with some just finally coming in where they shaved part of his head in the ER. At least he was dressed and not still in his pajamas. Usually that only happened when Sam or I forced the issue. He had spent far too many days in his pajamas vegging out in front of the television and not doing any of his physical therapy exercises with the other nurses. No one wanted to brave his ire.

"I can get by without it. See." His head trembled a little on his neck. The doctors said the tremor was probably just from weakness and lack of muscle strength. We had feared neurological damage. They didn't rule it out completely but said they didn't think it was enough of a consideration to run more tests. And God knows Charlie'd had way too many tests.

"The trouble is, doing it that way doesn't strengthen the muscles that need it. I know you hate to struggle with the cane, but if you'd try, you'd get better at it."

Marie looked at Charlie with a big smile. "I don't mind helping you, Charlie. You've got time."

I did roll my eyes then. Time was exactly what Charlie didn't have. The doctors said if he missed the window for regaining muscle strength, he'd always be an invalid.

"Marie, have you read the doctor's orders?" They stated clearly that Charlie needed to use the cane to get up and down and walk around the house by himself.

She gave me a dirty look. "I've been busy."

I walked over to the television and picked up the sheaf of papers. When I turned back, her face flushed with anger. I handed the orders to her.

"For God's sake! She helped me up once or twice. Big deal." Charlie's face reddened also.

"When you read those, you'll see he's to use the cane to get up and down by himself and walk short distances around the house without help." I tried to make my voice soft and not sound as if I was scolding. "It's important to his recovery. As the PT exercises are. And the diet."

"Aw, hell! What do those doctors know anyway?" Charlie

yelled. "They're full of shit. I don't need them or you telling me what to do."

Marie stood there just holding the sheaf of doctor's instructions, paying no attention to them, glaring at me.

I thought I'd been superrestrained. What I really wanted to do was throw something to get her attention and yell, *What kind of a nurse's aide comes in for a whole day and never reads the doctor's orders for the patient?*

I turned to Charlie. "The doctors know how to get you back to getting around by yourself and living on your own."

"I can do it by myself. Don't need doctors telling me what to do." Charlie's usual big-man bragging said I needed to get through to him somehow.

"I haven't seen any signs of you getting better. If you keep it up, you won't get better at all. Then I'll have no choice but to put you into a nursing home. Is that what you want?"

Marie's eyes widened at the anger I returned to Charlie's.

"I don't want some wet-behind-the-ears doctor telling me what I can and can't do," he yelled.

I tried to keep my voice even and calm, never easy around him. "Don't you want to get better? Do you want to be disabled, in need of a nurse forever? Because that's what will happen if you don't start doing what the doctors tell you."

"Nobody tells Big Charlie Bannion what to do," he roared.

I shook my head, disgusted at myself for trying to get through his bullheadedness. "Fine. Keep going the way you are. Refuse to do what the doctors say, and we run out of options. Get it through your head. Either you get well or give up living in your own home. There's no way around that."

I turned to Marie. "Please read those instructions from the doctors. You're paid to help him do his physical therapy exercises and the other things the doctors want him to do to recover, including respecting dietary guidelines. If that's something you can't do, we need to know so we can have the agency send someone else."

The angry red drained from her face. "I'll read them. There's no reason to go to the agency for someone else."

"That's fine." I turned to Charlie. He'd fallen back into his chair and looked at me as if he'd never seen me before.

"I'll go home now. It's past time." Marie handed me back the sheaf of papers.

I nodded. "Good night, Marie."

I saw her out the door. I knew, when I turned, Charlie'd lay into me. I knew, when he did, I'd finally blast his head off.

After shutting the door, I said, without turning to face him, "I think it's best if I don't stay with you this evening. I'll call someone else to get you ready for bed."

"Hell, who're you going to call? Sam's at work." Charlie blustered, but I could hear a tremor of fear.

I turned to look at the angry old man. Maybe that's what he needed—to be well and truly scared at what his future could be. I certainly was. "I don't know who. But if I stay longer, one of us is likely to murder the other."

His face swelled like a fighting cock's. "You'd like that. To have me dead. I'm just a burden to you. An old cripple."

I sucked in a deep breath that didn't do any good. I exploded. "Don't start that shit, Charlie, or I'll tell you just what a burden you are. What a giant problem it is having to deal with Sam constantly when I want him out of my life. That's why I left him in the first place. I left this city to get away from you. Don't start with that *poor old me* shit. It won't work tonight."

He flared up in response. A well-practiced dance between

us, sharing the same hot temper as we did. Why was it I only inherited Charlie's weaknesses? "If you really want to get away from
me, go ahead. Get away. I don't need you. I can get along without you."

"You can get along without me? Get out of the chair. Get yourself ready for bed if you're so independent."

He struggled to stand. I wouldn't help him. Cruel as it seemed,
the cane was within reach of his hand. If angry enough, he'd pick
it up and stand on his own. Just to show me. Nothing else seemed to
work.

As he struggled to stand without the hated cane, my cell
phone rang. It was Karen. "Someone's skulking around the house.
Ignacio made me come upstairs. He's sitting downstairs in the
dark with his rifle."

"Shit! I'll be there quick as I can, Karen, but I'm in the city.
I'll call Joe. He'll send someone. Ignacio's doing the right thing.
With lights out, he gives no good target and keeps his own night
vision clear."

I hung up and dialed Joe. He'd been laughing until he picked
up the phone. He promised he'd send one of his guys out to Karen.
He was stuck taking care of family, like me, so I tried not to sound
disappointed. His guys were good, but if I couldn't be there to
protect Karen, I'd like Joe there for her. I was grateful she had
Ignacio and his trusty rifle guarding her.

I hung up and turned back to Charlie, who had fallen back into
his chair.

"What's going on?"

"A killer who thinks Karen saw him is at her farm." I walked
over and pulled him out of the chair. "I'll get you to bed so I can
head back."

I rushed him into the bathroom, planting him on a chair at

the sink to brush his teeth while I set out clean pajamas and his evening meds. My mind was at Karen's farm while I raced to get him clothed, medicated, and in bed with his emergency alarm around his neck.

I could see Ignacio in the dark by a window, alert, watching for movement, walking around the house's windows himself, while Karen, still not fully recovered from her injuries, sat upstairs, terrified. I wanted to get my hands on the bastard who was after her, but first I had to put Charlie to bed.

I worked in silence, faster than ever, my thoughts on that little farm of Karen's, until Charlie was down for the night. I put the night-lights on, left the light on in the bathroom with the door slightly open, and set his cane beside the bed for him.

"Charlie, I'm turning off the lights and leaving now. Is there anything you need before I go?"

He shook his head. I hurried out of the bedroom, switching off the overhead light as I left. At the front door, I heard his voice in the dark room behind me. "You get this guy, Skeeter. You get him. I'll be better tomorrow." He sounded afraid.

"That's good. We'll both be better, keep our tempers, do what we're supposed to."

"Yeah."

Locking the door behind me, I didn't feel good about this night's visit. Wasn't much I could do about it now. Really, there wasn't ever much I could do about it.

I ran to the car and swung it around to head back the way I came as fast as I could. I hadn't heard back from Karen. I told myself that was a good sign, if someone had hurt Ignacio and broken in, she'd call in a panic. It didn't feel good, though. I headed for the highway at top speed. Someone was out in the dark trying to hurt people I loved.

# CHAPTER 7

I broke speed limits all the way back across the river. I didn't head into Brewster because Karen's farm sat between KC and the town. Quickest to cut off onto a winding country road. I blessed those teenage years night-driving Oklahoma mountains as I ran full out on this dark road that snaked its way to a junction with Karen's long straight drive.

When I reached her farm drive, I could see her house and Ignacio's trailer. A dark figure carrying something long darted between the two. I hit siren and lights, hoping to keep whoever it was from doing further harm. As I pulled up, a shadow ran for the woods. Behind me as I leaped out, a town police car drove in, siren and lights blaring.

Ignacio stepped out on the porch, rifle in hand. "We're okay. Get him!"

I continued to run in the direction the figure had taken. I'd seen a dark figure, outlines blurred with rapid movement, melt into the thicket of brush and trees that served as a winter wind-break for the house. Behind me, I heard Joe's officer running. Good. I'd have backup if I could find this phantom.

At the edge of the small woods, I stopped, looking for signs of entry. There should be broken branches, disturbed vegetation. But it was too dark to see.

A bright light sprang up over my shoulder, focused on the brushwood border where I stared. "Thanks," I said without turning. No visible sign of entry. Any disturbance looked old and natural. I'd have sworn he went in there. "Can you move it to the right?"

"Sure." Joe stood behind me, swinging his Maglite to the right, keeping it tight on that edge where undergrowth met meadow. No obvious signs there, either.

"Hell! Try the left." As I spoke, the beam of light veered to the other side and slowly moved along that border. Nothing.

I shut my eyes, listening for sounds of someone moving through that thicket, twigs snapping underfoot, bushes rustling. Nothing.

I opened my eyes to take one last look. The figure'd disappeared into that scrub woods, leaving no trace.

"Where the hell'd he go?" Joe stepped up beside me.

"In there, I'd swear. Unless he sprouted wings and flew over it." I straightened from the bent position in which I'd been inspecting the ground and the undergrowth.

"We lost him." Joe switched off his Maglite. My eyes kept tossing up memory of the spot of light as they adjusted to the dark again.

I wanted to hit something. Joe looked as frustrated and angry as I felt. "How come you're here and not one of your guys?"

He shrugged. "When I called dispatch, they were both out on calls. I can't call anyone in on overtime. The mayor's been all over me about that. So I packed Julie off to Mrs. Nieman. But damn, wish I could have had someone here earlier. We might have caught him."

I smiled. "We had the best out here tonight and still lost him."

He gave me a rueful smile in return. "Let's go back and hear the whole thing from those two at the house."

I nodded and started to follow as he turned toward the house. Behind me, I heard the slightest rustle deep within the thicket. Just an animal. I stopped a second and waited for another. Nothing. I shook my head at myself. I was such a bad loser.

I looked through the dark in the direction of the road. "Let's check the road. It swings by pretty close. He had to leave his car somewhere. Probably headed for it when he ran from us."

Joe thought a second and nodded. "We can use my car. It's behind yours."

Back at the farmhouse where our cars waited, Ignacio still stood on the porch, rifle in hand. Karen had come down and turned on the lights in the kitchen. The rest of the house remained dark.

"Did you find him?" Ignacio asked quietly.

I shook my head. "We'll look for where he parked his car. The road runs fairly close behind that stand of trees and brush on the north side of the house."

He nodded, looking out into the night, on alert again. "I'll see that Karen is not hurt if he comes back while you're gone."

"I think he ran for it," Joe said. "Two cop cars out here. He's not about to try anything else tonight."

I wished I felt as confident as Joe. We headed for his car. The presence of one police car in the farmyard should keep whoever it was from making another attempt while we were gone. He couldn't know how many of us there were. Hunting an injured woman on an isolated farm was a far cry from doing the same with an armed farmhand and several cops with guns and radios.

As we reached Joe's car, I heard a car start in the distance and roar down the road. Beams from the headlights bounced as it passed the far end of the long farm drive.

"Let's get him!" Joe leaped in, starting his engine as I jumped in the passenger seat. The other car's lights dimmed with distance. By the time we'd reached the intersection of Karen's drive with the county road, they disappeared. Joe turned in the direction they'd gone—toward the city—and we pursued. Joe wasn't nearly as fast on the pitch-black meandering roads as I could be. I wished I'd jumped into the driver's seat instead. No sign of the car as we drove. Whoever it was had a head start and my facility with twisting roads. We reached an intersection where our road met two other county roads. I knew we'd lost the car.

"There's no telling which way he turned," I told Joe. "He hit it full speed down to here and turned off. One way or another."

Joe idled the car. "I'm willing to try one of these roads at random, but I think we'll be wasting our time."

"If we had some light, I could tell which road he took from the surface." I didn't want to give our opponent this match.

"You'd need sunlight for that," he said, a wrinkle forming above his nose between his eyebrows, "not just a flashlight, no matter how powerful."

I nodded glumly. I knew he was right. Whoever it was had gotten away clean. "Let's head back."

We drove back in silence, frustrated and disappointed. As we pulled into the farmyard, I looked at Joe's sober face. "We didn't catch him this time, but we kept him from hurting Karen. I appreciate your being here. I know it's not easy. Julie and all."

He looked over and gave a tired smile. "We'll get him. Just not tonight."

Karen joined Ignacio on the porch as we parked.

"No luck?" Ignacio asked.

I shook my head. "He ran full speed out to that intersection with county D and B. We lost him there."

"It must have been Mel. It looked like him. Not tall like Sam or Jake." Karen looked drawn and haggard with the bandage on the back of her head. She held on to the porch railing for support.

I made my voice as gentle as possible. "I don't think it could have been Mel. Whoever this was could really run. Whoever it was made it through that copse of trees and thorn bushes in the dark, carrying a rifle and making no noise. I don't see Mel doing that. Do you?"

She stared at me for a long moment before taking a deep breath. "Maybe he hired someone. I think Mel's involved. He knows who killed Jake. If Leonard knew, Mel would know."

"Karen, let's go inside. You need to sit." Ignacio held out his left arm for her to take for support and led her through the kitchen door, still holding his rifle in his right hand.

Joe and I followed them into the lavender air of the kitchen. Ignacio laid his rifle on the counter and settled Karen into a chair at the table, adjusting her position for comfort as if he couldn't stop touching her. Joe pulled up a chair.

I threw myself into another. "What a night!"

Ignacio gave me that quiet grin I'd seen the night I brought Karen home from the hospital. Was it just last night?

"You need coffee." He looked at Joe with a question on his face. Joe nodded. When Ignacio looked at Karen, his smile softened. "You need a hot cup of yerba buena tea."

"Karen doesn't—" I started to say she didn't have coffee, but he pointed toward a coffeemaker sitting on the counter with half a pot of coffee. "Where did that come from?"

"His trailer," Karen answered listlessly. "He couldn't live without it."

"Ignacio, you're a lifesaver."

He smiled shyly. "It's good Mexican coffee. American coffee is . . ." He held both hands out in a helpless gesture. Joe and I burst into laughter.

Joe pulled out his notebook. "What first alerted you to the presence of this intruder?"

Karen laughed. "Nacio's watched like a hawk ever since Skeet brought me home last night."

Ignacio nodded, the creases at the corners of his mouth deepening and extending farther toward his chin. I wondered how old he was.

"I have watched. Tonight after we ate and the dark started to come, I sat on the porch with coffee. Suddenly, too quiet. No birds or insects. In the field, this means some predator. So I went in and locked the door, turned off the lights so I could see better without giving a target. I saw someone run between the goat shed and the sheep barn with something long, like a rifle, in his hand. He hid behind the sheep barn. I told Karen to go upstairs and call you."

Ignacio ran water in the teakettle, set it on a burner, pulled out a cup and tea bag.

"What's yerba buena?" I asked with concern. "Will it be okay with the meds she's taking?"

Karen laughed, almost like her old self. "It's just peppermint."

Meanwhile, Ignacio moved to the coffeepot with two cups and filled them. He handed them to Joe and me and sat in front of another half-full cup on the table. "I watched a long time before he moved. This is a patient villain. Another might have stopped watching."

Joe and I nodded. "He has skills," I said. "Made it into those thorny woods without a trace. At least, nothing we could find at night, and he stayed still until we went back to the house."

Ignacio stared down into his cup of coffee, frowning. "He's a serious threat to Karen. I think he won't rest until Karen is dead and unable to identify him."

"I can't identify him," Karen cried.

"I hoped circulating the rumor you'd lost your memory would keep you safe, but apparently not." I tried not to look at the friend I'd failed.

Joe crimped one corner of his mouth. "All it takes is a couple of minutes' research online to tell him those memories could return at any moment. Our killer's not a fool."

I caught myself tearing at my hair and pulled my hand away. "I'm getting a picture of someone with lots of dangerous skills. Someone who knows how to take advantage of circumstances at a moment's notice. I don't like it."

"I looked out the window upstairs when Nacio was watching below, but I couldn't see anything in the dark." Karen turned to face me. Ignacio stared at her intensely. "Knowing someone out there intended to harm me. Like in a horror movie. Evil out there, and I couldn't even see where it was coming from."

# CHAPTER 8

"Angie records people with her phone sometimes. Its camera takes still photos and videos. She's shot some brilliant video that she wants to put together into a film. Black humor. Very anti-establishment stuff, of course. Anarchist, just about, Angie says." Brian swallowed a link sausage, chewing only three or four times.

"Of course," I muttered, staring into my mug with eyes that hadn't spent enough time closed overnight.

He gulped down a glass of orange juice. "She thinks Liz is evil and has weird photos of Liz dressed like a soldier or ninja. Angie wants to be an independent filmmaker. She'll let me be her assistant. She's really brilliant."

Brian had been going on about Angie all morning. He'd been asleep by the time I made it home last night. He hadn't had a chance to tell me about his new enthusiasm then.

I should have been paying closer attention to what he said. I had broken down and bought a book on parenting (might as well have said *mothering* on the cover, since that's what it dealt with). The author made it clear that keeping the channel of communication open was vital. You had to listen to your kid, always know what was going on with him. I liked to think Brian and I had a good clear channel of communication, so I didn't believe one morning of being preoccupied with who was trying to kill my best friend would make a real difference.

"She's got film-editing software, and she's going to teach me to use it. Isn't that great?" He stuffed his last buttered-and-jellied biscuit into his mouth all at once, barely chewing before he swallowed it with the last of his milk.

"You'll choke one of these days doing that." I got up to go for more coffee. "Don't take such huge bites. Slow down and chew." I almost bit my tongue as I heard my mother's words coming out of my mouth.

He ignored me. "These were super biscuits. You're getting good at baking."

I smiled. "I'm getting good at buying a better quality of frozen ready-to-bake biscuit."

Brian grinned and shrugged. "Whatever. As long as they taste good. Make more next time, okay?"

He gathered his plate and glass to take to the sink, leaving the dirty silverware on the table, as always. Before I could say anything, the phone rang.

Ignacio's voice was deep and rough. "Karen's driven to town. She wouldn't listen to me. She's going to open her store today."

"After last night? Is she crazy?" Brian turned to stare as I shouted. "Was she even in any shape to drive?"

"She is stronger but still shaky, though she tried to hide it. She will be in danger. I told her. She ordered me to take care of the animals. That's my job, of course. But who will watch over her? Keep her safe?" Ignacio's low voice caught as he rushed out the last words.

"I'll talk to Joe. We'll try to keep someone watching over

her while she's in town." I hesitated, thinking of the problems that would entail. "It won't be easy. Why'd she decide to do this now? She's not even physically fit yet."

"She's a stubborn woman. She was frightened last night. She didn't sleep well. It bothers her that she was so frightened." His voice grew heated. "Anyone would be frightened to have someone stalking them with intent to kill." He paused to take a breath, and his voice dropped back to normal. "She's proving something to herself."

"All she's proving to me is that the blow to her head addled her wits. I'll stop by the shop on my way to Brian's school and make sure she got in okay. When I get to work, I'll call Joe. We'll see if we can't keep her alive. Thanks for calling."

"*De nada*. Just keep her safe. Please." His voice dropped to a whisper before he hung up.

"What is it?" Brian looked scared. I reminded myself his whole family was gone because of violence.

"It's okay. Karen just decided to drive into work today. She shouldn't really be up and driving." I cleared the table in quick movements as I spoke.

"Someone's trying to kill her, too," he said matter-of-factly, moving to help me load the dishwasher. "You won't let them, will you?"

I smiled at his huge overconfidence in me. What would happen when I failed him? I hoped he'd learn to forgive me for being human.

"I'll do my damnedest to stop them—if she lets me." I flipped my dish towel at his head. He grinned and ducked. "Pack up. Let's get going. We have to stop at Forgotten Arts on the way." I looked at the empty table with its scattered crumbs and grabbed a paper towel to sweep them into my hand for the trash.

*I'll clean it when I come home,* I told the memory of my mother's voice in my head.

We took precious minutes feeding Lady and Wilma and packing for work and school. I began to worry that Karen would find the killer waiting for her before we could get there. I reminded myself the murderer couldn't know she'd come into town today. The element of surprise was on her side.

When we pulled up in front of Forgotten Arts, Karen's station wagon was already parked in back. I could see its nose peeking around the side of the building. I'd tell Karen to pull it farther in so none of it showed to the casual passerby.

An early train hooted and clanged through town. The square was empty, except for a few cars at the Herbal for breakfast and in front of the Lynches' bed-and-breakfast. We walked through the unlocked front door, setting off its bell. Karen came through the door from the back rooms, carrying a rainbow of handspun yarn.

She started at the sight of me. Some hanks of yarn slid from her grip and hit the floor. "What are you doing here?"

I let out the breath I'd been holding. "Why are you here instead of at home healing? Why not paint a target on your back? Do you have any idea how tough it'll be to protect you if you come into your shop?"

"What do you expect me to do?" Karen's face turned red, one more sign that something was seriously wrong with her. Trained to control her expression, even when her emotions were engaged, she seldom showed embarrassment or anger.

"I can't just sit upstairs in the dark, letting you and Nacio risk your lives to protect me," she cried. "My life's been turned upside down. I'm going to reclaim it. I can't do that at home in bed."

I covered my eyes with a groan.

Brian said, "You want to be preemptive, right?"

"Correct." She turned to look at him. "I'll see you for your session after school today."

That sounded like the old Karen, concerned with responsibilities in the here and now. My shoulders straightened a little as Brian nodded. Maybe she'd make it through this and become again the Karen I'd always known.

"Skeet, if we don't make it to school on time, can I—"

"Who says?" I interrupted Brian. "Get in the car."

I turned back to Karen. "I don't suppose you'd stay in the back of the store while your students run it? Because someone's trying to kill you?"

"Not in the least interested." Karen turned her back on me to tumble the brightly colored hanks of yarn over a small loom and stack of old books in an artistic display. "I'm back to my life."

I marched to the door in angry exasperation. "I hope you can keep it."

After dropping Brian at school and letting my office know I'd be tracking down leads, I pulled over and parked on the road to Wickbrook to call my ex.

"What's up? Please don't tell me Charlie drove off the new nurse." Sam sounded as if he might be laughing, but part of him obviously feared that's what my call was about.

"He didn't, but I may." I stared through my window as cars hurried past me on the way into town. "She brought him cheeseburgers and beer and wasn't doing any exercises with him. We might as well pay a teenager to babysit him." As I thought of the damage the saturated fats and salt might be doing to his already damaged arteries, my voice grew intense.

"Maybe there was a reason. Maybe she's heard how he was to the others, so she's trying to start off in his good graces." I could see Sam brush away the seriousness of the problem with a sweep of his hand and a big smile designed to distract me. That was his way with problems.

"Feeding him salt and saturated fat? Putting him back on the booze? That might put her in his good graces but not in the doctors' or mine." My mind brought up Marie Doerr's sullen face. Did she have any intention of following the doctors' orders?

Sam was silent. What could he say?

"Check real closely tonight. She hadn't even read the doctors' orders. There should be no trace of fast food fats and beer or hard liquor. She needs to have had him doing his exercises, getting up and walking by himself with the cane. You know the drill. If not, we have to get rid of her and get another." I cringed at the thought myself and knew Sam was rolling his eyeballs. I didn't see where we had any other choice.

"Wait a minute." Irritated, Sam didn't like facing bad choices any more than I did. "You know how hard it's getting to find someone to work with Charlie."

I shook my head, though he couldn't see it. "Doesn't matter. If she's feeding him stuff the docs said will kill him and giving him booze, if she's not helping him exercise and rebuild his muscles, she's no good. We're better off putting him in a nursing home. Neither of us wants that."

Sam took a deep breath. His voice turned smoother, placating. "I'll go in early and check. It'll be all right."

I hung up, knowing there wasn't much I could do. I had to put Charlie's situation out of my mind and work this murder case. I had to track down Sid Ambrose to have him analyze Jake's autopsy report.

Turtle Creek ran through the heart of Brewster from the river at the old train station and on through the wildlife sanctuary. Its best fishing, according to Sid, was on the stretch after the sanctuary that ran through what was now being turned into Wickbrook. Sid wouldn't be happy to see me with an autopsy report.

Sid sat in the shade of a massive straw hat. He needed it. Though we finally had a breeze, the sun still raged above us.

Wearing sandals and wrinkled off-white pants and a shirt, Sid sat with closed eyes in an old metal-framed lawn chair at the edge of the bank, holding his fishing pole. He should have been sitting at a river or the seaside in tropical climes rather than in the middle of the Midwest. Periodically, he breathed out a gentle snore.

I touched him gently on the shoulder. "Sid?"

Without a start, he opened his eyes. "What are you doing here? Not bringing troubles to infect my peaceful place, surely?"

I laughed. "You know me too well. I need your help."

He fixed one stern eye on me. "Give me one good reason why I should let you invade my sanctuary."

"I'm out of time. This killer's after Karen." His face froze, so I blurted out the rest. "He thinks she can identify him, but she can't. Last night, he stalked her out at her house. Joe and I drove him off, but we couldn't catch him. He's a pro."

"You think it's someone tied to this?" He pointed to the papers in my hand, rattling slightly in the breeze.

"Yes. Leonard was killed right after saying Jake was murdered. His death, the attack on Karen, and this stalking are all tied to that." I stared back toward the center of town. "Karen's at her shop, just waiting for the sword to fall. Joe's trying to send one of his patrolmen past her every half hour. We can't do any more to protect her. My guys have to be on campus, except Gil and me investigating."

He straightened himself upright and pulled in his line. "So what have you got for me?"

I sat on the ground, legs dangling off the creek edge, and handed him Jake's autopsy report. "Read this and tell me what you know of the guy who did it, please. Whether or not there's a possibility the victim could have been killed by other means than the fall."

Sid took the report from my hand. "Whose body?"

"Jake Wise."

He shook his head sadly as he began to read. "I was out here by that time. Didn't know they'd given his autopsy to this idiot. I tried to get rid of him before I left, but he had clout somewhere."

"Something seemed wrong about it. Like someone was taking the path of least resistance."

"That's his way. Do what's easiest. Avoid exercising those precious few brain cells."

He turned back to the papers in his hand. I watched a little blue heron downstream, where a pile of tree limbs and rocks created a small pool on the left side of the creek. The peace of the water started to fill me, but an image of Karen alone in her shop invaded my mind. All peace fled.

Sid pursed his lips and whistled soundlessly. "I can't tell for certain without seeing the body. Some of these injuries could have come as easily from a physical attack as the fall. The broken neck sounds as if it were from twisting rather than smacking against marble edges. That's certainly suspicious and calls for further examination. The idiot didn't see it or didn't want to do the extra work it would entail if he admitted it." He shook his head in disgust. "No way to tell now."

My breathing tightened. Someone had probably knocked kind, caring Jake down those stairs and snapped his neck to ensure his death. I had accepted the cover-up and gone on with my life. I could have kept Homicide on the case to track down the killer of that most decent of men.

"Either someone who didn't belong was in the courthouse that night, or someone who was supposed to be there killed him." I looked toward the western horizon beyond the Missouri River.

"I'm sorry. I know you were close to Jake." Sid took out a big handkerchief and wiped sweat from his face and neck.

I shook myself back from the past. "I've got to worry about Karen now. I won't let the person who's gotten away with Jake's murder do it again. Not with Leonard's and certainly not Karen's."

Standing, I gave Sid a rueful smile. "Sorry I threw this nastiness into your peaceful retreat."

He waved a big hand in front of his face. "I'll be back to fishing in a little while. More than you can say, I suspect."

"This is someone we know. It has to be." I turned for a last look at the heron in its shallows. I was in deeper waters with a current growing stronger by the minute.

He nodded. "That makes it easier and harder both."

Driving away, I knew he was right. Easier because all suspects were within reach and known to me. Harder because none seemed likely. Except perhaps the mercenary soldier Terry Heldrich. And his boss, Walker Lynch, at one time connected with the human trafficking task force.

I checked on Karen on my way back from the creek. The calm, rational Karen I'd known had vanished to be replaced by this angry, obsessed, and emotionally fragile woman. I didn't know if I dared to tell her anything about Jake's death. She was already certain that Mel had had a hand in it and Leonard's in some way. I was afraid to spark violent words or actions against Mel. Suddenly, I had to worry about violence with always-rational Karen. The world was sadly out of balance.

I remembered Gran explaining the world depended on balance. Anything that threw off its balance must be put right, or there'd be frightening consequences. "Even small imbalances are dangerous," she'd said. "Creation itself depends on right thinking, right action, harmony, and balance." I knew she was right. Everything was getting more and more out of whack. I could feel the world around me spiraling into chaotic violence. It was my job to make it right again.

Karen waited on a loom-buying customer as I entered. I wandered around the shop, fondling skeins of alpaca and mohair and worrying. I picked up an intriguing hand-painted blue and violet merino and smoothed its softness against my cheek. The bell over the door tinkled behind me. I whirled to find Helen Lawson walking toward me.

"Just who I want to see." She smiled, but her eyes weren't part of it. Her face looked drawn and pale against her long lilac dress.

Karen's customer was someone I didn't recognize, probably one of her growing fiber-arts clientele from the city. She bustled out the door, loaded with packages of yarn and a small tapestry loom while Karen held the door for her and closed it behind her with a jingle. She flipped the OPEN sign to BACK IN A MINUTE.

"Okay, that's it for a while." Her voice had regained its life. Her face looked whole once more. I could have cheered, except I didn't want to draw attention to anything that would send her back to obsessed grief. "Let's sit down. I'll bring us some of Dolores's raspberry iced tea. She sent me half a gallon by one of her waitresses after the breakfast rush."

With a big smile, she headed to the back room for the tea. Helen sat in a wicker chair. I took a rocker. Had it been the act of returning to her daily routine that brought Karen back to her senses? Whatever it was, a weight lifted from my chest.

"Why were you looking for me, Helen?" I asked in a cheerful voice.

She looked around furtively. "I heard that Leonard's murder might be related to Jake's death."

I put my finger to my lips. "Don't talk about that in front of Karen. The trauma of the murder and attack were a shock to her system. She's starting to recover. She loved Jake very much."

Helen's lips trembled for a second in sympathy with Karen's grief. "Jake was great. His loss must have been terrible for her."

"I didn't know you knew him." How would they have come in contact? I didn't see Helen in trouble with the feds.

Her smile didn't reach troubled eyes. "I worked with immigrants. Prime target for human trafficking."

I nodded. Of course.

She continued, staring inward. "I brought Jake some cases. He didn't have the resources to work them. Investigating trafficking is an expensive, long-drawn-out process. I thought he gave up. I didn't know him well then."

She smiled again, rolling her eyes. "That man never gave up on anything. He just rethought it. He figured out how to get those resources. He put me on the advisory committee when he first initiated the task force because he wanted someone who dealt with it on the ground daily. We lost a great man when Jake died."

I heard the door to the back room and waved my hands to signal Helen not to say any more about Jake's death. Then I hurried over to help Karen with her tray of glasses.

"Don't worry. I'm fine. I can carry three glasses of tea without damaging myself."

Karen's long braid, normally neat and smooth, sprouted strands of hair along its length. But her face was almost back to its usual color and liveliness. I had to restrain myself from picking her up and carrying her in celebration through the shop.

Once we were all sitting, sipping iced raspberry tea—delicious but sadly caffeine-free—Karen turned to Helen. "Why were you looking for Skeet?"

I didn't dare shake my head at Helen with Karen right there. I hoped she'd make up another reason.

"It's about Leonard's murder," Helen answered. "I knew something few people did. It was told me in confidence, but after this, I want the person investigating his death to know."

I breathed a sigh of relief. Helen fidgeted slightly, situating herself so she didn't look directly at Karen. "You probably knew Jake had put me on the advisory committee for his human trafficking task force. I encountered it regularly in my work with refugees and immigrants."

She rushed through the last phrase as if worried Karen would be jealous of her contact with Jake. I could have told her Karen didn't have a jealous bone, muscle, or tendon in her whole body.

Karen looked puzzled. "I don't think I realized you'd also known Jake back then." She smiled at Helen. "It makes good sense. Jake was always sensible."

Helen smiled back mechanically. "We went to Walker Lynch for money. From his foundation. That was my idea. He funds organizations that help the people who are the primary targets of traffickers."

She took a drink of tea and choked as it went down too fast. I got up to help, but she waved me away. "I'm fine."

She took another tiny sip and stopped her throat-clearing. "Walker agreed to support the task force with his foundation. That allowed Jake to get government support, too. The task force came together. Jake started work on a case that spanned several states and multiple companies. The more he found out, the more excited he got. He thought it would be a huge organization when he traced all the threads back to their owners."

Karen nodded placidly.

Helen gave her a wary look. "He told me about it because I brought him the original cases that led to it."

I wondered if Helen was a jealous woman herself and projected it onto others. Matt was quite a hunk, after all. She was so ill at ease discussing her friendship with Jake, as if she worried Karen would erupt over it.

"One day, he was upset. He'd found signs hinting that Walker was involved at the most protected, highest levels. He didn't know what to do." Helen's hands twisted around each other. I could tell she didn't like talking about this.

"I didn't know that!" Karen said at the very moment I asked, "Why didn't he go to Mel?"

Helen shook her head forcefully. "Walker and Mel were too close politically. He talked to Leonard, but Leonard told him to drop it. Just not follow it. Said it would end Jake's career. Jake believed Leonard and Mel were on Walker's payroll. That's why he worked so late. No one was around to spy on what he was doing. Jake told me this days before he died."

"Why didn't you go to the police with this?" Karen's voice was fierce.

Helen looked down at the floor before raising her eyes. "I'd been overstressed, and I had a collapse about the time he died. I was in the hospital. I wasn't able to do anything."

She had a shamed look and twisted her hands again. "When I came home, I didn't think Jake would want me to run around talking about his suspicions. Then, we moved out here for a lower-stress life."

"Jake's suspicions weren't anything the police could use," I reassured her. "There wasn't anything you could have done. It's okay."

"No it's not." Karen's voice was overloud in the small shop. She turned to me with that frenzied excitement I'd come to dread. "You see. Jake did know things. Mel's involved. Somehow. My Jake knew it so they killed him."

Helen jerked back in her chair as if Karen's last sentence struck her physically.

I held my hands up, palms outward, and used my slow, calm voice. "It's not Helen's fault they killed him. If she'd told the police what she knew, they couldn't have used it."

"They could've arrested Mel. You could arrest Mel. Make him tell everything he knows." Karen was back in that world of hurt she'd first entered Sunday night.

"We don't arrest people without evidence. Someone's hunch told secondhand won't stand up in court. You know that. Just stop and think, will you? Think for a minute instead of just feeling." I lowered my voice again because I realized it was growing louder. "I know you loved Jake. So much. He loved you. But step out of all that pain to actually think about the situation."

Helen shot out of her chair. "I'm so sorry. I'd better leave." She ran out the door.

As the bell chimed behind her, I turned to Karen. "You aren't the only one hurting. Helen's dealing with guilt and shame over her breakdown. She feels she's let down the people who need her. Now, you add guilt about Jake's death?"

Karen dropped her gaze to the floor for a second. When she lifted her eyes again, her jaw hardened. "I'm sorry, but this shows Mel's involved. If you need evidence, get it. What are you doing here?"

I gulped air for a second. "Watching over you because Joe can't spare an officer. Trying to make sure the person who killed Leonard and Jake doesn't get you."

I stood and headed for the door, turning back to her as I opened it. "If you'd stay home where Ignacio could keep watch, those of us trying to solve this case could get more investigating done."

I slammed out of the shop. On the way to my car, I resolved to call Elizabeth Bickham, the new U.S. attorney for western Missouri, and ask a few pointed questions about the trafficking task force's progress since Jake's death.

# CHAPTER 9

When I reached campus, Gil and Trish had also returned from running down leads. Frank joined us in my office before the whiteboard.

One of Trish's assignments was to find out which of the party guests Sunday had military backgrounds or memberships in shooting clubs. And which had registered guns.

"I'm fairly certain whoever killed Leonard wouldn't have done it with an easily traced gun. A person with a registered gun is likely to have learned to use it and might have another unregistered." I looked at my team to see if they agreed. Frank nodded, as did Trish.

Gil looked doubtful. "We'll miss anyone with only unregistered guns."

I shrugged. "True. We won't know about those guns anyway, will we?"

His face flushed. "I guess not."

I laughed. "Don't feel bad. You get points for playing devil's advocate. Good argument. That's another assignment for you. Try to find out if someone has a gun who shouldn't."

"There are definite surprises on my list." Trish licked her lips nervously. "Terry Heldrich has three handguns and a rifle registered."

"Not surprising with the background we figured for him. I'm surprised it isn't more." I wrote the number under Terry's name on the whiteboard list.

"I couldn't find out much about his military background. Everything seems to be classified."

Frank whistled. "We figured that. All you have to do is see him to know he's special forces. This sounds like a lot more."

"At first, Joe and I thought he must be a bodyguard," I said. "But Walker claims he's more. After talking to him, I believe that. He's smart. He'd be good at strategy and planning. Finding out information."

"Think he's a spook?" Frank looked wary.

I shrugged. "Or has been. Trish, who's next?"

She consulted her list. "Mel has a .22-caliber handgun."

I nodded. "He, Leonard, and Jake each bought one after an attack on a U.S. attorney in Utah a few years back. I remember."

"He also was a marine during Vietnam. Two tours of duty. Won a sharpshooting medal and medals for bravery."

"Being a Vietnam vet played a big part in his campaign for state attorney general," I reminded them.

Trish frowned. "I thought the sharpshooter medal was worth consideration."

I wrote it on the whiteboard. "That's exactly the kind of thing we're looking for. I can't see Mel as a jarhead. Puts him in a whole different light."

"He still is." Trish looked at her notebook. "Colonel in the Marine Corps Reserves."

"He's probably kept his shooting skills," Gil said. "They train all the time."

Maybe Mel deserved a closer look. Karen's hunch about his involvement might pay off.

"Randy Thorsson also has a .22 that he bought around the same time," Trish continued. She looked up from her notebook. "Said he bought it because of the Utah attack, too."

Frank made a face. "As if they'd come after him."

We all laughed. Randy hadn't endeared himself to any law enforcement personnel—with the exception of his political henchman, Sheriff Dick Wold. We all hoped Randy would find a plum job for Dick and get him out of our hair, too.

"Randy was drafted at the tail end of Vietnam," Trish continued. "It was over before he finished basic training. He still claimed Vietnam veteran status in his state senate campaign." She frowned in disapproval.

I laughed. "Some politicians will outright lie, so why wouldn't he claim technical truth?"

Gil shook his head. "I know what she means. There's a whole generation of vets who went through that hell and came home to be ridiculed and forgotten. Seems a cheat to try to steal some of their glory for his political career."

Frank burst into a laugh that turned into a cough. He was smoking too much but refused to hear anything from me about stopping. "They're all cheats!" he finally managed.

I signaled to Trish to go on and walked to my desk for a bottle of water for Frank.

Trish turned back to her notebook. "Walker Lynch had no guns registered."

"He has Terry. He hardly needs to own one himself," Gil pointed out.

"I ran Reverend Matt and his wife. I learned they'd lived in Kansas City and might have known Leonard or Jake." Trish looked for approval. I nodded.

Frank laughed again. "You think the good reverend and his ex-nun wife might be killing folks?"

Trish's face turned deep red. I squashed my impulse to jump in. She'd have to learn to deal with old-style guys on her own or lose points. And Frank was pretty old-style.

She turned back to her notes. "Reverend Matt has no gun. Said he's turned away from that whole world. Whatever that means." She looked puzzled. "He was an army chaplain."

"I expect he's a good shot," I explained. "Before he became a minister and chaplain, he was a ranger."

Frank pursed his lips. "I didn't know that."

Gil shook his head. "Somehow I can't see Reverend Matt killing people. In the army or now."

"With kindness, maybe." Trish grinned at her little joke and turned back to her notebook. "Bob Lynch has a handgun and rifle. Says he used to trap and hunt but hasn't had time in years."

"I don't know if he could hit anything," Frank said. "Bob's clumsy and ham-handed. Kathy's the real brains of those two."

"I didn't think either of the Lynches knew Leonard or Jake. So why'd you run them?" I asked.

Gil spoke up. "I added Bob to her list. I learned he worked as a bailiff in KC's federal court for years, saving up for the B and B."

I nodded, adding Bob's name to the whiteboard list. I relied on Gil's investigative skills. Young as he was, his abilities and instincts were top-notch. "Excellent. I'm glad you're both looking beyond the list we started with. We don't want to overlook anyone."

"The surprises were the women. Call me a sexist pig," said Trish with a little laugh. "I'd never have figured Liz Richar to own two handguns, a military rifle, and a membership in a shooting club. She's also taken survival training."

"You're kidding." I turned and stared. "I've taken survival training courses before. They're frigging tough. How did Liz manage to get her nails done and keep her hair perfect deep in the woods grubbing by hand for edible roots?"

We had a laugh at the image. My cop sense went off in the back of my brain. Why would Liz bother with guns, gun clubs, survival training? Something was off with that.

Trish turned back to her notebook and continued her list. "Helen Lawson also owns a handgun, bought when she worked late nights in KC."

I nodded. "I can see that. She worked in the Northeast. Lots of gang violence there. Did she ever use it? Could she?"

"She said she grew up hunting with her father and brothers." Trish smiled. "I don't know how much stock we ought to put in that. She's never fired the gun. Said she had no need."

I twirled the marker in my hand. "She seems a truthful sort. However, I learned today that she knew Leonard and Jake when she worked in the city." I added her name to the list of names down one side of the board.

Gil looked as if he'd remembered something. "One day, we were talking in the Herbal—"

Frank interrupted in a heavy-handed joking tone. "When you should have been on duty, I'll bet. Sucking up to Dolores."

Everyone laughed, except red-faced Gil.

"I was talking with Helen," he continued. "When she first became a nun, she went to Guatemala as part of a mission. She worked with indigenous tribes in danger from the government."

Gil's father was from Guatemala, though his mother was from Texas and he was born here. Made sense he and Helen would chat about Guatemala.

"She talked about hunting for meat for the village. So she's probably a good shot." He looked at the whiteboard. "That gives us six party guests with guns that we know of."

We looked for other connections among our list of people who knew Leonard and Jake. We went over all the questions, trying to answer any of them even in part. We added new ones.

Afterward, I placed a call to Elizabeth Bickham, the woman who'd replaced Mel as U.S. attorney. She was in a meeting. I had to set an appointment for a phone conference in two days. Busy lady.

Answers were in short supply, questions growing. No matter what we did, we couldn't get anywhere. Another sign things were out of balance with my world.

The cherry on my day came with a call from Joe.

"I'm sorry, but I have to pull my guys off swinging by Karen's. Got a burglary and vandalism that may connect plus two highway pileups."

I hit the desk softly with my fist. "You've gone over and above already. Thanks, Joe. Hope the crashes aren't too bad."

I'd run out of resources to protect Karen. I thought about our friends. Annette had a deans-and-directors meeting with the chancellor. I would usually have attended as a director. This murder would exempt me. That meeting would swallow the whole afternoon because this interim chancellor loved to talk. No help there.

Miryam? Mother Earth Books sat next door to Forgotten Arts. I'd ask Miryam to keep an eye on Karen's place, call me when anyone entered. If it was someone on our suspects list, I'd head right over. That might be the best I could get. I left immediately for Miryam's bookstore.

In Mother Earth Books, the incense-filled air and Indian flute music should have calmed my overstressed mind but didn't. Miryam's gray-and-white-striped, long-haired cat came to me, rubbing against my leg. He'd have made three of Wilma Mankiller, but my little street urchin would have wiped the floor with him. She was tough. Cernunnos was just pretty and fat. I'd never seen him move. He was usually in a stupor from overeating. He must be hungry.

In the back, I heard something. So did he, obviously, and he headed for it with all the lumbering speed he could muster. I beat him to the doorway.

"I thought you'd come when you heard the can opener, sweetheart." This was obviously addressed to Cernunnos. Miryam bent to scoop food from a can into his dish.

"Thought for a second you were talking to me," I said.

Miryam laughed. "What are you doing here when you've got a— I know! You want me to help detect again! That will be great."

I began to have second—and third—thoughts.

"Come into the office where we can be confidential." She whispered the last word.

I followed her into the little office behind the bookstore. I knew Miryam spent little time there. Her business partner, Professor Carolyn Ehrlich, did accounts and inventory. The room was all business, unlike Miryam.

"I have a favor to ask," I began.

"Whatever it is, I'm glad to do it. Shall I follow someone? I was an actress. I can become another person no one would recognize." She beamed as she spoke, obviously imagining a standing ovation.

"I want you to stay right here, as usual." I gestured back through the doorway to the store.

Her face fell. I had to smile. Miryam could be maddening at times, but she was endearing. "Karen's at Forgotten Arts. I want you to keep a close eye on anyone going in and out over there. Anytime someone shows up, call me on my cell phone."

"You think someone will try to hurt Karen?" Her excitement returned, tinged with concern.

I made fists at the thought. "Yes. You're my first line of defense. Call me when anyone goes over there. I have a list of names I'm checking. If it's one of them, I'll hurry over to make sure they don't hurt her."

"I'll sit and work by the window with my phone, so it won't look suspicious. I'll be on stakeout." She bounced on her toes, fluffy blond hair rising and falling with her movement. "This is exciting. We're working together again to catch a murderer."

Her last contribution to catching a murderer had been photographers' names and the mention of an amethyst geode. I didn't get my hopes as high as hers obviously were. If she helped me keep Karen safe, that would be huge.

I put on my serious face. Not hard. I'm basically a serious person. "This is important. Someone was at Karen's place last night stalking her. I think Klamath's killer's afraid she'll remember and identify him."

She clapped her hands in delight. "He wants to silence her."

Her attitude concerned me. "Karen's in real danger."

Miryam put on her own serious face, much better than mine. "Don't worry. She's safe with me on the job. I won't let anyone slip past me."

I smiled. "Thanks. I knew I could rely on you."

Oddly enough, that was true. If Miryam set herself to this task, she'd do it thoroughly.

On the way back into the store, I leaned down to pet Cernunnos as he ate. He might be slow and dumb, but he was gorgeous, fur like silk beneath my hand.

Miryam walked on through the doorway from the dimly lit storage area into the brighter shop where Walker Lynch waylaid her. She saw him coming and turned to retreat back toward me. He stepped around her to face her. Since he now stood with his back to me, I could see Miryam's face but not his.

"This is a nice surprise. Don't you look lovely?" His voice sounded cold and mocking.

Miryam did look lovely in a peasant dress with embroidery, smocking, and ruffles. Everything I never wore.

A door in Miryam's face closed instantly. All her enthusiasm, charm, and vivacity disappeared. I'd seen something similar on the faces of children facing their abusers in court. Their faces just shut down.

Walker didn't seem to notice the real Miryam, my friend, was no longer there. I wondered what he'd done to her. He had to have done something awful to prompt that reaction.

"What are you doing here?" she asked abruptly.

"I came to see you." Something unpleasant in his voice made him seem to threaten her in some way. "Your beauty makes another conquest."

"Go away." She shrank into herself, face still wooden. "I'm not interested."

He started a loud, booming laugh. "Since when are you not interested in a wealthy man? I'm half Harry's age with twice as much money." He laughed again.

I stepped forward into the lit bookstore. "Walker." I kept my voice neutral and touched Miryam's trembling arm.

The gesture gave her strength. Perhaps by reminding her she wasn't alone with him. He couldn't do anything to her here.

She shook her head. "You could never interest me. Never."

I felt like I'd walked into the middle of a melodrama with a gloating villain. Miryam was terrified of Walker, and he was gloating. He knew he frightened her and liked it. I didn't.

"She's told you she's not interested. She's asked you to leave. Why don't you?"

He looked at me for the first time. His eyes had been locked on Miryam the whole time. "What have you got to do with this? I didn't think you swung that way. I know she doesn't."

Through my hand on her arm, I could feel Miryam's trembling increase. I practically bit my tongue, holding on to my temper. "She's my friend. You're being a jerk. Why not go somewhere else and think better of it? You don't endear yourself to anyone with this behavior."

Walker smiled again. I wondered why I ever thought his smiles pleasant. He reminded me of a cat playing with its prey.

"You sound like you're telling off one of your freshmen." He shook his head in a patronizing gesture. My free hand clenched into a fist.

Taking a deep breath, I matched his unconcerned tone. "Because that's what you're acting like."

Walker snickered, raising an eyebrow. "Miryam knows better than that, don't you?" He turned his gaze to her closed face. "You have reason to know I'm a man full-grown."

He reached to touch her face. She shrank back visibly. I moved to stand between them.

The door in the front of the shop opened with a tinkle of chimes, slamming back against the wall. The sound drew our attention. Terry Heldrich stood, legs apart, ready for action, staring at his boss.

"Someone wants you, Walker." I gestured toward the door

with my head. I wanted to break Gran's taboo, point directly at him, then out the door to force him to leave Miryam alone. If I thought I had the power Gran worried about, I'd have done it.

Turning, Walker saw Terry, then faced us, all sign of the predator gone. The pleasant habitual mask dropped back in place. "It looks as if I will leave. Later, Miryam."

Terry remained at the door until Walker passed him on his way out. He gave me a direct look carrying heat—warning, anger, something—before following Walker outside.

I remembered thinking Terry a dangerous predator. He was definitely not harmless, but I'd take my chances with him over his boss any day. Terry didn't seem to like doing damage or hurting people. It would just be all in a day's work. From what I'd just seen, Walker got high off pain he'd inflicted. Of such stuff were serial killers made. I hoped Walker never took that final step. With his money and power, he'd be a profiler's nightmare. I remembered Jake's belief that Walker was behind a huge human trafficking scheme.

We watched in silence as the two men got in the Lexus and drove off. Next to me, I could feel Miryam's trembling increase and then leave her body, draining out of her. I felt more than a little shaken myself. Yet nothing had actually happened.

I turned to my friend. "For God's sake! What did he do to you? To make you so terrified?"

She shook her head in vigorous denial. "Thanks for standing by me. So much. You don't know what it meant. But I can't tell you anything. I'm sorry. I just can't. I'll watch out for Karen. Like a hawk. There are really bad people around. I won't let her be hurt." She spoke at twice her usual speed.

The wooden look was slowly leaving her face. But her usual bright spirit didn't return. Instead, she looked drained and haunted. She patted the hand I'd laid on her arm before gently peeling it off. "Thanks for the strength you gave me. If you hadn't been here . . ." She shuddered a little. "Watch out for him, Skeet. He won't like that you stood up to him or that I did. He's a bad man. And a bad man with money and power is just . . . hell." On the last word, her voice dropped almost an octave.

"Tell me what this is all about."

"No, sweetie. I can't. I'll get some work to do by the window." She turned and walked back to the office. Her whole body looked different, older, slower.

I knew that what Walker had done to Miryam had been something awful. I recognized that look on her face. I'd seen it too many times. I might never find out what had happened, but he wouldn't do anything else to her—or anyone else I could protect.

# CHAPTER 10

A train moaned shivery heartbreak in the distance as I drove from Miryam's bookstore to the campus to meet with Jeremy. The chancellor wanted an update. We both preferred to do it through Jeremy.

Parking behind New Admin, I realized my dread of seeing Jeremy was weaker than usual. I laughed at myself. A simple matter of scale. Jeremy had embezzled from the university and nudged a mentally unstable accomplice toward suicide. Like Terry, though, he wasn't the true predator Walker was.

For Terry, it was business. For Jeremy, expediency. Neither was a sociopath. I might arrest one or the other of them one day, but not for the kind of frightful crime that brought up the memory of my FBI course ever since I'd encountered Walker in true form.

I couldn't just forget what I knew about Jeremy, but maybe it would lie quieter in my mind. Since he was determined to play a role in my life, that would make things easier.

As I entered New Admin, the train hit town rattling over the tracks that crossed to the side of the square below Chouteau

University's hill. Its whistle lost the haunting quality, simply sounding like another complaint about the heat. The air-conditioned air inside the building was a relief. I took the elevator to Jeremy's posh fourth-floor offices.

Smiling broadly, he ushered me over to his conference table, looking out on Old Central's gargoyles and, below them, the town square's antique buildings resembling a doll's village with the Missouri River a silver ribbon in the background.

"You can stop the constant smile," I said. "It's unnerving."

His smile grew broader. "Good. My smile's one of my best tools. I keep it sharp and ready to use." He laughed, shaking his head. "Marquitta, you always know how to skewer my pretenses."

I looked around at the kilim rugs on the floor and his collection of sea glass on built-in bookshelves that matched his desk. It all coordinated with his well-tailored figure.

"You certainly do well for yourself." I could hear the disapproval in my voice. I hadn't meant it to come out that way.

He shrugged eloquently. "I must have something to compensate me for this primitive climate. How do you stand the heat, Marquitta? In New England by this time, trees are turning and nights grow cool. Here, we just cook."

I thought maybe Liz Richar's shrug thing was something taught in Ivy League schools because Jeremy had the same shrug.

I rolled my eyes. "You sound like you just moved here. You've been in Missouri for years. Surely you're used to the weather."

"Never. A place where you only have spring for two days and three minutes before temperatures turn scorching. Where the heat only stops searing you when it freezes and dumps ice and snow. This is not a place for civilized beings." He looked out the window, a bleak expression on his face. I wondered what he saw.

136

"The longer I'm here, the harder it grows to stay." His voice was hushed. "I miss New England. It's been my family's home for generations. A couple of trips to the Cape every year aren't enough any longer."

I should have felt pleased to see him unhappy. I wasn't. I came from a people who still grieve over a homeland we were forced to leave almost two centuries ago. I knew how longing for a lost place can eat a hole in the soul. The land plants ties in us. They give us strength. If we're torn away, we bleed through those ripped ties, sometimes forever. It's never a good thing to have lost your home. I sat in silence with him as he stared out the window and grieved for his home. That was all I could give him, respect and silence.

Shaking his head slightly, he turned back to me. "You have a disastrous effect on me, Marquitta. Making me want to tell the truth." He laughed abruptly. "As you can imagine, that's never a good idea for me."

I joined in his laughter for a second—until I thought how awful it was never to be honest with anyone. My laughter died out.

Jeremy smiled at me ruefully. "Never mind my distress. The chancellor's impatient. Tell me what's happening with the case."

I took a deep breath. There was no reason I couldn't give him the outlines of what we'd learned, to share with the chancellor. This time no one on the campus was involved, except possibly Mel, who hardly counted, since he'd just started. I brought him up to date.

"Liz Richar? A lot of money there. Walker Lynch?" He looked disturbed. "He's extremely wealthy, which makes him powerful. More powerful than Liz even. Watch yourself, Marquitta." He shook his head lightly and smiled. "Why should I worry? I know you'll succeed. You always do. Which of the suspects will you tackle next?"

"Is that enough for the chancellor?"

He threw his head back with laughter. "That's my girl! You never give me an inch. That's probably enough for the chancellor."

I rose. "Good. I have to get back to my job."

He rose with me, steering me to the office door by my left arm as if I couldn't find it on my own. "Be careful. Watch your back. The less you have to do with Walker Lynch, the better." His long face showed concern.

"That's one thing we agree on. The less I have to do with Walker, the happier I'll be."

Early that afternoon, I parked at Bob and Kathy Lynch's Grand Hotel Bed-and-Breakfast and climbed the steps to the broad front porch to ring the bell, feeling as if this Tuesday would never end. Inside, I heard something hit the floor. Kathy cried, "Oh, damn!" A flurry of activity followed. Finally, footsteps approached the front door where I stood in the aching heat. At least the solid porch roof shielded me from the blinding sun. Looking up, I found a delightful surprise. Puffy white clouds painted on the sky-blue ceiling.

"Hello!" Kathy whisked the door open, freezing when she saw me. "What is it?" Thinking better of her greeting, she put her smile back on. "Goodness, come in."

"Thanks," I said, entering the old hotel Kathy and Bob had turned into a bed-and-breakfast. What had once been the lobby was now a living room with modern chairs and sofas mixed with antiques. The combination worked.

"You've done a beautiful job with this, Kathy."

A smile wiped the worry and fatigue off her face. "Thanks. It's a total labor of love." She gestured to a couch. "Want to have a seat out here? Or come into the kitchen with me?"

I could tell she'd prefer that, so she could get back to work. "I'm here to see Bob. Is he around?"

"Oh." She looked flustered. "Is it trouble?"

Why was that her first assumption? "No. He worked in the Kansas City federal courthouse. I hope he'll give me some idea about who had it in for Leonard Klamath."

She looked relieved. "I'll send him out to you. Shouldn't take long."

As she bustled out of the room, I sat in a comfortable wing chair and leaned my head back, eyes closed, listening to the faint background music of instrumental guitar and smelling wood polish and rose potpourri. Underneath all the room's scents lay a hint of wood smoke. It had been too hot for months to light a fire, but more than a century of wood fires in the hearth had imbued the walls with the scent.

Heavy footsteps clomped down the wood-floored hall. I sat up with open eyes as Bob Lynch plodded into the living room, his face scratched by briars or thorns. Suddenly, I wondered if he'd been at the farm running from me, unlikely as it seemed.

"Skeet! Good to see you. Kathy says you want to know about folks who might have had it in for Klamath. Right?" Bob gave me a big smile, but his eyes searched my face intently.

Smiling, I nodded. "Tell me what you remember about Leonard Klamath and people involved with him at the courthouse."

Bob's smile grew warmer. With visible stiffness, he sat on the edge of a sofa.

"Have you hurt yourself?" I asked.

He waved a negligent hand. "Nah. Just sore from cutting

brush in the back all yesterday. The back garden's an overgrown tangle of trees and thornbushes. Yesterday I overdid."

"Lot of work, that. You really throw yourself into it." I gestured across my face.

"Oh. My wedding ring slid off into the bushes. I went in after it. You'd think it'd give me extra points with Kathy. Don't think that'll happen." His hearty laugh had a ring of falseness.

I smiled, wondering if Bob Lynch had slithered through thornbushes at Karen's farm last night. Fantastic to think of gregarious Bob sneaking around in the dark with a rifle, but suddenly I could see it.

"Do you have a rifle?"

He looked startled. "Sure I do. Used to go hunting. Haven't been able to get free since we bought this time, energy, and money sinkhole." He gestured at the walls around us.

Restoring this old hotel into a bed-and-breakfast was apparently not a labor of love for Bob.

"What'd you want to know about Klamath?" he asked abruptly.

"How long did you know him? How well?" I softened my voice, trying to set him at ease. Bob was definitely nervous.

His tense expression smoothed, and he settled onto the sofa. "Not as well as some of them, like Jake Wise."

I perked up at the mention of Jake's name. "Why was that?"

"Leonard did mostly white-collar, financial crime. Most cases were settled out of court. He didn't try cases much. Not like Jake, always trying some case. A workhorse, that guy." He leaned his head forward. "If you ask me, Melvin exploited the hell out of him."

He shook his head. "Probably why he died. He hadn't been himself for weeks. Curt. Not noticing things he always noticed.

Working late. Dizzy from overwork. Falling down those stairs. Hell of an end for a good man."

"What kind of things did Jake stop noticing?"

"He always knew everyone who worked there. Made no distinctions, U.S. attorney, secretary, janitor. He said hello, asked how things were going. Really wanted to hear the answers. Not like Melvin and the other big shots. Jake noticed if you were upset or sick and asked about it. Tried to help if he could."

That was the Jake I'd known as an adopted father.

He smiled, remembering. "Everybody loved the guy."

A wave of pain swept over me. This beloved man would never again give me a hug or be there for me to run to when life got twisted. I shoved it down deep inside me.

Bob's face grew somber. "For a month or so before he died, he didn't answer when you said hello. He'd walk by without asking how you were. He didn't notice one of the court clerks crying one morning when her dad had died. Another time when one was real sick."

"Jake would have noticed?" I asked, knowing he would. That was who Jake had been.

Bob nodded vigorously. "Oh, yeah! He'd notice and get her released from work so she could go home. It wasn't like him. Melvin piled so much on him he couldn't take it anymore. His body broke down, and he fell down those damn marble stairs."

I changed the subject. "Did you ever know anyone who had a grudge against Leonard? One of the people he sent to prison?"

He shook his head. "Hell, no. Why? They got short sentences at country club places and went on their merry ways. If Jake had prosecuted them, they'd have done hard time and paid back money. Not Leonard. He was probably on the take."

"Really?"

Bob looked suddenly wary. "What do I know? It seemed that way. I didn't know anything. I was just a bailiff."

This bailiff noticed a lot of things more highly placed people missed.

"Is there anything else?" He stood up with a groan. "I've got to fix the toilet in one of the suites before they check in tonight."

I stood also. "Thanks a lot. I'll see myself out so you can head back to your plumbing."

"Don't want to, but guests got to have working toilets." He headed back down the hall with a heavy tread.

I'd learned about Jake's final days—and about how he and Leonard were perceived by those beneath them on the org chart. I still wondered if Bob was the phantom at Karen's farm. His facial scratches and back injury made him a real possibility. Still, I couldn't see Bob going through thornbushes without leaving a trail.

I let myself out as promised and stopped right outside to make notes. When I turned to leave, I saw Terry Heldrich sitting in the porch swing watching me the way I'd seen big cats watch small prey in nature films.

"What are you doing here?" I was embarrassed at being observed while unaware.

Terry laughed. His attention, usually assessing unknown dangers in his surroundings, fixed on my face and caused me to stay flustered.

"Actually, I should ask you that. I'm a paying guest after growing tired of the married couple's battles. Checked in last night." He smiled, lighting up his face. I tried not to notice his soft lips. He patted the seat beside him. "Sit with me. You're red in the face from the heat. Sit and rest."

My hands flew to my cheeks. Hot. They must be flushed. I didn't like that.

"Sorry, Terry. Too much to do to sit in a porch swing." I made my tone brisk.

Rising from the swing, he sauntered over to me without taking that intense focus off my face. He moved like a big cat, too. Embarrassed again, I dropped my gaze from his face. It landed on the tattoo peeking out from under his short sleeve. It looked like a Mariner's Compass quilt done all in black on bronze flesh. Quickly, I moved my gaze back to his face.

"I just want to talk with you, Skeet. Spend some time with you." His dark eyes remained focused on my face, making me uncomfortable.

I looked down at my notebook and pen. "I have questions to ask you."

He threw his head back and laughed. "Ask me what you want. Then I'll ask you what I want. Is that how this game is played?"

"I'm not playing games. I'm investigating a murder." With relief, I heard anger invade my voice. I could handle this. Just another arrogant man.

"Why would you think I have anything to do with your murder, Skeet? Strange name for a woman. But it suits you."

I tried to clear my head. Stay in control. He pulled me deliberately off topic to make me react. An angry outburst wouldn't help. "What time did you leave the party Sunday night?"

His smile crooked down one corner of his mouth. "I left with Walker after your sheriff came back to tell us to go home. Whatever time that was."

Did I believe him? If anyone among the suspects could kill at the drop of a hat, it was this man. But had he? He'd turned his guns over for testing without hesitation. They'd come up clean and been returned.

His eyes ran up and down me, returning to my face. His gaze was like a palpable touch. The corners of his mouth quirked further. "Why would you think I'd bother to kill Klamath? I hardly knew the man."

I looked down at my notebook. I wanted to be able to read this later. Still writing, I said, "Your boss knows him well. He might have wanted Leonard dead."

"He'd have to bloody well kill him himself then, wouldn't he?" He reached out to lift my chin. "I've killed before but not for profit. I'm not Walker's weapon, Skeet. If he wants someone frightened, hurt, or dead, I wouldn't put it past him to have some Neanderthal do it for him. I do more sophisticated things for Walker, things he couldn't get elsewhere. That's why he pays me."

I believed him. Immediately, I scolded myself for gullibility. It sounded good, and I'd begun to like Terry a little. But he was dangerous. At the very best amoral. He'd killed. He admitted it. Not some innocent man for me to believe every word coming out of his mouth.

"Duly noted." I didn't see him move. I looked up into his eyes to find him directly in front of me, only inches away. He breathed harder than I'd have expected from that short move. So did I, I suddenly noticed.

Shit! I recognized this—intense looks and ragged breathing. It had been like that when Sam and I first got involved. Not what I needed or wanted. Never with this man.

He moved his hand toward my face. Part of me wanted to see the chemical reaction when it touched my skin. I was older and smarter than I'd been when hormones sucked me into Sam's life. I dodged his hand, heading for the porch steps. "Thanks for answering my questions."

My foot was on the first step when I felt his hand on my shoulder.

"You can't run away from what's between us. Not forever."

Shielding myself firmly, I looked up. "I never like it when someone tells me I can't do something. It drives me to go ahead and do it. Take your hand off."

With a deadly smile, he slid his hand from my shoulder slowly down my arm. I shook it off and continued down the steps.

It'd been too long since I'd had sex. That was all this was. Nothing else. If I were to get involved with someone, it would be Joe. Sweet and nondemanding. If I wanted sparks in the dark and heartache in daylight, I'd just go back to Sam. Already had one problem like that on my plate. Sure didn't need to add another.

Anyway, how could I know he hadn't offed Leonard as part of his daily duties for Walker? Terry was still high on the suspect list. He was turning out to be more dangerous than I'd realized.

# CHAPTER 11

My next stop was Helen Lawson's fair-trade import store, the World in Your Hands. Before opening the orange door in the center of tiger stripes brightly painted over squares of primary colors and escaping the heat that left me sweating through my clothes from my short walk, I looked across the square toward Forgotten Arts, but the courthouse blocked my line of vision. I hoped Miryam kept close watch over Karen. I did see Terry leaning against the bed-and-breakfast porch watching me. He'd put on his hat before stepping into the sun, and he gave me a cocky salute.

Quickly I pulled open the shop door and slipped into the cool air inside, determined to put Terry out of my mind and concentrate on what I was here to do. Ridiculous name. Terry. Not at all fitting for someone who thought he was so bad.

Helen rang up the purchases of two older women. As they headed out the door, she called after them, "Thank you. Be sure to come back."

"I'm so glad they're gone," Helen said once the door closed. "They've been here over an hour. Picking up one thing after another. Always acting like the price was outrageous. I explained over and over we sell things at a cost that allows the artisans a living wage. Not like the places that exploit them because they're starving. They've picked over every single thing in the store."

Helen did look stressed. Her lilac dress was creased and wrinkled, her hair even more droopy than usual, her face washed out. I remembered she'd moved here because of a stress breakdown.

"Why not take a break?" I suggested. "The streets are deserted right now. Only mad dogs and Englishmen—and campus police chiefs—go out in the sun." And that stupid Terry, I added to myself.

Her laugh was halfhearted, all the tired joke deserved. "You're right. Sit down. I haven't got raspberry herbal tea like Karen, but I have ice-cold water."

"Just as good. If I have to drink something without caffeine or chocolate, make it water. Can I help?"

Shaking her head, Helen disappeared through a curtain of long beaded strands. I wondered why it felt so peaceful before realizing there was no piped-in music. Helen had only silence in her place of business, a surprising relief.

When she came back through the beads with two glasses in her hands, Reverend Matt opened the front door. He smiled at me, but when he saw Helen, his face lit like a beacon in darkness. I had to grin. True love, that was for sure.

"Aha! Caught you sneaking in a rest." His eyes laughed as he tried to hold his mouth in a stern line that quivered with the smile trying to burst forth.

He took the glasses from Helen's hands and gave one to me. Then he looked back at Helen. "I'm so glad to see you paying attention to your own needs."

He hugged her with the arm that didn't hold the glass. "Sit

down, sweetheart. Here." He handed her the glass and pulled over a chair and ottoman, settling her into it as if she were a fragile grandmother or wealthy great-aunt.

Helen rolled her eyes, lips tight. "That's enough, Matt."

A sheepish look crossed his face. "I just want you comfortable. I only want you well and happy, love." His tone held a hint of pleading.

Helen looked exasperated and uncomfortable. "That's all right, but don't hover."

"Of course," Matt replied, chastened.

The tableau that played out in front of me made me uncomfortable. Matt didn't seem to be doing anything wrong. Most women would be delighted to have their husbands take such good care of them. He didn't seem domineering, just caring.

Helen frowned. "Skeet and I were chatting. Would you mind?"

Reverend Matt's head jerked slightly, as if she'd struck him. "Of course not." He gave me a pained smile. "Sorry for interrupting."

He headed for the door but at the last minute turned back to give Helen a pleading look. "Don't work too late, please, sweetheart. I'll come help you close."

At Helen's nod, he left the shop. She turned to me, frown lines clearing.

"You didn't have to run Matt off." I'd wanted to speak with Helen alone, but I hated to be the reason for friction.

Helen waved a negligent hand. "He pops in five or six times a day. Checking up. It . . . gets old."

I could understand that. I'm pretty independent myself. I'd have problems with someone constantly checking on me. "Let's talk about Jake and Leonard. I'm trying to get a handle on this murder."

Her face stiffened slightly at the mention of the two victims. Had Helen pulled the trigger on Leonard? Was it her crawling through the bushes on Karen's farm? She'd hunted in the Guatemalan jungle as a nun. It seemed possible.

"Yes, Skeet. It's important to find out who killed Leonard."

"And who killed Jake."

She stared at me intently. "Jake? Are you saying he was murdered?"

"Accidental death was what we thought at the time. We know now it was murder." At the end of this case, I'd have proof he'd been murdered, and I'd have the culprit. I hoped.

Helen's face fell into sad lines. "But Jake was so wonderful. How . . . ?"

She was truly devastated to learn of Jake's murder—or perhaps that it had been discovered?

I pulled out my notebook and pen. "Let's talk about human trafficking. How did you run into it? Why did you turn to Jake about it?"

Helen looked toward the yellow wall covered with bright woven wall hangings and a collection of necklaces made of big, colorful beads in animal shapes, as if she were seeing through the wall and into distant lands.

"Human traffickers target the most vulnerable populations—runaway and abused children, new immigrants, the homeless, the devastatingly poor."

I nodded. "The usual victims of crime."

She looked over at me and leaned forward. "They offer jobs and sometimes homes and safety. That's how they lure the victims in. They stick them in crowded rooms the traffickers' company owns, keeping all their wages for 'rent and expenses.' They take away their ID."

A big factor, especially with immigrants. "So the victim has no ID or money and is in deep debt to the trafficker?"

She sighed. "They keep their slaves completely isolated except when they're working. They contract with big corporations for labor and provide slaves to work, often under unsafe conditions."

"Slaves?"

Helen grew angry. "That's really what they are. These traffickers are really slavers. Sometimes the slavers put brands on them." She twisted her hands together, her voice growing harsher. "No one uses those terms today. We like to think slavery's gone. Certainly in America. We whitewash it and call it human trafficking."

I always thought of trafficking as involving sex or babies. America still wants prostitutes, younger than ever, and babies to adopt instead of the thousands of older kids without families. This was new. I scribbled in my notebook before looking up.

Helen stared at me intently, leaning toward me. "These monsters have whole families caught in this slavery, and the children work like the adults—if they're lucky."

"Why 'if they're lucky'?" I asked.

Helen's face twisted. "If they don't get taken for sex slavery." She looked as if she'd like to physically attack those responsible.

"Of course." I couldn't believe myself. How did sex with kids become *of course*? Still, I knew that demand had been exploding. Saw ugly reminders on the streets all the time. "How do they keep people in such total servitude? Don't they try to run away?"

Helen tilted her head. "Slavers use fear. Of the immigration service, of the law—saying they owe all this money and can be thrown into jail—and fear of physical violence. Beatings and rapes are often punishments when someone tries to escape or tell what's going on. Killings, too."

"This is going on large-scale?" Earlier, Helen had said Jake thought Walker headed a big trafficking network he'd discovered.

"It's a multimillion-dollar business. Maids and janitors for hotel chains. Window cleaners. Roofers. Meat processors. Factories and sweatshops. Hardworking laborers who can't complain about unsafe conditions or wages or overtime. Every big company's dream workforce." She couldn't spit out her bitter words fast enough.

I laid a hand on her wrist. "Take a minute and breathe."

She ignored me. "Sometimes the work is worse than just hard, unhealthy, and unsafe." She twisted her hands again, looking into that far distance beyond the brightly colored walls. "Sometimes young women and girls, occasionally boys, are forced into prostitution. That's particularly brutal. Some of the worst involves torture and live Internet pornography. Sometimes death."

I couldn't believe this former nun could describe such things. She got more and more wound up as she spoke. She looked as if it wouldn't take much to make her explode. She'd told me Jake thought Leonard was on the take to keep investigations away from human trafficking. Had she followed him to the Caves and executed him?

"How did you learn about this firsthand?" I hoped my calm voice would ease the tension obviously building within her.

She shifted her eyes to the far wall, staring through its pink surface. "I had a family go missing. Last time I saw them, I sent the father to a company hiring laborers. Wanting to check out how the interview had gone, I found their apartment empty. It never was, with four kids, a grandmother, and two parents." She closed her eyes for a second, seeing once again the abandoned apartment.

I thought I knew what happened.

"I checked with the company I sent him to." She stopped and looked at me wildly. "I sent him. They trusted me, and I sent them there."

"Not your fault, Helen. You didn't know." My words were futile. How did you live, knowing you'd sent trusting victims to a slaver?

"The company said Ezam never showed up. However, the neighbor said Ezam came back all excited because they had a great future now. Told him I was wonderful and he should come see me." Her voice choked to a stop.

She began to cry—hard, racking sobs, the way someone who hates to cry does. I knew. I cried like that when I couldn't help it. The sobs were the only sound in the place. I'd have welcomed background music. But there's no music that makes a good background to hard, angry tears.

Finally the sobbing stopped. She rubbed the back of her hands across her eyes and face. "I'm sorry." She still had a shudder in her voice. "It's hard to remember."

I waved off her apologies. "It would be hard for anyone. Was that when you went to Jake?"

"Not until the oldest daughter's body turned up, beaten and raped and branded." She touched the top of one breast. "The police didn't do anything when I reported them missing. But one officer remembered me when they found this body. He called to see if I could identify it. I could."

She rubbed her hand across her eyes again. "I'd heard about sex trafficking. Probably some TV show. I went to Jake. He investigated the company, found weird stuff, but nothing he could connect to human trafficking. That investigation led him to a bad case involving torture. Just one young girl, mentally ill from the torture and drugs. She'll probably be institutionalized the rest of her life. Men all across the country were involved. The task force eventually put them in prison."

"I remember. That case made all the papers in the state."

"Jake believed they got the girl from the company I told him about. He couldn't prove that final link. Trafficking is hard to prove. Takes money, man-hours, sophisticated equipment and more. He decided to set up the task force. I suggested he go to Walker Lynch for funding."

"You two worked together on plans for the task force?" I looked to see if she'd calmed down. She avoided my eyes. That made me curious. I leaned forward to show interest without a word. An old trick. Stay quiet, and people tell you amazing truths.

She saw me watching her and quickly turned her head. The silence built.

"Trafficking was an obsession with us. We shared an obsession no one else had. We met late. After our day jobs were finished. To work on it together."

I kept my face expressionless.

"We didn't mean to fall in love." She looked up blindly, nothing but pain in her eyes. "At first, it was just me. Or he was better at hiding it. Later, both of us. We were crazy. He said he loved his wife. I didn't care by that time. No, I couldn't believe he could make love to me the way he did and love someone else."

Strategy wasn't keeping me silent any longer. Shock was. Jake? That faithful, loving husband? An affair?

Helen's words came tumbling over each other now, as if she needed to tell someone. "We were insane. Twice, he let me in a secret door at the courthouse to make love in his office. Sleazy motels. Backseats of cars. The hood of mine once. Under bushes in parks. Up against a brick wall in an alley in the Northeast at midnight."

She shook her head as if, even now, she couldn't believe she'd done these things.

"That was after we started fighting. He tried to draw back. I'd call him to me, try to seduce him, and we'd fight. In the middle of it all, he'd take me until we were both shaking and ashamed. And I couldn't get enough. I couldn't let him go."

I sat, stunned. Jake, closest thing to a saint I'd ever known. I'd have bet my life on his fidelity. With this drab ex-nun. In such passion. No, call it what it was. Lust.

Tears started streaming down Helen's face without any sobbing. Unaware of them, she talked on.

"He was stronger, though. He walked away. Wouldn't return calls, e-mails. Wouldn't see me. Over. For him."

She paused, startled by her words. "But it's never been over for me. Never."

Her voice echoed in the room's stillness. For the first time, she looked at me, as if just aware I listened. "Then he died. When I heard of Jake's death, I tried to kill myself. Wound up in Research Psychiatric for a month."

She paused a second. I tried to think of something to say to get out of there, away from her. Her face twisted.

"Matt quit the job of his dreams and moved me out here to take care of me." She spat out the last words as if she hated them.

Now, loud sobs joined the tears. I sat next to her, frozen.

Jake. How could he have done such a thing? Not even a falling-in-love thing, but a hot-hot-sex thing. With an ex-nun, for God's sake. Karen. This would kill her. The man whose death she was going crazy trying to avenge. Karen could never know this. Never.

I looked at Helen with hostility, a sad, middle-aged woman.

Jake took a big part of her into the grave with him. I had to pity her. There was nothing else left to give.

Reeling, I left Helen after calming her and promising I'd never tell what she'd confessed to me. As if I ever wanted to tell anyone. I wanted to unlearn everything I'd heard from her in the last hour.

So I went to church.

Brewster First Methodist Church was lovely old brick with a white wooden spire and lovely old stained-glass windows. Periodically, the board had to decide whether to sell the quite valuable windows to make needed repairs on the building. So far, they'd always found another source of needed income. I'd heard that was growing more difficult.

There's nothing quite like a small-town Protestant church on a weekday in summer. The air-conditioning was off, but darkness, punctuated only by the stained-glass light, and silence shut out summer's heat, along with the town and its problems.

I wasn't a church member, but Gran and my mother were churchgoers. I'd grown up with these peaceful spaces. Christianity came early to the Cherokee, hit hard, and stuck. Gran saw no contradiction between church and the old ways. Most of the tribe felt the same, either placing more weight on traditional ways, like Gran, or Christianity, like Coreen.

I had to question Matt. First, I'd sit on this wooden pew to let his church's peace ease the pain Helen's confession had dealt me. I still loved Jake like a father, even knowing this. Love or no, it hurt to learn he wasn't the man I'd thought him. So I breathed quiet church air. Almost as good as going to water.

Later, I headed through the door beside the chancel to the church offices. At that moment, Matt popped his head out of his office. "Louisa, have you seen my calendar? I had notes in it for this sermon." When he noticed me, a smile lit his face. "Come for a visit, Skeet?"

I smiled back. "A short one, Reverend. Need to ask a few questions."

Reverend Matt spoke to me, then to his secretary. "Come in, Skeet. Louisa, would you find my calendar?"

I moved into the inner office as Louisa clicked down the hall.

Smiling, Matt pointed to a chair facing the desk. "I'm glad to answer your questions. Easier than writing this sermon."

I smiled. "Did you know Leonard Klamath before the party Sunday? You lived in KC when he was assistant U.S. attorney."

Matt shook his handsome head with another confused look, keeping his hazel eyes fixed on my face. "I didn't meet him even there. I'd never seen the man before."

I raised an eyebrow. "Helen knew him from her time in Kansas City."

Matt lifted long, aristocratic hands. "Helen knew him through her work. I'm ashamed to say I never paid the attention I should have to her work."

He twirled his desk chair a quarter turn away, staring out the small window set in the side wall. "I love my wife. Right after I met Helen back East, I knew she was the one for me. Took three years to make her agree." He threw his head back in a laugh. "Tough on the old ego."

His laughter was infectious. I couldn't help laughing with him.

"After we married, I took the tenure-track job out here, obsessed with my career. Helen found work similar to her job in Boston. I got swallowed up in academic politics, trying to publish so I'd get tenure." He rubbed his right hand over his broad forehead. "I neglected her. When she needed me most, I neglected her."

I offered a polite disavowal, thinking of Helen's tale.

"It's true. I almost lost her. I couldn't have survived that." His eyes gleamed with unshed tears. "She was so stressed and unhappy she almost died."

I didn't think the stresses of her job almost killed her. Who knew? Perhaps they—and Matt's neglect—made her more vulnerable to what sprang up between her and Jake.

"You made a great sacrifice for her," I pointed out. "Giving up your faculty position. Becoming a small-town minister."

Eyes flashing with scorn, he snapped his fingers. "I'd sacrifice more than a hotshot career to keep Helen healthy and happy. She's truly the core of my life."

I thought of Karen, for whom Jake was the foundation of life. Jake had been the center of the shattered woman I'd just seen, leaving her in fragments. Now, this nice man didn't realize the woman at the core of his life was nothing but shards.

I changed the subject. "Did you know Jake Wise when you were in the city?"

Reverend Matt's jaw tightened. His eyes darted away. He took a breath. "I knew of him. Helen was . . . involved with him on the human trafficking task force. I heard about him."

I glanced at my notebook. "What time did you leave the party Sunday night?"

He looked up, figuring times in his head. "After Joe came back to get Brian and head to the hospital. By the time we left, Jeremy was shutting things down. It must have been between eleven-thirty and eleven forty-five."

"Who was still there then, Reverend Matt?"

"Jeremy, of course. Melvin was still there looking for his

wife. Walker Lynch and his man left shortly before we did. Randy Thorsson was still there. Kathy Lynch couldn't find Bob, either. She and Melvin joked about what they'd do if they found them together." He rubbed his eyes and closed them while I scribbled the names he mentioned. Opening his eyes again, he shook his head with a frown. "I don't know who else. Lots of people were still there when Joe came back. It took most of us a while to leave."

I nodded. "That's what everyone says. Each of you has memories of different people. We'll put together a portrait from everyone's testimony."

He glanced at his watch. Irritation washed over his face and fled. "I have an appointment. If you've more questions, could we take care of them later?"

Packing my notebook away, I stood. "Thanks for your time. If I need anything else, I'll let you know."

He stood also, putting on his sport coat, straightening his tie.

As I started out the door, he called my name. I turned. "Thank you for befriending Helen. There aren't many people here she can talk to. I'm glad you and she are becoming friends."

His smile lit up the handsome face that had half the women in town drooling—the only thing on his mind the unfaithful, broken-hearted woman he loved obsessively.

"Take care, Reverend Matt."

Walking out of the back of the church, I thought about the Lawson marriage. It looked like the happiest in town. Like many things in this case, the truth was worlds apart from the appearance. A murder always opened a can or two of worms. Sometimes the worms turned out to be snakes.

# CHAPTER 12

My next stop was Forgotten Arts. Brian walked from school to Karen's shop for counseling sessions the afternoons he didn't have music class. Miryam had called to tell me Brian and Angie had entered the store. No one else. Besides Cherry, Karen's student manager.

"You can't count her, now can you?" Miryam had said breezily.

I'd pick up Brian and check on Karen. Maybe persuade her to let Cherry run things and go home.

Inside the shop, neither Karen nor Brian could be seen, secluded in Karen's office in back. Angie messed with wicked-looking wool combs, five-inch-long sharp tines curving from the wood handle, playing keep-away with Cherry, who kept trying to grab them.

"Those aren't toys. Wool combs are dangerous. Real sharp." Normally cheerful Cherry sounded seriously annoyed. She made another grab. Angie swept them out of her reach with a loud laugh, coming dangerously close to Cherry's face.

"Angie! Put those down." I walked over to them. "You almost cut Cherry."

"Or what? You going to pull your gun and shoot me?" Angie waved the tines in front of my face.

The only safe place to put your hand on one of those was the wood handle, both firmly in Angie's grip. They could have been arcane tools of torture. Karen had shown me how they were used to separate and smooth long fibers in preparation for spinning.

I glared at Angie for a second. While I had her attention, Cherry crept up behind her, grabbing her wrists.

"Shit!" Angie started to struggle.

"They're too dangerous to let some kid play with," Cherry said.

"Who are you calling a kid? I'm fifteen. I've probably been around more than you have, college girl."

While they called names back and forth, I took three steps forward and grabbed Angie's arms, pinching inside the elbow. This loosened her grip on the combs. Cherry caught the handles and pulled them away. I let the angry teenager go, as Brian and Karen entered the shop front.

"Be careful with those wool combs." Karen's voice rose as she saw our little tableau.

"Angie, you don't want to mess with those," Brian added. "You could cut yourself pretty badly."

"Who took these out of the box?" Karen asked, irritated.

"She did." Cherry's face was red with anger. "I was taking inventory to see what to order. When I turned around, she was messing with them. She wouldn't put them down when I told her. Skeet and I had to wrestle them from her."

Brian stared from Angie's scornful face to my exasperated expression. He looked over to Karen, but her face also showed anger. She wagged her index finger in Angie's face. I flinched, not only from Gran's teachings but because I'd never seen Karen do that before, as if to grind her finger into Angie's face.

"In my shop, young lady, you put something down if shop employees tell you to. Those are dangerous." Karen's voice trembled with anger she tried to control.

Angie sniffed, drawing herself up with fake arrogance. "I was just playing. They're vicious-looking. You could do major damn destruction with them in a gang fight."

I tried to hold back my own anger and impatience but failed. "How would you know? You've never seen a gang fight."

Angie bristled. "I have. Lots of times, Supercop."

I laughed. "Where? At the first private school you went to or the second? Out there in the rich suburbs. Quit being ridiculous, and behave."

"Don't call her ridiculous!" Brian moved to stand next to Angie, as if I'd threatened her. "You have no right to talk to Angie that way."

Great! Brian and I were having our first argument over this gangsta wannabe.

The bell over the door jingled, but no one paid any attention, caught up in the tense situation.

"Someone needs to talk to her that way," I told Brian. "Better me now than some real gangbanger later. Then it'll be too late."

"What's going on?" Mel walked up, frowning. "Angie?"

"I'm standing up to the cop bully who manhandled me," Angie said in a self-righteous voice.

Mel turned to me, face reddening. "You manhandled my kid?"

I rolled my eyes. "She took dangerous tools from their box and waved them around, refusing to put them down. She could have hurt herself or others."

Karen moved to stand between Mel and me. "Who are you to come into my shop and start yelling, you murderer?"

For a second, Angie's hard mask dropped, her face displaying fear. Brian looked confused and wary. Cherry's mouth dropped.

Karen's words stopped Mel for a second. He looked around, trying to figure out who Karen addressed. Then he turned back to Karen, voice angry, face still confused.

"Who are you calling a murderer? What's going on in this crazy place?"

Karen moved close to Mel and jabbed at him with her finger, stopping short of his chest. I was afraid she'd miss or lose that last bit of control and start physically attacking.

"You! George Melvin! Murderer of my Jake. Your best friend. Some friend! Murderer of Leonard. Another friend. Attempted murderer of me. Who knows who else you murdered, monster."

I groaned. Karen had finally lost it. I didn't know how to save her from herself. Brian stared in shock. Cherry looked appalled. Angie resumed her cocky façade, looking smug. I wished I'd smacked her while taking the combs.

"Karen." I set my hands on her shoulders to calm her.

Mel's face swelled bright red. His answer was a roar. "What shit! You're insane. I never killed anyone, except in war. Jake got dizzy and fell. Leonard was a drunk. You can't believe him. Someone probably killed him because he was an ass."

"More lies! Liar!" Karen shook her head wildly. "Get out! Right now. Out. Out." She swept him toward the door with her hands.

"Angie, come here." Mel had been pushed back to the door. "We're leaving."

Angie sauntered past us with a look of satisfaction on her face. Brian's face sank. I wanted to shake her and say, *See what your troublemaking* brought? I wanted to tell her, *Leave my boy alone.* I wanted to lock Karen in her back office until she calmed down. I couldn't make any of this better.

Karen kept sweeping her hands at Mel, crying, "Out, killer!"

Mel backed through the open door. People stepped out of shops and stopped on the sidewalk. "I'd sue you for slander, but you'd plead insanity," he shouted, grabbing Angie and pulling her to his car.

Karen stood in the doorway, screaming. "You leave. Don't ever come back, murderer."

A crowd formed in the street. I pulled a sobbing Karen back into the shop by her shoulders. I closed the door, and she threw herself into my arms.

"I hate him. Why is he still alive when Jake's dead?" Then sobs overtook her.

I held her, looking over her head at Cherry, eyes wide with shock. She'd never seen Karen like this before. Neither had I.

Beside Cherry, Brian looked stunned, trying to get his mind around the sudden about-face his afternoon had taken. My own afternoon had been an emotional roller coaster, as well.

"Karen, come on." I supported her to the nearest chair, stroking her shoulder to calm her.

I looked up at Cherry, whose lower lip quivered. "Please make Karen a cup of hot mint tea." Glad of an excuse to flee, Cherry sped off to the storeroom's little kitchen.

Karen finally gave up all effort at fighting and sobbed. I preferred even angry Karen to broken Karen.

"Things will get better," I murmured. "Part of this is letdown from pain meds, temporary depression. Go home and sleep. Tomorrow you'll feel better."

She sucked in a quavering breath, bringing her tears under

control. "How, Skeet? Will you bring Jake back from the dead? Leonard? How can I feel better tomorrow? They'll still be dead. That murderer still walking around free."

She was back on the attack. I thought of everone who'd dumped their emotions on me today, from Karen earlier to Miryam and Walker to Terry to Helen and Reverend Matt. I wanted to be as unruffled about it as Karen usually was. Only I didn't have her training. Mine was in standing up for myself and fighting back.

"Answer me! Just how can I feel better tomorrow?" Karen shouted. Something crashed in the storeroom. I figured Cherry wouldn't bring out that cup of tea anytime soon.

I looked at my friend, thinking how ugly she looked. I was shocked to think such a thing of someone I loved.

"You're not the only one hurting, not the only one who loved Jake." My words shocked me. I couldn't go there. I couldn't bear for her to learn about Jake and Helen.

"I loved Jake," I continued in a softer tone of voice. "I'm try-ing to be as reasonable as he was. A man's been killed. Possibly another killed earlier. That's where my concern lies. And the pos-sibility the killer's trying to kill you. These are what I'm dealing with. Your outbursts don't make it any easier. Are you trying to keep me from solving these murders?"

Her mouth opened and closed. "I . . . No. Not trying to keep you from that. You know—"

I made my voice gentler. "This kind of thing makes it harder for me to do my job. Stop and think. Be the Karen you always were, and you'll see." I hoped I was getting through. I might be.

She looked up, strands of white hair flying around her face, her broken heart in her eyes. "I can't be that Karen right now. All I can do is cry and scream and want that man to pay for killing Jake." Her voice rose with each sentence.

I tried to make her understand. "I don't know that Mel killed Jake. Neither do you."

Jaw stiffening, she glared at me. "He was involved. I know he was."

"You don't know he was involved in Jake's murder." My voice sounded angry even to me. I lowered it. "You're guessing. Or you want him to be involved. You can't know it without evidence. Just as you didn't know Jake was murdered until Leonard told you."

She stared at me, stricken, her face crumbling. "I didn't know. I believed it was an accident. I should have felt something was wrong. I didn't try to avenge Jake." She was headed toward another crazy outburst, but tears overwhelmed her.

Cherry crept out of the storeroom with the cup of tea. I gestured with my head toward her weeping boss. She carefully offered Karen the tea. "Drink this. You'll feel better with something warm in your stomach."

Karen looked up through tears at the good-natured college student and took the cup. "You're not seeing me at my best. I'm sorry."

Cherry leaned over to hug her. "This is an awful time for you. I can't imagine how bad you feel. Your friend killed. Finding out your husband was, too. Someone trying to kill you. I wish I could do something to help."

Her words made me sick. I was Karen's best friend. She'd been my help and support through the years. Why couldn't I suck it up and be a better friend to her now? No matter how she behaved.

"Thanks, Cherry." Karen took the cup of tea and drank.

"Let's close the shop early," I said. "Go home to eat and sleep."

"Skeet's right. Everything's easier with a good night's sleep, my mom always says." Cherry's face had brightened at my words. She looked her normal self.

Karen looked apologetic. "I'm tired. Maybe that would be best."

She looked exhausted. I, too, felt exhausted after this day.

"Great," said Cherry. "I'll lock up. Let Skeet take you home."

"I drove my car this morning." Karen lifted her hands helplessly.

"I'll take you home, then get Joe to follow me to the farm as I drive your car. I'll ride back with him." I wanted to keep her car in town so she'd be stuck at home, but I knew that wouldn't fly. At least she wouldn't drive in her current wobbly state.

Karen stretched out in the back of my car, and Brian rode in front with me, stiff and silent. I guessed we'd have an angry conversation once we dropped off Karen, but I put it from my mind, to concentrate on taking Karen home. This tired, I could only think of the task in front of me. Other trouble could wait its turn.

We drove in silence to the farm. I hit the horn lightly, and Ignacio hurried out to help Karen inside. Once they were safely in the house, I headed for home.

The silence of emotional and mental exhaustion had settled over us for the trip from town. Now, only Brian and I rode in silence turned hostile. I waited for the storm to break.

"You had no right to treat Angie like that."

I looked at Brian, stiff and staring ahead. "What she did was foolish and dangerous. You didn't see anything but the end. She almost slashed Cherry's face with the wool combs. You know they're no toys."

He shook his head angrily. "You just don't like Angie. She knows that."

She probably thought no one but Brian liked her. "I don't dislike Angie. Sometimes I dislike her behavior."

He turned his face to stare out his window at the land rushing past. "She's right. You're a control freak."

"Sounds to me like Angie doesn't like me. Don't you think?"

He shook his head vigorously, trying to shake out my words. "You turn it all around! You don't like Angie because she's different. She's not . . . a homogenized commodity."

I shrugged, knowing he quoted Angie. "I don't like it when she's rude and hurtful to others. I don't like it when she does stupid, dangerous things to show off."

"She's not stupid. She's brilliant!" He faced me. "You don't know her."

I nodded. "That may be. I think she's smart, but she doesn't show me that side. All she shows me is bad behavior she thinks is cool. It's not. It's stupid."

He held his hands over his ears. "Stop saying she's stupid. She's not."

"You say she's brilliant. I don't think waving sharp, dangerous tools near someone's eyes is brilliant. Sorry about that." I wished away the sharp edge to my voice. I felt a headache's approach.

"You don't cut anyone any slack. Not Angie, not Karen. If you don't like what they say or do, that's it. You need to be more tolerant. Everyone can't be perfect like you." His voice took on Angie's sarcastic tone.

What he said hurt. I knew how imperfect I was. I felt sure Angie'd filled his ears with my failings.

"I've never claimed to be perfect. I try to be tolerant with Karen. She's under emotional pressure. Angie deliberately acts out, then wants us to give her a pass. No thanks." I turned my head to watch him stare sullenly at his lap. Near town, I could hear a distant train that would rumble through downtown shortly. Clouds moved in. Maybe we'd get rain to break the heat straining everyone's nerves.

"Do you like it when Angie does that kind of thing? Doesn't it bother you?" Behind my left eye, I felt a stabbing pain.

He shook his head slowly. "You don't know her situation. That Liz is awful to her. Her mom's suffering. Angie's miserable, so she gets mad." The anger seeped from his voice.

I touched his hand briefly. "And she strikes out at everyone. But she's hurting herself. I give her a lot more leeway than most people will. She's damaging herself with this behavior. No one will like her."

"I like her." He stuck his chin out.

I smiled at his loyalty. "You're very special. If she wants to have friends, if she wants people to sympathize with her tough situation, she needs to change her attitude."

I pulled onto our street. Maybe I'd beat this headache, after all. "She's playing right into Liz's hands."

"I know." He looked helpless and unhappy. "It's hard for her. She's real mad."

I parked in front of the garage in back of the house. Thunder rumbled in the distance. "She's also afraid. Do you know why?"

He looked puzzled. "I don't think she's afraid. She's the bravest person I know."

"She may be brave, but she's still afraid. I see it in her eyes when she lets her mask down for a second. Ask her what's frightened her. I may be able to help."

We sat in silence before getting out of the car. Walking to the back door, I smelled that ozone that heralds rain. Maybe we'd get some relief.

I had to call Joe and drive Karen's car to her home before I could pick up Chinese for supper. I'd have to keep the headache at bay that long. Maybe the time apart would give Brian time to think about what we'd discussed. I hoped our fight was over, and rain would clear the air.

I was angry, too. Not at Brian, Karen, or even Angie, but with this person who'd come into my house and my town, committing murder and tearing apart so many lives. This person claimed friendship with Karen and me, then betrayed it in the worst way. I needed to get my hands on whoever it was. Exactly what I intended to do.

# CHAPTER 13

After General Tso's chicken and shrimp lo mein with Brian in a subdued atmosphere, the welcome sound of thunder accompanied me to my bedroom. Maybe a good thunderstorm would clear the tension from the air and my head. Lady followed me like she did before Brian moved in. Wilma Mankiller appeared from the bedroom and led the way back in. Brian was upstairs doing homework and playing video games. The animals avoided him, sensing his anger.

The older homes of Old Brewster had plenty of space. My bedroom had room for my grandparents' big old bed and dressers, a chair with a table, and lots of bookcases. I took off my jacket and shoulder rig, removing my gun from its holster and storing it in the locked drawer of my bedside table. When I finished undressing, I hung my black pantsuit in the closet and draped my turquoise hand-knit shell and socks over the chair for hand washing.

Sitting on the quilt Gran gave me for high school graduation, I pulled on jeans and a T-shirt. Thunder cracked outside, much closer. Lightning brightened the room momentarily. Lady whined, thrusting her head in my lap, while Wilma whipped under the bed. I sympathized with them a few minutes, then headed back to the kitchen.

No working upstairs on the computer during the storm. I'd make some hot chocolate with whipped cream. Sit on the couch and knit on the alpaca lace shawl for Gran's birthday. Put on some Eric Marienthal. Untangle the strands of motive and opportunity in these killings.

My mind replayed the past two days—what I'd learned from Mel and Liz, Walker and Terry. Walker. I'd planned to interview him again today, but my time was eaten up. Tomorrow I'd get the truth out of him. My forehead wrinkled at the prospect.

Terry, I didn't want to think about, but his face popped into my mind. I didn't like men with mustaches or long hair. He could take his face and get out of my head. He was trouble. Especially in ways that had nothing to do with these murders. He was the perfect murderer. All the skills and experience. But I heard him saying, "I've killed before, but not for profit." Those words had the ring of truth. Unfortunately, I wasn't going to be able to put him in jail, which would solve all my problems nicely. I shook my head to send his face flying.

The sad case of Reverend Matt and Helen. He, loving so much. She, loving so much, but someone else. Jake's infidelity and what it would do to Karen if she ever found out brought on my headache in earnest. Karen must never find out.

The phone rang, and I wondered who'd call this late.

"It's me," my ex said. The trouble in his voice goosed the headache up a notch.

"Sam, what is it?" I couldn't handle anything more.

"When I got here tonight, that damned Marie had brought Charlie another cheeseburger and a pack of cigarettes." I could hear the disgust and anger held back in Sam's voice. Marie was lucky he hadn't blasted her with it.

My head started a double throbbing. "Is she trying to give him a major heart attack or stroke? What's wrong with her?"

He growled. "I've got a pretty good idea. She was sitting in his lap when I got here. With her arms wrapped around him. I told her not to come back."

I had a troubling visual of what he'd said.

He snorted in contempt. "She's decided his pension and savings look awful good, and she doesn't care what we or the doctors say. She's out to marry him. I'll bet my next paycheck."

I closed my eyes as the headache rolled across my skull. "It makes sense. Cheeseburgers, beer, cigarettes, no exercises, a little slap and tickle. I'm glad you sent her packing."

I pictured Marie luring poor Charlie into marriage, being so good to him, letting him have everything the doctors forbade, not like his mean daughter, until he had another stroke or heart attack and left her his pension, savings, house, and car. I should ask the company to check her records. If I ever got clear of this case, I'd run her through the computers, see if there was anything on her in other jurisdictions.

Sam's anger was cooling. He sounded tired. "I'll arrange with the agency for someone else tomorrow. There'll be someone new tomorrow evening."

I'd have to be there early once more. I hoped they had someone for us. We were running out of nurses. "Tell the agency what she's doing. The woman's a menace."

"We may have this problem again." Sam's voice carried heat again. "We'll have to watch out. Charlie probably looks like a good bet who needs a wife."

My headache deepened into two pulsing pain points behind

my eyes. "I wouldn't mind if he did marry—if anyone could put up with him. But I don't want it to be someone who wants his little bit of money and won't be good to him."

Sam sighed heavily. "We'll have to keep our eyes open while he has to have these home nurse's aides. I never thought to worry about it before this woman showed up."

Funny how good he could sound even when his voice dragged with fatigue. I'd find something to thank him for his help with Charlie, but not what I knew he'd want.

"It's probably not an issue with any of them but this one. I'll get there early tomorrow night."

"Sorry. I know your hands are full with this murder right now. How's it going?"

The headache ground its way through my skull. "Don't ask. This is all tied up with Jake's death. And the shooter's trying for Karen."

Would my brain explode when the headache grated all the way through the skull? I tried to remember if I had anything to knock it out.

"That must be awful for you and Karen, sweetheart." His voice dropped into its whiskey-smooth timbre. "If you need help, babe, just call."

I sighed. When Sam started calling me "sweetheart" and "babe," it meant I'd have to start pushing away. I was in no shape to do it kindly tonight.

"Thanks, Sam. Charlie and I appreciate all the help you give with him."

He chuckled and used his oh-baby-I'm-the-best-thing-you've-ever-seen voice. "I'd do anything for you. Don't you know?"

Nothing I could say to that. So I said nothing while my headache decided it was Sherman and my skull Atlanta.

"I have to go, Sam. I'll get there early to meet the new nurse."

"Sleep tight and dream of me." He chuckled again.

"Not likely." I hung up the phone.

I certainly didn't need Terry sniffing around, trying to start something. I had enough trouble with the man I'd never get completely out of my life as long as my father lived.

The headache might let me crawl down the hall to the medicine cabinet. The night didn't look promising for sleep. Tomorrow would be hectic. First on my list, keep murderer from killing Karen. And try to get my son not to hate me and my father to do what he needed to do to stay alive. I had a full docket.

Since sleep was elusive, I headed out to run at dawn. Get a start on the day rather than tangling sheets. The storm had washed heat and humidity from the air. It could have been a crisp, clear autumn morning as dawn's pink and gray turned brighter yellow. Partway through my first lap, a high-pitched scream turned me toward a female red-tailed hawk plummeting to earth to lock talons into a squirrel. She flapped great wings twice to lift and carry her prey up to the top of a light post beside the river trail, where she sat with him securely held by both sets of talons. She turned her head to fix me with one eye. I nodded politely in respect. Satisfied, she began to feast, and I continued on my run.

I viewed an encounter with a hawk as a good sign. This one was tinged with death. The natural way for a hawk to act and a natural end for a squirrel, it was still a good sign—perhaps with a warning in it, a reminder that the strong live by preying on the weak. Gran said the Cherokee didn't go on vision quests. They never had any problem seeing visions and looked constantly to signs in the world around them for illumination and help on their path.

Picking up the pace, I put on a burst of speed until I was where I should have been without the hawk. I settled into my steady distance-eating trot alongside the whispering river, trying to slide into that hypnotic peace running by the river always brought, but it escaped me. Instead, I moved to a state of fierce alert. Apparently, my body and mind thought the hawk had been a warning.

Ahead of me, I heard another runner's steps, rare this early. Probably Reverend Matt. Normally, I'd put on speed to catch up for a friendly race and conversation, but I was reluctant to give up the solitude.

I followed thirty feet behind him around the circuit. As he approached the parking lot, I could see Matt clearly. Scenes from yesterday skipped through my head. His painful love probably had him tossing in bed. He decided to run it out of his system so he could work. I'm not romantic like Annette, but I thought his love was the kind of love men had in the movies and books.

He climbed into his car and drove off. I had another circuit to go to get my miles in. I turned into my second time around the long riverside park and tried again to lapse into that effortless, one-with-the-world state running by the river usually brought me. My cell phone's ring pulled me out of it.

"Someone's in the shop. Waiting. He tried to shoot me." Karen's voice was frantic, hushed.

"I'll be right there. Call 911." I took a deep breath and charged straight across the park to my lone car in the lot.

Sobbing for air by the time I reached it, I unlocked the door and hit the street, siren screaming, lights flashing. Traffic was no problem this early, the light still that gray earliest morning light. What was Karen doing at Forgotten Arts this early?

I hit the courthouse square in minutes. Terry, barefooted and

175

bare-chested, hair flying, raced down the street from the bed-and-breakfast with a gun in his hand. I squealed to a stop in front of the shop and leaped out as Terry also arrived.

"I heard shooting. What's going on?" Only slightly breathless, he cautiously moved to one side of the door.

I had my own gun out and stepped to the other side of the slightly open door. I gestured with my foot. Terry nodded. I kicked it wide and moved through, gun out, to stand beside the door on the inside wall of the dark room. Terry jumped in to take the other side and flipped on the light.

A spinning wheel lay knocked over on its side, wheel still slowly rotating. Several stacks of yarn had been knocked down and two small looms thrown to the floor. As if someone had moved through too quickly in the dark. I crossed the room to the back doorway that still held darkness.

"Thank God it's you!" Karen came stumbling out of the dark toward me.

"Watch your gun, Terry! Where was he?" I asked Karen, who sobbed onto my free shoulder.

"Take her outside," Terry said. "I'll check the back."

Karen shook her head wildly. "He was here. In the front. Waiting for me. I stooped to pick up yarn I dropped opening the door from the alley. That saved me. The bullet went whistling over my head."

Outside, a siren sounded and shut off abruptly. I knew Joe only had one guy on the deep night shift, and God knows where he was on his patrols when the call came in.

Karen shuddered against my arm. "I slammed the door to shut off light and crawled away from it to call you. I've been hiding back there ever since."

"He was probably trying to rob you." Terry looked at us. "You surprised him. He could have hunted you down back there and left you dead, easy as not, otherwise. Just some petty thief without the brains to be allowed a gun."

I shook my head. "Someone's been trying to kill Karen ever since she walked in on the murder of Leonard."

Terry laughed. "I hope when my time comes they send that killer after me. Totally incompetent!"

"For which I'm grateful," Karen said, regathering her composure.

Larry Prenter came through the door in a rumpled Brewster City Police uniform, with a Stetson on his head instead of a uniform cap. "What's the problem?"

"Someone broke into Forgotten Arts and tried to shoot Karen."

He looked at Karen. "You hurt?"

Karen shook her head. "No, he missed because I stumbled coming in the door."

Larry took Karen over to sit at one of the tables for his official report. I was grateful it wasn't my jurisdiction. I had taken my shoulder holster and gun in the car when I ran, as always, so my gun was there for me to grab before I ran inside. My holster was still in the car. I had nowhere to put the gun away.

With a big grin on his face, Terry watched me reach for a holster that wasn't there. Nothing between that and his waist. My face burned as I stared at his naked chest.

"I'm truly impressed." He looked as if he'd burst into laughter any moment. "You keep your weapon available when you jog. But where? In that outfit, the holster should be apparent, but it isn't."

I wore the old T-shirt and shorts that I always wore running. Suddenly, the outfit in which I never had problems talking with Reverend Matt seemed too skimpy.

"In the car." The sweaty T-shirt clinging to my chest bothered me. As did the sweat glistening on Terry's muscles. "Your own dress is a little informal."

He laughed at that. "Like what you see?" He indicated himself with an exaggerated showman's gesture. "I was still in bed when I heard shots. Threw on pants and grabbed my gun."

His face sobered. "Two shots fired. She's very lucky. Or he's an incredibly bad shot. Or someone was just trying to scare your friend."

I nodded, looking for a place to sit while I waited for Karen. "That's what I'm dealing with. Someone with scary skills. Only, sometimes he doesn't use them. Then, next time he's a ninja we can't keep up with or find."

Terry frowned and stepped closer. "Two killers? One who's unstable? Neither's a good prospect for you to face." He gazed at me, keeping his eyes on my face. "Someone's playing cat-and-mouse with you. Be on alert. Your friend may not be the real target."

I shook my head. "I—"

"Listen!" His suddenly hard voice overrode mine. "You must be careful. Something's twisted beneath the surface of your little town." He put his hand on my shoulder. It burned through shirt, skin, and muscle into the bone itself.

After a long second, I turned away. "Thanks for your concern. I'll be careful. I'll start by restoring my gun to its holster."

I headed toward the door. I couldn't hear him behind me because he was barefoot and moved like a hunting animal, but I knew he followed me. What he'd said made me decide to strap the shoulder harness over my flimsy T-shirt. I must have made a bizarre sight, but it felt right.

When I looked up, he nodded. "Don't think any place or situation is safe."

I shrugged. "Don't want to leave it in the car with some dangerous nut running around." I searched his face. "Speaking of dangerous nuts, is Walker still out at Mel's or gone back to the city? I need to talk to him."

Terry's smile fled his face. "Watch yourself with him. He's not trustworthy with women." He stared for a second, then shrugged. "He's at the bed-and-breakfast now. He also decided to leave the battling couple. You should find him there. We're not due at Mel's until eleven."

He took a long step, moving closer. My feet wanted to reciprocate with a step toward him. I forced myself to step back.

Joe's car peeled down the block to pull up in front of us. He jumped out, hair still wet but combed, face unshaven. "Skeet, what happened?" He looked at Terry. "What's he doing here? Like that?"

Terry chuckled and bowed a deep European bow to both of us, swinging his arm back ceremoniously. "Since I'm no longer needed, I'll go dress."

"That's a good idea." Joe's voice hardened, along with his face. "And put that gun up. Do you have a permit?"

"Yes," I said automatically.

"Of course," said Terry at the same time. He turned and looked at me with a mocking question in his eyes.

"Three handguns and a rifle." I kept my face blank. "We checked gun possession for everyone at the party who knew Leonard and Jake. A surprising number have them. You have a surprising number of them."

He shrugged. "They're old friends."

I nodded, turning to Joe. I could feel Terry moving away down the sidewalk but refused to watch.

"What was that freak doing here?" Joe asked, his voice more rumbly than usual.

I tried to make my voice light and matter-of-fact. "He heard the shots at Karen and came running to help."

"How do you know it wasn't him?" His shaggy eyebrows pulled together into a deep frown.

I smiled at him. "I arrived before he got here. He's not our guy."

"Why not Heldrich? If anyone around here's a cold-blooded killer, he is." He examined my face suspiciously.

"I don't know what he is." I laid my hand on Joe's arm. "He could do it. That goes without saying. I'm not sure he would. Actually, I doubt it."

He turned to gaze at the horizon across the river. "Maybe you just don't want it to be him."

I rolled my eyes. "All right. Motive, means, opportunity. Show me if you've got anything that makes him guilty because I have nothing." That Joe seemed willing to pin something on Terry because of personal dislike disturbed me. That wasn't Joe. "It'd be easier if Terry were the one because he's not from here. He's probably killed people for the military and the government. We can't just settle on him because he's easy or you don't like him."

He glared at me. "But you do?"

I stared at him for a second or two before turning around to march into Forgotten Arts. I'd collect Karen, take her home, and return to my own home to shower and drop Brian at the high school on my way to work. My life was packed with people and obligations without adding any man's demands. And right now that was what I was getting from Sam, Terry, and Joe. Joe, who'd always seemed so accepting, so free of that kind of stuff! Larry'd better be finished taking Karen's statement because I was ready to leave and in no mood to brook an argument from any man.

# CHAPTER 14

After taking Karen home, I gave up breakfast to get an uncharacteristically silent Brian to school on time and myself into the office before making the trip to the Grand Hotel B and B to interview Walker. I wondered if Bob and Kathy were driving Walker nuts with ancestry questions as they had at the party.

Walker was upset when Bob insisted he talk about his family. Kathy said almost all American Lynches were related. Bob asked if Walker was from the Southern Lynches or Lynches from the East. Was Walker nervous about anyone looking into his background? What would they find if they did?

I dropped Brian off and headed to the office. My guesses about the Lynches embarrassing their wealthy namesake transformed into curiosity about what Walker hid. While in the office, I left Gil and Trish a message to check on Walker's past, tracing him as far back as records would allow—with special emphasis on his money. I'd assumed Walker inherited money that he built into a financial empire. But no one knew where Walker's money came from. People love to talk. They love to talk about other people. Most of all, they love to talk about other people's money.

No one talked about Walker or his money. Was Jake right that Walker was behind a huge forced-labor business? Jake was a pro and wouldn't make a charge like that, even privately, without having good reason. Was Walker's money illegal? Was that why no one talked about where it came from?

The sun had already burned off the puddles from the night's showers and turned the air steamy when I parked in front of the Grand Hotel B and B. In the front porch swing again, Terry read a paperback, his chest now covered by a canvas vest full of pockets that would be handy for trekking through the Amazon. His bare arms showed large, intricate tattoos on both biceps. The left arm had a mandala. I knew the other had a mariner's compass. Once again, I wondered why Walker needed someone with his skills.

"Looking for the boss?" he asked in a wry voice.

I climbed the stairs to the porch reluctantly. I'd already had too much Terry this morning. Didn't need more trouble. "I need to interview him again."

"Language, Skeet, use precise language," he scolded with that corner of his mouth crooked. "You want to interrogate him."

I rolled my eyes. "Sometimes you sound like a Brit. But I think you're American. Which is it?"

He laughed. "Both, of course. Father American. Grew up all over the world. Educated in the finest British schools. When I went to school." His amusement ebbed as he spoke, replaced by a wistful look.

I looked away. Why should I care about his sad childhood. On task, Skeet.

I turned back. "What exactly do you do for Walker?"

"I make things happen." He laughed, dark hair swinging slightly. "I'm good at that."

When he saw I didn't laugh, his face and tone of voice grew

serious. "Walker decides he wants A to happen. I analyze each component to see what must happen when for that component to be achieved. Resources needed, licenses or legal documents obtained, et cetera. I set up a timeline of what to do when to achieve functional A." He ticked the components off on the long fingers of one hand.

"Then, I tell Walker what the cost—money, staff, legal fees, political clout, whatever—will be to go for A. If he decides he wants A under those circumstances, I set it in motion and make A happen. I'm basically a tactician. Nothing glamorous." He shot me a small grin.

I bit the inside of my lip as I thought about it. "What if A is impossible to achieve?"

Terry splayed his hands on strong thighs. I pulled my eyes away.

"It's always possible to achieve A. The cost may be too high. It may be a cost that can't be paid under present laws. It may be a cost that Walker's not willing to pay or that I'm not willing to be part of, but A is always possible to achieve."

I shook my head. "That's sheer arrogance. Plenty of things are just physically impossible."

"I said it might be a cost that can't be paid under present laws—of physics as well as political entities. Laws change all the time, even laws of physics. Have you read any of the new quantum physics?" He moved a step closer to me, the canvas vest making a deep, rustling noise with his movement.

I frowned, thinking about Walker and what Jake had been certain he was doing. "I assume laborers are part of the resources you mentioned."

Terry stared at me, puzzled. "They're often the largest part of the equation."

"Do you have anything to do with hiring or supervising

laborers?" I moved a step away from him to regain the distance I'd originally had.

He twisted his lips, looking perplexed rather than angry. "That's done by other people in the organization."

So Terry wouldn't know if Walker was engaged in human trafficking. No help here. Plenty of danger to avoid.

I moved to the door and rang the doorbell. Kathy must have been near because she opened it immediately. "Skeet!" Her eyes widened, troubled again to see me. I made a mental note to run a check on Bob and Kathy.

That was a policing problem for modern small towns. Unlike a nineteenth- or early-twentieth-century town, we knew only what others told us about themselves. They'd not lived all their lives with their family among us for generations. They could make up identities or change things in their history.

"Good morning, Kathy. I'd like to talk with Walker."

"Come in." The fear that peeked out of Kathy's eyes for a flash of a second receded. "Have a seat. I'll let him know you're here."

As I sat in the living room, she hurried over to the old hotel-lobby counter that ran across one side of the room to pick up a phone and call Walker. "He'll be right down. I'll go back to my baking, if you don't mind." She practically ran from the room. I hoped because something in the oven was close to burning.

Once again, I sat in the cool, dark living room with its wood smoke and potpourri scent and faint Spanish guitar music. I replayed the scene with Miryam and Walker. Who was this man really? What had he done to Miryam to terrify her?

I heard his feet on the stairs before I saw him, a heavier tread than you'd expect from his trim form. He came in smoothing his hand over his short hair, dressed like an Ivy League grad student.

"What is it, Skeet?" He smiled warmly. Remembering the Walker in Miryam's bookstore, I refused to be fooled.

"A few more questions." I gestured to a chair, and he sat. "Before he died, Jake Wise began avoiding you. Can you tell me what prompted that?"

Walker smiled easily. "No. I've never known what led to his sudden dislike. I asked Mel to find out if I'd upset or offended Jake, but Jake refused to talk about it. If you find out, I hope you'll tell me. It's always bothered me." His smile faded as he spoke. His face had an earnest, sincere look I'd have believed in the past.

My cue to smile, say something reassuring. I didn't. "What can you tell me about the human trafficking task force?"

He shrugged gracefully, but his façade slipped for a second. I stared into scary, dead eyes before he slapped his normal mask back on. "An important initiative. According to Jake, human trafficking preys on the most vulnerable. As a society, we must fight it."

This caring-citizen pose made me want to puncture his shield of complacency. "Jake believed one of your subsidiary companies was involved in human trafficking."

His eyebrows lifted in surprise. "That's false. Jake was more stressed than we realized if he was creating persecution fantasies like that. I'm sorry no one was able to get him the help he needed in time."

His voice grew colder and harder with each word, flattening and losing its ordinary timbre. "Don't repeat such nonsense, unless you're willing to pay substantial damages in a slander suit."

The real man appeared, not at all caring, just embracing the disguise civilized behavior provided him to cruise under the radar we have to alert us to the predator.

"Are you threatening me?" I stared at his face, undergoing the same transformation as voice and words, cold and hard, what Karen would call flat affect.

"I'm warning you. Unsubstantiated rumors can damage me and my businesses. I'll protect myself against them. Slander's an ugly thing. Courts demand an ugly penalty from those guilty of it." His smile was unpleasant.

"I haven't repeated this to anyone but you," I said. "I asked you a question. You immediately threatened me. What am I to think about that?"

His chilling smile grew larger. "It doesn't matter. You're no KCPD hotshot any longer. No longer on the way to becoming the first woman chief. No longer someone I need consider because of power you might someday wield. You're just a campus cop in a tiny town."

I got up to leave. I had goose bumps from his eerie transformation and the knowledge that, if someone else walked in, he'd immediately turn into Walker, good guy.

"If Jake was right, you'd better watch it. I have this intense distaste for slavery."

Dead eyes watched me. "Is that a threat?"

I shrugged, and it wasn't one of his or Liz's movie star shrugs. It just said, *I don't give a damn*. "Only if you're a slaver. If not, you've nothing to worry about."

His eyes narrowed. "You're as insane as Jake."

I turned and walked out the front door, those eyes boring into my back as if they focused through a gun sight.

Outside, Terry still lounged in the porch swing, reading. He looked up with a smile as I slammed the door behind me. The smile faded. "Why so grim?"

"How can you work for that man?"

Terry held out his hands in a "don't be angry" gesture. "He pays extremely well. I don't have to like him."

I shook my head in angry denial. "And how does he come by his money? Tell me that."

"I make a hell of a lot of it for him. Quite legally." He stepped closer.

I moved back. "Including the money from human trafficking? Did you set that up?"

"No. I've nothing to do with slavery. Seen enough of that in other parts of the world." He grimaced.

"News flash. It's going on right here. Your boss is probably up to his eyebrows in it."

"You need to be careful what you say about Walker. He could ruin you." Terry's voice was harsh with concern. "Worse, he could have you hurt."

"This is someone you choose to work for?" I stalked away from him and down the steps. "If Jake was right about Walker—I think he was—I'll prove it and see that man in prison if it costs me my job and takes me years. If you're still with him, you'll go to prison, too."

He followed me to the top of the steps. "I know some of his business doesn't bear scrutiny, but I've nothing to do with that part of his empire."

I snorted in disbelief. As if a man with his experience thought he could work for someone evil and keep his virtue intact.

"Don't bother washing your hands, Pontius Pilate, because that blood's going to splash you anyway," I said as I left him behind.

An old-fashioned, working-class bar, Art's Bar and Grill was one of the few original inhabitants of the courthouse square remaining, along with the pre-Civil War—era courthouse itself. Its inside walls were unfinished timbers of the original building. Trendier businesses on the square wanted Art's gone, along with the two bail bondsmen on either side, but Art Williamson refused to leave.

I entered a different world from the bed-and-breakfast. Instead of potpourri, the dark, cool inside smelled of wood, beer, and the biggest hamburgers in town. My stomach growled.

Gil and Trish occupied one of the substantial wooden booths at the back. Twyla Koenig, wrinkled and rawboned with wiry red hair twisted on top of her head and pierced by a pencil, indicated them with a wave of the towel she used to wipe tables near the front. "If you want something other than your regular, tell me now."

"That's great, Twyla. I'm starving. No breakfast."

"That was pretty stupid, wasn't it?" Twyla never sugarcoated her words. She finished cleaning her tables as I slid into the booth next to Trish.

"What's up?"

Trish took out her notebook. "I've got everything there is on Walker. Not much, at all."

Gil looked surprised. "When did you do that? We haven't had time yet."

Trish blushed slightly. "I was staying after work the other day and got to wondering about him. Guy's mysterious. I ran him. Took hours. He really covered his tracks."

I smiled at Trish. "That's great. Proactive. Gil, she might make a real investigator, after all, huh?"

Gil nodded, looking glum. Trish flashed me a grin. Average height for a woman, she was ten years younger, only twenty-five, but we were the only two women on the campus force. That almost always made a bond.

All my life there'd been only a few women doing what I did, going through the academy, working the streets, making detective and Homicide Squad, heading a whole division. We few usually shared something major. Whatever else might separate us, we were in this together among men who sometimes hated us, often didn't want us doing what we were doing, and always had trouble figuring us out.

Twyla came over with an icy Diet Coke for me and refilled Trish's and Gil's drinks. "Your burger'll be here in a minute."

Gil was halfway through a chili dog, and Trish was making headway on a pork tenderloin. Just looking at them made me wish I'd ordered those.

Once Twyla left, I turned to Trish. "Tell me what you discovered about Walker?"

"First of all, there's no Walker Lynch. Not until fifteen years ago. He just appears, wealthy, getting wealthier. Right away, he's a big philanthropist and starts moving in society circles."

"So where'd his money come from?" Gil's investigative instincts were pushing out his bad mood. He was one of the blessings I always counted when things looked bleak. I could rely on Gil.

Twyla bustled up, slammed down my burger and onion rings without a word, and hurried off to take beers to two guys sitting at a table in front.

Trish shrugged, raising her eyebrows. "Where'd Walker come from?"

I frowned. "He didn't spring full grown from the brow of Zeus. He has another name, background. Find it."

I turned to a suddenly scowling Gil. "You're my money expert. Follow his money. Find out where it comes from." Gil's double degree in accounting and criminal justice had tracked down a big embezzlement scheme against the university earlier.

"He'll have that info protected big-time. It'll take feds to get access to his financial records." With a wave of his hand, he dismissed the probability.

"True." I pulled my hand from my hair. It was probably a bird's nest again. "Thursday I'm talking with the new U.S. attorney. Maybe she can help."

Gil perked up. "If she gets me access to records, I'll track him."

I laughed. "I've just got to be sure not to lose you to the feds when they see what you can do." I reached across the table to slap him on his arm. "Can't let that happen."

He grinned, bad mood gone for now. "They'd pay better."

"But they wouldn't let you stay in Brewster. We've got that secret weapon, Dolores." I winked at him. He laughed and turned red.

I took a bite of burger and washed it down with Coke. Trish's face had fallen during my exchange with Gil. Did she feel left out as the newbie on the investigative team? We wouldn't keep her for long. Young, smart, and ambitious, she'd be gone those twelve miles to the city police force in no time. While we had her, I intended to use her to the fullest.

"We don't need the feds for you to track him down before he became Walker. You're straight out of training. All those identity-tracing techniques are fresh in your mind, right?"

She flashed an eager smile. "It'll cost. If you're willing to spend money and time, you can track down anyone."

I nodded. "You can spend money within reason. I'll talk with Frank about budget. You check with him on what you can spend without coming to us again for approval."

Gil tilted his head and gave me a doubtful look. "What if Walker's not behind the murders? How can you justify spending time and money on him then?"

I remembered Walker's arrogance, sure no one could touch him for trafficking. "He's bad news. If he's not involved in these murders, he'll be into something else. We'll keep going. In pieces of downtime with bits of my discretionary fund. We may join the human trafficking task force. Lots of good PR for the university there."

He gave a hesitant nod, looking at Trish, as if his real problem was the greenhorn investigator I'd put on the trail.

"Once this case is over, Trish won't get much chance to use her training unless you or I are gone. This'll keep her hand in." I smiled at Trish, who beamed at the prospect.

Gil nodded slowly. "Makes sense. I'm like you. Got a bad feeling about this guy."

He'd finished his meal, and Trish pushed hers away, half eaten. "I shouldn't get the tenderloin, except when I can take left-overs home. It's enough for two meals." We both laughed.

"I found the car that spooked our killer in the Caves," Gil said quickly. "A librarian came in to work on a project without her keys. Turned around right before the Caves and drove home for them. When she returned, the place was blocked by crime scene techs so she just went home. Never saw anything."

I nodded. Bystanders seldom saw anything.

Gil stood and grabbed his bill. I rose to let Trish out. I sat back down to my own lunch, and Trish followed him with her bill to the register in front.

I thought of joining the human trafficking task force. I could spin it so the chancellor and Jeremy would approve. If this new slavery was spreading from the big city to the boonies as it had elsewhere in the state, who knew when it'd hit Brewster. Best be ready. College students were often desperate for money and infamous for impulse choices. It wouldn't be just Joe's problem.

As if he'd heard my thoughts, Joe walked straight back to my booth. "Mind if I join you?" He looked hesitant, unsure of his welcome.

He had reason after the way he behaved this morning. But my resentment melted. Joe was the nicest guy I knew. "Have a seat. I'm finishing lunch." I bobbed my head toward the other side of the booth, and Joe slid in.

"I want to apologize for this morning," he said when seated. "I had no right to act like that."

I wondered if this apology was serious—*I won't do it again*—or placatory. Sam was real good at the latter. "That's true. You had no right. Don't do it again. Apology accepted." I swallowed a drink of soda.

"Let me explain—" he began.

"You can't. There's no good reason for wanting to pin crimes on the most convenient suspect, evidence or not." I stared. If I'd said that to Sam, there'd be fireworks. I had Joe pegged differently. I'd find out if I was right.

His mouth tightened, eyes narrowed, as he stared at me. After a second, his face relaxed. "You're right. It's not my normal way of behaving."

I relaxed. I'd gauged Joe correctly. "Just want to make sure that doesn't change."

"Terry rings all my warning bells. He's big-time trouble."

I shrugged. "I'm more worried about his boss, the one calling the shots. I don't put much past Terry, but he'll only exert himself if it's worth his while. If Walker's not paying, he's not playing." I stared at Joe's decent face, trying to see if I'd made my point. "It's Walker we need to worry about. He holds Terry's chain."

His lips tightened to a narrow line. "Because he does what he does for pay doesn't give him a free pass to commit crimes. Not in my town."

I sighed. "What crime has he committed in your town? Just exactly what's he done?" I laid my hands on the table. "He came running to Karen's rescue with a licensed gun. I've found nothing to tie him to Leonard's murder or Jake's. Good motives for Walker, but nothing else to tie Terry to either. He's got a .357. He turned it over. No problem. Not the gun that shot Leonard."

Joe shook his head angrily. "I've got nothing on him. You're right. Let it go."

I stood and grabbed my bill. "Good. Settled. I have to get back to work."

He looked unconvinced. "Yeah. Me, too."

We walked to the cash register together. After a second's hesitation, Joe walked out while I waited to pay. Who did I think I was fooling? Nothing was settled.

# CHAPTER 15

I spent the afternoon checking where all of our suspects were at the time of the attack on Karen. Most of them were home in bed or just getting up, all but Reverend Matt in his after-run shower.

Kathy Lynch gave Bob a fierce alibi. "He was in bed. Right beside me. I'd know if he left."

Mel was sleeping, as was Liz, but neither could alibi the other since they had two different suites of rooms—on different sides of the house. Liz was intent on having privacy. Mel had never been in her suite. She visited him in his. A convenient kind of marriage.

Randy was actually up, packing. He was leaving his wife of thirty years while someone tried to kill Karen. His wife stated that she couldn't verify his story. Exhausted from the night's battle, she slept until long after he was gone.

Helen made breakfast while Reverend Matt showered. Walker slept through everything, shooting and sirens. Though Terry in the room next to his heard shots and ran down the street to help.

None of the stories could be proved or disproved, except

Matt's and Terry's because I'd seen them both that morning. Kathy and Matt might swear their spouses were where they said they were, but I knew each would lie. Heaven only knew what Matt wouldn't do for Helen.

Now I made my second trip out to Mel's house, this one personal. After the cold reception I'd had earlier, I didn't relish returning. But Brian had gone home with Angie after school. Without letting me know. For the second time. I was not happy.

Angie came to the door again. At least this time she wore clothes, though the sleeves were cut off her T-shirt to display her wild tattoos.

"You here to arrest Liz?" Real hope hid behind her scornful tone.

Brian showed up behind her. His eyes darted away from mine, and he shrank inside his clothes for a second. He knew he'd broken the rules. Angie caught his eyes. He stood straighter, eyes turned defiant.

"Come in," Angie said in a world-weary voice, waving her hand in a languorous gesture from an Oscar Wilde play.

Before I could reply, ear-piercing curses erupted from the hall on the other side of the great room. "You're such an idiot! Pathetic excuse for a man! Hell, you have no idea how a real man acts."

Her movie-star appearance at odds with her fishwife voice, Liz entered the room, followed by Mel's roar. "Where do you think you're going? You can't talk to me like that and walk off." He appeared behind her, rushing to catch up. "Come back here."

Liz turned to him. "Why don't you make me?" She laughed, just short of a cackle. "You can't even try, can you? You cretin. How'd I ever make the massive fucking mistake of marrying you?"

Angie shrank back as the words hit the air like sharp weapons. I wondered if she had to listen to this all the time. No wonder the kid was so brittle.

Mel bellowed an almost incomprehensible answer, his face turning dangerously red. Angie straightened her shoulders and slapped a furious look on her face. The two combatants were oblivious to the kids—and me. They were locked into their battle, focused completely on each other.

"You'd better watch that foul mouth of yours. It'll get you hurt one of these days. You don't want to push a marine too far." Mel's ruddy face turned scarlet with fury. I hoped he wasn't going to stroke out. "You make me want to punch you."

Liz laughed her horrible laugh again. This laugh wasn't practiced or sophisticated. It was pure primitive hate. "As if you could, you bulbous worm. I'd have you on the floor under my heel so fast. You'd probably like that, wouldn't you? Spike heels in your chest and a whip in your face. You'd—"

"That's enough." I stepped into the room, shouting over their battle cries. Both kids drew close to me. "You've got kids right here. The door's open. What are you thinking?"

They stopped mid-scream and turned to where I stood in front of the now-closed door, kids next to me. I put my arms around the kids' shoulders and pulled them closer.

"What are you doing here?" Liz screeched. "How dare you walk into my house and lecture me, you—"

"I came to pick up Brian." I yelled right over her. "I ought to take Angie, too. Get her away from this crap."

Mel's mouth had been open to add his own outrage to Liz's. It snapped shut. The high color drained from his face.

Liz's face twisted as she looked at Angie. "Take the nasty creature. Do! It'll be heaven to be free of her."

Mel laid a heavy hand on her shoulder. "Stop now, Liz. You've gone too far. We both have."

"Maybe you have, but I haven't gone nearly far enough." She tossed her model's mane.

Angie pulled away from me on the attack, her voice quavering. "What will you do? Take me out in the woods and hunt me? You like really big game, don't you? You could cut off my ears and keep them in your locked chamber, wicked stepmother."

Angie's words were the first to penetrate Liz's rage. Her eyes grew round. She rocked back on her heels. Then her eyes narrowed to a sharp, threatening focus on her stepdaughter.

Paling further, Mel's face sagged with fatigue. "Enough. Skeet's right. We're all out of control." He slid his arm around Liz's shoulders. She grimaced but leaned into it.

Brian shivered and moved farther into my arm.

"I just started." Angie's voice grew brasher as she moved forward.

"Don't," Mel warned. "We need to calm down."

"Yes, you do." I shook my head. "I'm taking Brian home." I turned to Angie. "Will you be all right?"

She gave a brittle laugh. "In the loving arms of my family? Where could I be safer? If you find my corpse pierced by stiletto heels, you'll know where to look, won't you?" She glared at Liz, who sniffed and drew her head higher.

"Try not to be so melodramatic." Turning abruptly, Liz glided out of the room, followed by Angie's voice. "Melodramatic? I thought you were rehearsing for the Wicked Queen in *Snow White*."

"Angie, enough." Mel bowed his head, shaking it hopelessly. "I'm sorry about this, Skeet."

I stared at him until he sensed my gaze and lifted his head to

197

meet my eyes. "Are you sure Angie's better off here than with Denise? That was pretty raw and cruel just now. If this goes on all the time, what do you think it's doing to her?"

He looked alarmed. "No. It's not like this all the time. Of course it's better than life with that addict."

Angie rolled her eyes dramatically. "Thanks for the touching concern, Supercop. I can take care of myself. They wouldn't let Denise have me anyway."

I didn't like it. I had no choice but to take Brian and leave.

Once in the car and headed home, I turned to him. "I don't want you coming over here again. You didn't ask permission. You didn't leave any message about where you were going. You broke house rules."

"It's better to ask forgiveness than permission, Angie says." I could see hurt in Brian's eyes. The rest of his face showed only anger. "You expect me to abandon Angie? Who knows what they'd do to her if I wasn't there?"

It was futile talking to him when all his loyal instincts were aroused. "You're my responsibility. I don't want you following her into trouble."

He held his arms out to me. "You see the way they treat her."

"Yes, it's awful." I stared at the road. "No wonder she acts out."

At the next red light, I turned to face him, making my tone as serious as I could. "I don't want you in trouble because of her. She's going to be in serious trouble soon, I think." I winced at the memory of Angie's face when Liz screamed at her.

"I won't abandon her. She knows bad stuff about Liz. I'm afraid of what they'd do if I wasn't there." He folded his arms across his chest with a mulish look on his face. It was the same look I saw in the mirror when I was being a stubborn fool.

"What does she know about Liz? Does it involve Leonard's murder?" That was wishful thinking, just like Angie's belief she knew Liz's secrets. At most, Angie might know about the affair with Randy.

He shook his head. "She knows where Liz keeps incriminating evidence." His voice took on that bitter note of quoting Angie.

I softened my voice. "Understand, Bri. The law's on their side. Unless they hurt her, I can't do anything. It stinks, but that's it. If Denise gets cleaned up and tries for custody, I can testify what Angie's had to go through. Other than that, I can't do anything."

Feeling a huge sense of failure, I stared at the road. "She'll act out and get in worse and worse trouble. One day it'll be major trouble with the law. I don't want you with her then."

Sticking his chin out, he glared at me. "I won't stay away from her."

At another red light, I turned to him again. "If you get in trouble with the law, they'll take you away. Put you back in the foster system. I won't be able to get you out."

Fear moved across his face, followed by the same stubborn look. "You believe the crap they say about her. You just want to throw her away."

I closed my eyes for a second before opening them to a green light and driving on. "I care, but I've no control over Angie's situation. I care even more what happens to you. There I do have some control."

He shook his head vehemently and bit off his words in a cold voice I didn't recognize. "Not as much as you think. Unless you're going to lock me up, I'll keep seeing Angie."

I didn't know how to answer that, so I drove in silence. What in hell was I doing with this defiant teenager? Who did I think I was, trying to be a parent?

. . .

The rest of the drive home was silent. I let Brian out of the car at our house. I knew—or hoped—he'd stay home with the animals to care for them. After our fight, I didn't really know what he'd do.

I wanted nothing more than to go with him. Try to resuscitate our relationship. But I had to head for my father's house in Kansas City. I was caught between two males who needed my help but wouldn't admit or accept it, rebellious son and belligerent father. Lucky me!

At least one worry was off my shoulders. Karen had agreed to stay home with Ignacio on guard. I respected Ignacio. He'd keep Karen as safe as he could. At risk to himself, if need be.

At Charlie's, I saw a half-rusted-out, navy Buick LeSabre and Sam's silver Malibu. Sam shouldn't have been there. What was wrong now?

Dreading the beginnings of another headache, I headed for the door. Sam opened it. "We've got trouble."

"I knew when I saw your car." Inside, I turned to him. "What is it this time?"

He recoiled at my tone. "Whoa! Bad day already?"

I shook my head. "You wouldn't believe it if I told you. What's up?"

"Skeeter. How are you? You're looking . . . real good. Come meet Erika." Charlie's voice came from behind me. I recognized the false cheer in it. He was in trouble and wanted to charm his way out. He hadn't been able to charm me in years. That didn't keep him from trying.

Turning to face him, I took a deep breath. "Charlie. How do you feel? Did you do your exercises?"

The small Latina who stood next to him smiled shyly at me.

"Yes, he did them today and walked with the cane around the house twice."

Expecting a disaster report, I blinked in surprise. "That's great. You must be Erika." I walked forward and held out my hand. "I'm Charlie's daughter, Skeet."

She took my hand in her own much smaller but firm grip. "Erika Adame. Pleased to meet you. Charlie speaks of you all the time." She looked into my eyes steadily. I liked what I saw.

"Only believe the good." I laughed. "I'm delighted to hear he did his exercises and used the cane." I looked at Charlie. "You'll be back on your feet in no time. Good going."

Sam laid a restraining hand on my shoulder. I knew that look. He was pissed.

"That's not everything, is it?" I felt the headache climb out of its lair and spread across the top of my head.

He frowned. "Marie Doerr showed up and bullied her way in."

"What did she want?" I shook my head in disbelief.

"Charlie. She took him out in her car." Sam's face grew grim. "Erika tried to stop them, but they both outweighed her. Marie had him out all afternoon. Erika called me right after they left. I damn near put out an APB, but Marie finally returned him. Left before I could get here."

I turned to Charlie. "Why'd you go with her?"

"Hell, she's a good-looking woman, just trying to be friendly." He couldn't meet my eyes.

"How many cigarettes, beers, and cheeseburgers did you have while out with your friend, who seems determined to kill you?" I glared at the fragile old troublemaker.

"I called the company. They'd fired her," Sam said from behind me.

I closed my eyes for a second against the day's craziness. "Charlie, she's no friend. She might hurt you to get revenge."

"Naw. Marie wouldn't hurt me. She likes me. A lot. Thinks I got class." Charlie's face softened, remembering.

"Shit. She thinks you've got money." Sam pushed past me. "You have to stay away from her." He turned to me. "I told Erika Marie's not allowed in here or to take Charlie out."

"So my own kids'll keep me a prisoner in my own home?" Charlie's voice started to rise in pitch and volume.

"Hold it!" I put up my hand in warning. "I am not going to get into an argument with you tonight. I've had too many today. If you want to see Marie, that's your right. But you won't see me. I won't come here to watch her kill you."

Sam looked sick. "Same for me, Charlie. She's bad news. If you can't see it, I won't stand by while she hurts you. I can't watch that."

Charlie's face had gone white. "I . . . don't want to lose you, Skeeter. Sam. No, don't want that. You're wrong about Marie. She likes me."

Erika backed away from our argument, appalled. Probably at our threats to abandon Charlie. Not how she thought family should act. Not how I thought family should act, either. We didn't have a lot of options.

At that moment, my phone rang. I moved into the kitchen to take the call.

"I've got damn bad news for you." Joe's voice sounded angry.

"What, Joe?" A lump of fear filled my throat. I saw Karen, bloodied and dead. While I'd argued with Charlie, the killer got past Ignacio, probably leaving him dead, too.

"I've got Karen and Brian. They broke into Melvin's house, helped by his daughter. His wife caught them and called me." The anger drained from Joe's voice, leaving only fatigue.

I stared at the phone in shock. "This can't be real."

Joe groaned. "I'm sorry. I'm not kidding. The wife wants to press charges. I've asked them to wait until you get here."

The headache covered the whole top of my skull now. "I'm on my way. Tell them. And Joe, thanks."

Hanging up, I hurried back to the living room to ask Sam, "Will you put Charlie to bed? I have to keep Karen and Brian out of jail."

His eyebrows rose. "Sure. What the hell—"

Charlie and Erika looked shocked.

"Don't ask. I don't want to think about it." I turned to Charlie. "We'll talk about this another time. Or if you decide to go on with this Marie, we won't bother. Now, I have to go."

I turned to Erika as Charlie sputtered. "Erika, I'm glad you've come to take care of Charlie. Things aren't like this always. I promise."

I turned and shot out the door to my car, heading back to Brewster, not to rescue Karen from a killer this time but from jail. With Brian. My headache grew and sent out tendrils to my ears, jaw, and back of neck.

Things weren't just out of balance in my world, but totally crazy. Chaos was invading my life, and I didn't know how to stop it.

# CHAPTER 16

I pulled up outside Mel's concrete bunker in record time. The house was lit up. I parked behind Joe's car in front. He called out from the side of the house. "Around here."

I hurried to where he stood, outside another door. Through lit windows I could see Mel and Liz standing on crimson carpet. Brian and Karen huddled on a white love seat facing the door across a black lacquer coffee table. Angie stood like a trapped rat in the far corner of the room against bamboo-textured wallpaper.

I turned to Joe. "What happened? I was at Charlie's—"

Joe's expression was grave. He always smiled at me. His smile's absence told me we were in deep trouble. "Brian told me. Hold on to your temper in there. Liz already said Brian should be taken from you for lack of oversight. Who knows what she'll say next. Keep it under control. Maybe we can get Brian out of this with no record."

I looked up at Joe's strong, serious face. "It's Angie. I know it. That damn Liz says hurtful things, and Angie acts out self-destructively. I told Brian she'd get him in trouble."

Joe held up his hands to stop my words. "Karen got both teens into it."

I groaned. "Has she finally lost it?"

He shook his head wearily. "Come on."

We walked into the room. Everyone turned to stare. I took a deep breath. "Okay, I'm here. I don't know anything. Someone please tell me what happened."

Wearing a leopard-print halter top with beige miniskirt and five-inch heels, Liz leaped first. "Your friend and your ward broke into my quarters to steal."

"We did not!" Brian shouted.

"We didn't take anything—" Karen began.

"That's a lie!" Angie leaped from her corner, as if to physically attack Liz. "You witch."

"Hold on." I moved myself between Angie and Liz in the center of the room.

"It's not the kids' fault, Liz." Mel pointed at Karen, who slumped on the love seat. "This one's nuts. First, she accuses me of murder, attacks me publicly. Then, she breaks into my house and drags the kids into it."

Brian looked at me with frightened eyes. Karen wouldn't look at me. Angie turned to her father. "It was my idea. Karen didn't sucker me into it. I left a window open for them to get in. They weren't breaking in. I live here. Though you'd never know to hear wicked stepmother talk."

Liz's nostrils flared. Her eyes turned mean. "You can't let them into my quarters, you little zombie. You have no rights over my space."

Joe turned to Angie. "You told them to come in that window?"

She nodded, eyes frightened, then quickly put on her sulky mask. "Why not? I live here."

Mel turned to her. "Why'd you do that, Angie?"

"She's an idiot juvenile delinquent, that's why. Send her to boarding school. You can't handle her. She needs professionals who know how to handle her kind." Regaining control of her face, Liz looked smooth and sophisticated again.

I walked over to Karen and knelt on the carpet. "Why did you do this? Why involve Brian? You know this could hurt my chances of adopting him."

She looked up at me with raw pain in her eyes. "Angie told Brian Liz had evidence. Against Mel. We came to find it for the police. I wouldn't harm Brian."

I kept my voice soft and low. "You know better than to involve Brian and endanger his adoption. How could you?"

She shrank from my words. "No one listens to me. If I could find proof . . ." She looked up at me, suddenly angry. "You haven't. You're still messing around. He's getting away with it."

I got up off my knees. "I'm looking for facts. Facts will lead me to the killer. Facts will put him behind bars. Feelings, guesses— they're no good. You used to know that."

"She's out of her mind," Mel growled. "Ought to be locked up for her own good, as well as mine."

Joe stepped forward. "No one needs to be locked up. No crime's occurred. Unless you want to press charges against your daughter, too."

Liz nodded vigorously. "Why not?"

"No." Mel swung his eyes from Angie to Brian and Karen to me and back to Joe. "We won't press charges."

"Speak for yourself." Liz turned to Joe. "I intend to press charges against the lot of them."

I stepped toward her. "Imagine how it will look in the Kansas City newspapers. Candidate's wealthy wife sends stepdaughter to jail. You'll have a dozen wicked-stepmother headlines all over the country before day's end. Political suicide. Is that what you want?"

She glared at me. I faced her down. "You know I'm right. You'll be so tainted no one'll even want your money."

She gave her patented movie-star shrug. "All right. No charges. But I want your word they won't try it again."

I sighed. "You have it. Karen and Brian won't get in your house again." I hoped. I'd see to it, if I had to tie them up and set Ignacio to guard them with his rifle.

"Good." Joe came over. "Skeet, will you take them home?"

I nodded. "Come on, guys."

Behind me, I heard a sharp intake of breath and turned. Angie's eyes held an instant of fear before the façade masked it. "Angie, if either of them hurts you or threatens you physically, you let Joe or me know."

Mel sucked in air to yell. I glared at him. "After everything I heard here today, I'd be remiss as an officer of the court not to remind Angie she has legal protection against physical harm."

Mel's face swelled and reddened. "I'd never——"

"Can you say the same for her?" I gestured toward Liz with my head.

He gulped visibly.

I felt sad for his predicament and my own. "Let's take you two home."

Joe walked out the door, Karen behind him, Brian and me together behind her. As we stepped into the dark and the door closed, I let out a shaky breath.

"We're around front," I told them.

"My car's down there." Karen pointed toward the backyard that ran into the wildlife refuge.

"It'll stay there for now." I hurried them along the walk to the front.

Karen balked. "But——"

That was the spark that set my head on fire from the inside out. "I don't want to hear it. Between us, Joe and I managed to get you off without an arrest or a charge order to Western Missouri Mental Health. We're taking you home and making sure you stay there. Out of trouble."

I hated to hear how hard my voice had grown. "You know as well as I do, after publicly threatening Mel and breaking into his house, you could be remanded to Western Missouri. You know how these things work."

Looking shaken, Karen turned and walked on to my car.

"That was mean, Skeet." Brian glared at me.

I tightened my lips. "Don't even go there tonight. You also have been so damn lucky. You don't even know. Are you trying to go back to that foster home from hell we got you out of?"

He shrank from me and shook his head, eyes grown large.

"Then head for the car, and don't give Joe or me any lip tonight." I gestured ahead toward the car. He followed Karen.

When we reached the cars, Joe said in a low growl, as forcefully as if he were yelling, "Karen, I've had enough. Don't make me regret not arresting you. If anything else happens, you'll go to jail or Western Missouri, friend or not." He pointed fiercely at her. "Forget about Mel. Let Skeet solve this murder. Go home. Go to sleep. You haven't been yourself since that hit on the head. Rest and get yourself back together."

He turned to me. Brian pulled back in alarm.

"Thanks for everything," I said.

He gave me an intense look. "Keep them out of trouble. Next time, I won't be able to do anything else. You know that."

"I do." My headache exploded and gave birth to a litter of little headaches that spread across my skull while big mama set up permanent housekeeping.

He smiled faintly. "We'll all feel better in the morning."

I sighed. "Couldn't feel worse."

He gave me his usual smile and headed to his cruiser. I unlocked mine. Karen and Brian got in. I stood at the driver's door, dreading the ride with the people dearest to me in the world. My universe was severely out of whack.


The trip to the farm was silent. I drove and battled the family of headaches homesteading my skull. Karen and Brian apparently didn't want a heated discussion while I drove pitch-black, snaking country roads.

We parked and left the car to go inside the farmhouse. Ignacio appeared as soon as we turned onto the drive, helping Karen, who seemed tired and weak, into the house. Brian and I followed.

"You wore yourself out," Ignacio said to Karen. "How was the movie?"

She huddled into herself.

"So that's how you got out without Ignacio calling me." I rolled my eyes.

"What? Karen was taking Brian and his friend to the movies." Ignacio looked back at me. "They'd be with other people. It should have been safe."

"We didn't go to the movie, Nacio." Karen's voice was flat and breathless.

"Where did you go then?" he asked, his expression and voice strained.

Inside the big, lavender-scented kitchen, Karen dropped into a chair like a puppet with strings suddenly cut. She looked up at me, raw pain still showing in her eyes. "I'm sorry, Skeet. You're right. I never should have involved Brian. I didn't think I could talk Ignacio into it."

"What have you done?" Ignacio's voice was sharper.

"It was wrong to involve Brian," I said in my firmest voice. "But it's illegal to break into Mel's house. You could have gone to jail. If you do anything like it again, you will. That ought to scare you. I don't see any signs of sane thinking."

Karen waved her hand dismissively. "I know it's wrong and illegal to break into someone's house, but Mel's getting away with murder. That's ten times worse, and if burglary will prevent that—"

I held up my hands in a stop gesture. "It hasn't. There's still no evidence against Mel."

"He's involved, Skeet. I know it." Karen slammed her fist into her palm.

I turned to Brian. "You said Angie thinks Liz has something incriminating. When I asked if it had to do with the murders, you said it didn't."

"I don't think so." Brian turned to Karen. "Angie told you she didn't think there was anything on Mel."

"Of course there is." Karen curled her small, capable hands into fists. "Whatever else she has, the evidence on Mel will be with it. Liz is cleaning up after him and protecting him. He's not smart enough."

"Karen, what have you done tonight?" Ignacio's voice was unusually strong and forceful, not his usual shy manner. He stared at her. She dropped her gaze, unable to meet his.

"I'm sorry, Nacio. I didn't want to lie to you, but I knew if I didn't, you'd call Skeet." She spoke to the floor rather than face his glare.

"You involved children? To do something illegal?" His voice was relentless.

Karen's voice, on the other hand, shriveled. "I know I shouldn't have. I'm sorry. I won't do anything like that again."

"How could you do this?" Ignacio's face looked as if it was carved out of unforgiving rock. "This is not you. This is beneath you."

Karen lifted her head to look at me, still avoiding his gaze. "I didn't think of what it could do to Brian's adoption. I never want to harm either of you. I love you both."

Sighing, I sat on the edge of one of the chairs so I wasn't looming over her. "No more. Stay home with Ignacio to guard you. Let me do my job. I'll find out who killed Jake and Leonard and do it so we can put the murderer behind bars."

Pausing, I decided to go all out. "If you'd found the most direct evidence of Mel's guilt, it would have become useless, illegally obtained. You'd make it possible for him to go free."

Karen's eyes widened.

I stood looking down at her. "Stay home. Let me work on this."

Ignacio still watched her face. Finally, he turned to me. "I'll keep watch for the killer." He turned back to Karen, who finally raised her face to meet his eyes. "If she tries to leave, I'll call." His voice was firm and determined.

Karen dropped her gaze to the floor. Silent tears ran down her face. I wanted to comfort her but was afraid to undo what I'd said. Ignacio set a dark hand on her shoulder. With the other, he patted her hands which were clutched together on the table.

"Get some sleep. Let sanity prevail," I said. "I'm taking Brian home."

Karen said nothing. Ignacio freed her hands but kept a hand on her shoulder. I gave Brian's shoulder a nudge toward the door and followed.

We drove in silence until we reached the house. As we got out, Brian stopped, eyes full of angry tears. "You're supposed to love Karen. And me. But you're not on our side. You should have been on our side, Skeet."

"If Joe and I hadn't been on your side, you'd be on your way to juvie, and Karen would be in jail. Who do you think talked them out of pressing charges? Who had to swear she'd keep you both out of trouble when she has no idea in heaven if she can?"

He shook his head, tears starting to overflow and clog his voice. "You should've been on our side, even if we were wrong."

He ran inside. By the time I made it into the house, I heard him upstairs in his room and knew he'd not be back down. I was at the end of my tether with no idea how to handle this boy I was responsible for and had come to love. So I did the only thing I could do. I called Gran.

# CHAPTER 17

I dialed from memory. Some things we never forget.

Of course, my mother answered. I closed my eyes against the headache trying to consume me. "Coreen, it's Skeet. I need to talk to Gran."

"You never called me back, Skeet." My mother has an exceptionally pleasant voice. Once as an angry teenager, I'd told her she should do phone sex to make money.

I hardened myself against the plea implicit in her voice. "I've been busy here with murders. It wasn't urgent."

"How could you possibly know that?" Good, she was getting irritated. Maybe she'd get off the phone and let me speak to Gran.

"You didn't mention any problem with Gran."

After a sudden intake of breath, the phone went silent.

"Please, Coreen, I need to talk to Gran right now."

"You have more family than my mother down here." Her voice held more hurt feelings. I could have cursed. "What if your sister or brother was hurt? Or me?"

Half sister and half brother. I wanted to correct her but didn't. I'd left after high school just before my half sister was born and hadn't been back, except to celebrate Gran's birthdays every few years. I didn't really know those kids, except from photos and letters from her and Gran.

She broke the silence on the phone. "I'll get your grandmother."

I'd hurt her. I never talked to her unless I absolutely had to because I always hurt her. I long ago stopped wanting to, but it still happened. Neither of us needed that.

"What is it, Skeet? What's wrong?" Gran's strong, old voice was a relief.

"Gran, how are you?" I wanted to sidle up next to her so she could swing her solid arm around me and squeeze my shoulders.

"Healthy and full of zip. What's wrong up there? Charlie? Or Sam?"

I laughed breathlessly. "They're both still problems, but the big one is Brian, the boy I'm adopting."

I had talked with Gran and written her about Brian, what we'd gone through, and what I was doing. She was supportive and helped me figure out how to do some things I'd had to manage.

Her voice was throaty and rough like some great old blues singer's. "Is he hurt?"

I almost wished I could say yes. Injury to the body would be easy for Gran to remedy. "Not physically. Inside, I don't know if he's more hurt or angry. Hard to tell."

"It usually is. Tell me." I almost saw her nod knowingly.

I brought her up to date on what had happened. When I finished, she laughed. My head jolted back. I looked at the phone in doubt before putting it back to my ear.

"Remember when you were Brian's age?" she asked. "Remember the hell you put your mama through? Because you were hurt and angry over the divorce and never stopped siding with that damn Charlie?"

214

I didn't feel good when I thought about those days. I'd since had abundant chances to see why Coreen left Charlie. I tried never to think about them.

"What goes around comes around." Gran's voice held a sorrowful note. "Now you have your own teenager who won't understand why you've made adult decisions. You're getting a taste of your own medicine. Now you know how your mama felt all these years."

I could feel tears start at the back of my eyes and throat. I pushed them away. "It's not the same thing. Coreen remarried and started a new family to replace Charlie and me. I've not done anything like that with Brian."

"What do you want me to say? It'll get better? It usually does. Unless he's as stubborn as you. That situation's never healed. I don't know when you'll stop hating your mother."

I shook my head as if she could see me across the miles. "I don't hate her. I've come to see she did the right thing, leaving Charlie. I've seen him as an adult. You know that."

"Hmmh." She didn't sound convinced.

"This isn't about Coreen and me. It's about Brian. How do I deal with this? I'm trying to keep Karen alive with a murderer after her, find that murderer, keep Charlie from killing himself, and deal with Sam every other night. It's just too much sometimes." I could hear the tears threatening again behind my voice and tried to control myself.

"You have your hands full, for sure. With Brian, you got to have patience. No way you can change his mind. He has to realize for himself that you love him and are doing your best. Give him room. I used to tell your mama that, but she wouldn't listen, kept pushing you. Always bounced back to hurt her."

I could hear her breathing over the phone. Somehow just that comforted me.

"Get yourself to water. You got a load of troubles. Take them to water. You'll see clearer how to handle them. As for Brian, you're out of luck, girl. I don't have any wild herb to treat that teenage misery. You just got to wade through it, honey."

I nodded silently. Deep inside, I knew there was no easy answer, but Gran so often did have an answer or cure. I turned to her with real hope.

"You got a headache." I felt as if she were in the room with me, looking at me. "Get some food in you. Something dairy. Get some sleep. Put all this aside. You can't do anything about it tonight."

"Thanks, Gran. I will." I tried to mask the hint of resentment in my voice. I'd hoped for answers or at least sage advice.

"Your problem is you need help, Skeet. You can't take care of all these people, young, old, cantankerous, without help. You got to learn to ask for help, even though you act like it would just about kill you."

"I thought that's what I was doing, calling you. Asking for help." Even I could hear the bitterness in my voice.

"And didn't get what you wanted, eh? No great magic to heal this." She laughed again with a tinge of sadness. "If I had something that would do that, don't you think I'd have used it on you and your mama all those years ago?"

"I guess so." The line was silent for a second. "Well, thanks. I guess you're right. I've just got to suck it up and deal with it."

"It'll be okay, honey. You just wait and see." Her voice had warmed and held real affection.

I rang off then, headache threatening to evict me from my own skull. Gran was right. I'd hoped for some miraculous bit of wisdom or healing that would make everything right again with Brian. Wasn't going to happen.

I went to my room to change, found some Advil in the bathroom, and swallowed it, realizing as I did that I hadn't eaten since my lunchtime burger. Gran was right again. Dairy, she'd said. I'd make cocoa. It was that kind of night.

In the kitchen, I topped the cocoa with plenty of real whipped cream and headed into the living room to knit and do some heavy-duty thinking.

Jake's death was the key to the whole puzzle, I felt. But it was impossible for someone to have killed Jake that night. No one with a motive was in the building, and there was no way to get in without the marshals knowing.

Wait. Something wasn't right. Something I'd heard the last few days as I questioned people. I ran those conversations back to see what was catching in my mind like a scratch on an old vinyl record making it skip at the same place. The headache pulled back into a throbbing behind my right eye.

I'd learned to pay attention when my mind played these memory tricks on me. It was trying to get me to see some detail or pattern I'd missed. Was this a pattern I was missing? A detail?

I leaned back against the sofa and closed my eyes, replaying the whole week, scenes with Liz and Mel, Miryam and Walker, Bob and Kathy, Terry—no, forget those—Helen and Reverend Matt, as well as the scene yesterday in Forgotten Arts.

I sat up and stirred the whipped cream into my chocolate slightly. Found the point that had stuck. Helen. Jake had sneaked her through a secret door up to his office to make love.

Putting away my knitting, I picked up the phone to call Bob Lynch. When he came on the line, I asked him if such a door existed.

"Sure," he said, sounds of loud television drama in the background. "A back door so the big shots can leave when there's lots of press out front. It's hidden away. Can't be opened from outside. Only someone inside can open it. I've had to go back to let in Melvin when there was a high-publicity case and the front was a media circus. It's totally safe. No one can open it from outside."

After the call was over, I ruminated on what Bob told me. It made sense. Jake let Helen in through that door. Had he let in his killer? Who? Mel? Who else would he let in late at night, bypassing marshals and safeguards? Had to be Leonard or Mel. Leonard was dead. I didn't think it had been him. But he could have known who it was—or guessed.

Who else might Jake have let in? Walker? He avoided him, wanted nothing to do with him. Why let him in the secret door? Terry? Only as Walker's representative. Again why let him in that door and bypass the guards?

Liz? He hardly knew her. Wait. If Jake was unfaithful with Helen, he might have been unfaithful with Liz. Any number of women. My beliefs about Jake had to be completely revised.

Helen? Supposedly he wasn't seeing her. What if she'd blackmailed him to let her in? Threatened to tell Karen? When she realized he'd never come back to her, she pushed him down the stairs. Perhaps in anger, not realizing what she was doing. She ran down to find him dying, panicked, and finished him off.

It explained the breakdown and suicide attempt. But why kill Leonard? I could see her pushing Jake accidentally during an argument. Not the neck-breaking afterward. Didn't fit Helen. I wasn't sure she'd even be physically capable of that.

It kept coming back to Mel. I wondered if Karen's fixation on him as the killer might be correct. Helen said Jake thought Mel and Leonard were on the take, paid to keep investigation away from Walker's human trafficking. He could have called Jake, said he was at the door. If Mel tried to silence Jake, he could have lost his temper, knocked Jake down the stairs, given him the coup de grâce. I'd seen his temper. He was a marine, still in the reserves.

Leonard could have known about it or even been there. His guilty conscience had eaten at him. As his drinking grew worse, he became a threat. Mel was the first of us to try to shut him up. He was furious with Leonard, more than the situation called for.

I began to think Mel might be the culprit. He could have been at Karen's farm the other night. As Gil reminded me, the Marine Reserves trained constantly. Mel was probably capable of running, hiding, and escaping. I was glad Ignacio had turned out all the lights, remembering Mel's sharpshooter medal.

No proof, of course. I'd have to dig for that. My headache reasserted itself, moving from behind the eye to spread throughout the skull. When would that Advil kick in?

Risen right to the top of tomorrow's docket was that phone interview with the new U.S. attorney, Elizabeth Bickham. I'd call in the morning to turn the phone call into an in-person meeting. The task force and human trafficking were behind this. Mel and Leonard were involved through covering up for Walker. Maybe this conspiracy was finally starting to unravel.

As I set my knitting aside, I smiled, headache or not. Unraveling was one thing I was really good at. I'd pull this whole plot apart, stitch by stitch. Mel was my loose end to begin pulling.

As I dressed to run in the morning, Miryam appeared with garden tools. Miryam awake at 5:45 A.M. was unheard of, but Miryam carrying shovels and trowels was a fever dream.

"Good, you're already dressed in old work clothes." She walked into my house through the door I opened to her knock, dragging a shovel and carrying a bucket full of trowels and work gloves. Miryam herself wore matching capris and top, white with red hearts and red binding at all hems and edges—hardly a practical gardening outfit.

Brian came out of the shower in jeans, carrying his T-shirt until he saw her. He struggled to pull it on over still-damp skin to cover up in the presence of a female. I had ceased to count in that category.

"And Brian, too." Miryam beamed at us as if we'd done something wonderful by simply existing. It was good to see the old Miryam back after the episode with Walker, but a little disorienting to see her act as if nothing had happened.

I shut the door and turned. "What the—"

"Skeet and Brian, I need your help this morning." She set down all the tools but one trowel that she kept in her hand. "There now, everything we'll need."

I walked over to look at the collection of gardening implements on my floor. "What on earth—"

"It's exciting, isn't it?" She grinned at us like a little girl. "I got permission from the mayor to dig up those old irises hidden away in the park. On the hill behind the campus."

"Where?" Brian asked.

Miryam smiled at us. "Around that old burned-out house behind the Caves. The mayor said they're tearing that down to build something for the park. All those lovely irises will be killed. I love to go over in spring when they bloom. I'll dig them up and plant them in my garden."

"You don't have a garden," I reminded her.

"I will once I have the iris roots planted." She waved a trowel like a torch over her head, Lady Liberty of the garden.

I smiled helplessly. "I'm glad you're rescuing irises and taking up gardening, but I've got a full plate of murders to investigate, so—"

"And Brian has school. That's why I came now." She laughed. "You can't imagine I'd be up at this ridiculous hour for anything else."

Brian and I looked at each other, equally puzzled.

Miryam rolled her eyes, as if we were very slow. "We'll dig them up before you go to school, Brian, and before you solve those murders, Skeet. Get a super-early start on it."

I could feel my frown. "You want us to dig irises at six A.M.?"

Brian grinned. "Sounds like fun. We'll be sneaking in to get them to safety just in time."

"Exactly. We'll be heroes of the Iris Resistance." She struck a heroic pose, holding the trowel out before her as if it were a sword.

I groaned. They turned reproachful eyes on me.

"Where were you going dressed like that?" Miryam pointed to my old T-shirt and shorts with a distasteful moue.

"Running. You don't dress up to go running for exercise. At least, I don't."

"You don't have to run for exercise if you can dig up plants instead. Healthy exercise first thing in the morning, right, Brian?" She winked at him. I saw his wink and accompanying smile and knew I was doomed to dig iris roots.

That was why we walked the overgrown trail behind the Caves across the boundary between university and Brewster public lands, looking for remnants of a nineteenth-century house that huddled among the overgrowth of shrubs and vines.

"You know what iris leaves look like, don't you?" Miryam asked anxiously.

I nodded, recalling the irises surrounding Gran's house in Oklahoma. You couldn't miss those blades spearing out of the ground.

"There's one," I pointed out. "Over there. We probably want

to get those that are farther from the house first. We might have trouble digging those closest to it if boards have fallen on them."

We set down the shovel, trowels, and buckets, which Brian and I carried. Miryam walked, hands free, extolling the beauties of early morning, which she so seldom saw. Brian and I put gloves on and knelt with trowels by the iris foliage I'd pointed out.

"What color will this one be?" Miryam asked anxiously, keeping her distance from the leaf-covered loam in which we dug.

"I don't know what color its blooms will be." I lifted out one root.

"Oh. I thought you might." She tried to sound as if she didn't really care.

"What difference does it make?" I struggled with another large tuber twisted deep in the earth, trying to pull it out without breaking it.

"Because I want a color scheme to my garden." She looked off to the horizon happily. "Purple and yellow and white and——"

Sitting back on my legs, I gave her a severe look. "If you want a color scheme, buy plants from a nursery where you know what color you're getting." I indicated the ground before me. "You won't know what color these are until they bloom."

"Oh." Miryam looked disappointed. Then she dismissed it with a wave of her hand. "Never mind. It'll be a garden quilt. A patchwork of irises." She smiled broadly. "I like that."

Sighing, I resumed digging. Soon Brian and I had a handful of iris roots in the bucket. We picked up our equipment and moved nearer to the skeleton of the old house. Kneeling, we started to dig again.

Miryam examined what we'd already exhumed. "I think I should be able to recognize these leaves now. I'll look for more."

I grunted, working out another stubborn root.

She wandered around, crooning a song in an unexpectedly pleasant voice. "What's that over there?"

"Be careful around the house." I didn't look up, keeping my eyes on the root I wrestled with. "The timbers are ready to fall at the slightest breeze."

"It looks like— Oh—" Her words were cut short by a scream.

I looked up immediately. She stood unharmed in a clump of low bushes, looking down at something. While I watched, she screamed again.

I got to my feet, grumbling. "What is it? A snake? You'll wake the whole town."

She turned to me, eyes wild, and shook her head, as if she'd screamed out her voice. I hurried over. At her feet lay Mel Melvin, staring sightlessly at the sky, one of Karen's wool combs embedded in his throat. Automatically, I knelt to check his pulse. His wrist was cold and as dead as the rest of him.

# CHAPTER 18

Since it was his jurisdiction, I called Joe to the crime scene. After driving Brian home, I called Karen to insist she stay on the farm. No need to remind people of her earlier threats to Mel. I also rescheduled my interview with Bickham.

In the afternoon, Joe asked Brian and me to accompany him to tell Liz and Angie about Mel's death. He thought it might make it easier for them.

Angie must have been peeking out the window. She opened the door before we knocked, happy to see Brian. "Only Liz is here. I already called her. Come on, Bri. We'll play computer games while the big people talk."

Brian looked uncomfortable. Joe said, "No!" in a sharp voice.

I tried to soften things. "Please stay with us. This is an official visit."

She gave a world-weary shrug. "Whatever. At least sit down, Bri. No need to stand all stiff and military like the supercops."

Brian shot me a panicked look.

"Good idea. We'll all sit." I followed her to the leather couch and chairs, taking a chair when she took the couch and patted the space next to her for Brian. Joe opted for a chair. A painful silence fell.

As Joe looked at the floor and cleared his throat, Liz made her entrance in a tailored suit with shorts instead of skirt or slacks. I despised that fad, but she carried it off. "What's this all about?" she said with obvious disdain. "I have a city board meeting in half an hour. I've no time to spare."

Joe looked at me. I glared back. This was a town murder. I wasn't breaking it to them. He took a deep breath. "Mrs. Melvin, please sit down. I have something important to tell you."

Liz's eyes flashed fire. "Ms. Richar, not Mrs. Melvin." She sat, model-perfect, on the arm of the couch, leaving an empty seat between her and Angie. "What's this important news? Get on with it."

I almost missed the flash of anger that crossed Joe's face. "I'm sorry to inform you both George Melvin was found dead this morning." He looked directly at Liz.

Angie gasped. "Was it his heart?"

Looking unaffected, Liz took a deep breath. I'd once seen a documentary with actors pulling out emotions and molding their features to match. I watched Liz shape an expression of grief the same way. "Found dead? He's in bed." She frowned. "Must be a mistake."

Angie looked willing to grasp at straws even tossed by her hated stepmother. "A mistake?"

I leaned forward. "It's no mistake. Brian and I were there when he was found. I've known your dad for years. I checked his pulse myself."

Angie's face melted into that of a frightened child. "Not Daddy. Please, no." Tears began to roll down her face, forming canyons in her thick foundation, smearing eyeshadow and mascara. She turned to Brian. He patted her hand and then her shoulder.

"I'm sorry, Angie." He choked on his own tears. Angie turned into his shoulder and began to cry in earnest, shoulders shaking. He slid his arm around her shoulders self-consciously, continuing to pat her.

"You mean Mel's lying somewhere dead?" Liz cried out. She now appeared dramatically shaken.

"He was stabbed through the throat," Joe replied. "Sometime in the night."

"We found him at about six A.M.," I added.

Angie was shaking her head against Brian's shoulder. "Someone killed him," she moaned. Suddenly, she looked up and asked through sobs, tears still sliding down her face, "The same bastard that killed Leonard? This followed us from the city."

"We don't know yet," Joe answered before I could. "We're waiting for the autopsy. We'll investigate—"

"What in hell do you mean, you don't know who killed him?" Liz's voice was a snarl of rage. "That crazy bitch, Karen Wise, threatened to kill him the other day in front of witnesses. Why aren't you arresting her? She killed my husband."

She wasn't acting. Her anger was genuine—someone had taken something from her. I bit back the retort that leaped to my lips.

"How do we know you didn't do it?" Angie cried, pointing at Liz. "You hated him. I thought you were going to give him a heart attack with all your screaming threats. Besides, you've got a new boyfriend."

"We don't know who did it." Joe's raised voice overrode them both. "We're investigating."

Angie's sobs returned. "What does it matter? He's gone. I was mean to him. I didn't want to be. I didn't." She threw herself at Brian's shoulder again. He resumed patting her with more assurance.

"Shhh. It'll be okay." His boyish voice crooned.

I tried to forestall Liz from another round of accusations. "Angie, would you like to stay with Brian and me for the next couple of days?" Not that I had any more idea how to deal with a grieving teenage girl than I had with Brian, but the kid needed someone.

She looked up from Brian's shoulder and nodded. "Thanks——"

"Absolutely not!" Liz shot off the couch arm on which she'd perched. "She belongs here. I'm her stepmother. Her guardian, now that Mel's dead. With Denise in rehab for the next three months. Not that she'll get Angie once she gets out. She'll just go back to her druggie friends."

"She won't!" Angie cried. "What do you care where I go? You hate me as much as I hate you."

Liz turned to Joe. "She's in emotional meltdown. We both are. Of course Angie belongs here with me. In times of grief, families belong together." She turned to face me with a hateful look. "No one has the right to take my stepdaughter from me."

Liz was, as always, looking at this politically. She could milk the public's sympathy as a grieving widow who insisted on caring for her dead husband's child. I looked over to Angie staring at her in horror, seeing the same vision I did. I could have throttled the woman.

"I'm sorry, Angie," I said. She continued to stare, shaking her head, unable to believe the future she faced. I wanted to vomit at the cruelty. Liz had custody of Angie. Anyone trying to help would be shut out at Angie's expense.

After we left, Joe said he was sending county crime techs to

Karen's shop to look for evidence of blood since Mel had been killed somewhere other than the spot where his body was found. I knew he had to do it, but I argued with him, fighting the desperate fear inside me that this could turn very bad for Karen.

Karen might have done all those crazy things she had, but I knew she could never take a life. Whoever killed Mel stole her wool comb to throw the blame on her. What else might he or she have done to make Karen look guilty?

Friday morning broke stormy. Temperatures dropped twenty degrees overnight the way they do in the Midwest. I'd spent hours at Karen's farm after leaving Joe, explaining that she needed to stay home and out of trouble while Mel's murder was investigated. Ignacio wanted to pack up and flee with Karen, certain she would be arrested. Obliviously certain that no one could think her guilty of murder, Karen stopped him before I had to. When I drove to Kansas City in the rain to meet Elizabeth Bickham, new U.S. attorney, I was bleary from a sleepless night and haunted by worst-case scenarios of Karen arrested for murder.

In Kansas City's federal courthouse, I passed through security to face the marble staircase on which Jake died. Closing my eyes as a wave of emotional pain overwhelmed me, I could see the man who'd shown me how a good father behaved lying at the foot of the stairs, injured and in pain. A shadowy figure approached to break his neck, taking all that kindness out of my world. I took a deep breath to bring my thoughts back to my task ahead and avoided the staircase on my way to the elevator.

With perfect posture and a short Afro, Elizabeth Bickham greeted me with the photogenic smile I'd seen in her picture on the U.S. attorney's Web site. Slightly taller than I, she was much thinner and dressed in an expensively tailored purple suit and four-inch heels. She towered over me.

A tiny assistant DA, always in stilettos, once told me about studies showing that height equaled power in people's perceptions. I wore duck boots for the rain and mud outside. Take ten power points from me right there. Bickham had a round conference table with chairs on one side of her office but chose to face me across her big desk. It went with the spike heels.

"I understand you wanted to talk with me about our human trafficking task force, Chief Bannion?" She regarded me intently with almond-shaped eyes, weighing my substance. She sat upright, rigid posture negating the warmth of that great smile.

"I want to involve my police department in the task force." I waited for the inevitable laugh or smirk. Most people not in law enforcement dismissed campus police.

Bickham's scrutiny of my face intensified. "I've heard of you," she finally said. "You might have been the first woman chief in Kansas City. Certainly would have been somewhere." Leaning forward, she pointed one perfectly manicured finger at me.

I moved uneasily out of its path, wondering if Gran wasn't on to something with her warnings of a pointed finger's power. Bickham dropped her finger to the desk and tapped the nail on it.

I shrugged. "It wasn't what I wanted."

She stared for half a second, eyes widened. Then the corners of her mouth turned up slightly. "Many would, if only for the power."

I moved back to my original position, now that her finger no longer pointed. "I'm not real interested in power."

She laughed, throwing her head back and hooting like a train. "Anyone who becomes a cop is interested in power. Don't fool yourself, and don't try to fool me."

I had to smile. "I'm not interested in *power over*—people or institutions. I want *power to*—fix things, make positive change."

She leaned back, relaxing her rigid stance. "That's why you want to join my task force?"

I stared straight at her. "I don't want slavery in my state or country ever again. I have a trained investigator, gifted at tracking money and financial crime. I have a newly trained but gung-ho and smart young officer, willing to log extra hours. We're working on a murder investigation now with some tie-ins to trafficking. I've seen enough to know my pristine little town and college aren't immune. Even if my murder plays out some different way, I'd like in. I want the power to help defeat human trafficking. At least around here."

Bickham looked at me for a long moment, then smiled broadly. Standing, she gestured toward the conference table. "Let's move over here, have some coffee, and talk about what we can do together. Skeet? Is that right?"

I nodded and headed for the conference table, noticing she'd left the killer heels under the desk and walked in her stocking feet to the table after calling for coffee. The day was looking up.

She filled me in on the task force, a national pilot. They'd already had more successful prosecutions of human trafficking than anywhere else in the U.S. "Mostly small operations. We know several large networks are growing wealthy from human trafficking, right here. It's near impossible to trace the top people, though. If we go after small fry, it's only an inconvenience and minor expense for the big operators." Her face twisted with frustrated anger as she spoke.

I inhaled deeply and took a chance. "Have you come across well-known names such as Walker Lynch?"

Her eyes opened wide. "You have come across our trail, haven't you?" She shook her head. "That name keeps popping up in the wrong places. I find that problematical. Nothing actually links him to trafficking."

I nodded and gave her a quick summary of my murders and

the investigation. "Even if Walker turns out not to be involved in these murders, I believe investigating human trafficking will reveal his involvement."

Elizabeth leaned back in her chair, considering. "I've heard of Jake Wise, of course. He started this task force when old Mel Melvin didn't really want it. I shouldn't speak ill of the recently dead, but from everything I've heard and seen, Jake should have been U.S. attorney instead."

I started to say Jake hadn't been political and caught myself. Elizabeth had to be pretty political herself.

As if reading my thoughts, she smiled. "I suppose he was one of those idealists who wasn't a politician?" I nodded. "I learned the hard way as a little girl that politicians influence and control our lives, usually for the worse. I wasn't going to be a passive bystander, so I went after my version of *power to*."

I shuddered. "I don't envy you. I'll take dealing with criminals to dealing with politicians any day."

"Just remember. No criminal has the power those with wealth and political clout have. The ultracriminals use politics to thrive unmolested." She stared at me intently. "Maybe you should run for office. Go after the really dangerous bad guys."

I held my hands up in a warding-off gesture. "No thanks. I admire you for taking it on. I suspect ordinary criminals are more my speed."

Elizabeth chuckled, then looked at me in frank appraisal. "You're willing to take on Walker Lynch. He's very politically connected. Lots of money and power. *Power over*. Dangerous. More than you can guess."

I laid my palms flat on the table and looked up at her. "I probably don't know how dangerous he can get. It doesn't matter. Call me a fool."

"Quixotic rather. You see behind the façade of this windmill. Welcome to the task force. I'll have my secretary add you to the list for meetings and memos. Let's meet again, just the two of us, once your murders are taken care of." She held out her hand, long and thin like the rest of her but strong, and we shook on our joint venture. "We might turn out to be dangerous together, even to Walker Lynch."

On the way back to my car, I felt good about the morning in spite of the chill rain still falling steadily and the traffic splashing me regularly. But walking through crowded sidewalks to the lot where I'd parked my car, I received two phone calls, back-to-back, to darken my mood.

The first, from Brian's school, asked why he wasn't there. He'd been getting ready for school when I left town for this early-morning meeting. He must have gone to Angie's. I told the school secretary he'd be in school Monday. She didn't like it. I didn't, either. I'd check in on both kids when I got back to Brewster and find some way to deal with Brian.

The second call came from Joe. "Stay calm until I finish. I've got a warrant for Karen's arrest." Joe's tone was sorrowful.

"You can't seriously think Karen had anything to do with Mel's murder." I wrapped my jacket closer around me, dodging a passing umbrella. A muddy SUV zipped in and out of traffic, splashing me.

"Techs found traces of Mel's blood in her shop. It's where he was killed." His voice rumbled in my ear.

"Karen's so small. How could she kill Mel and move his body?" I reached the parking lot and hurried off the crowded street, raising my voice above the whooshing of cars through rain.

"They also found blood on the dolly she uses for fleeces and floor looms." Joe's voice sounded sad. "Blood in her car. It was moved, then moved back, according to tire tracks."

I unlocked my car door. "Someone used Karen's wool comb, shop, dolly, and car. It wasn't her, stuck at the farm with her car behind Mel's house." Reassured by my own reasoning, I slid into the driver's seat.

Joe was silent. Perhaps I was getting through to him. "She could have driven that shepherd's car into town and back when finished."

I shook my head, then realized he couldn't see me. "Ignacio wouldn't let her." I slammed the car door, hoping Joe could hear.

He paused again. I heard him breathing. "The shepherd's keys weren't on the hook where he keeps them. Karen admitted she took them but claims she never used the car." Silence again. This time I didn't think I'd convinced him of anything. "She could have done it."

"What did Sid say? I'll bet the wool comb wasn't even the murder weapon. The killer used it to throw suspicion on Karen. And you fell for it." I could hear my voice rising with desperation and tried to bring it under control.

How likely was it the ugly things could actually kill? They were used to comb fibers, never intended as a weapon.

I heard the rustle of papers over the phone line. "Cause of death was the wool comb piercing the carotid artery. Didn't take long for Mel to bleed out."

I felt as if the breath had been punched out of me. "Shit. Ignacio can prove she didn't leave the farm."

"He slept in a room down the hall from hers. Hers was closest to the stairs. She could leave without ever waking him." Joe's voice was gentle.

"Karen didn't kill him." I could hear despair and uncertainty in my voice. "You know her."

Joe sighed. "So do you—and she's not been herself for days."

He was right, of course. "Other people had it in for Mel—Liz, Angie, his ex-wife. Liz is having an affair."

Joe said nothing.

"Besides," I said, relieved at what just occurred to me, "this murder has to be linked to Leonard's, and we both know Karen couldn't have killed him."

"Too many people know Karen threatened Mel. Some even know she broke into his house, thanks to Liz. Who's also been after the mayor about Karen killing her husband. She's called every politician she knows and sicced them on the mayor and me. Lots of bad feeling out there, Skeet. If she didn't do it, Karen would be better off in jail than out there with anger escalating. And she's really made it look like she did it."

It was my turn for silence. "When will you arrest her?" I finally asked, almost succeeding at sounding professional.

"I'm heading out now. Thought you'd want to be there. Make sure she gets a lawyer."

I knew what it cost him to call me. We do not call best friends of the accused to alert them we're arresting their buddies. He'd compromised professional standards for me. I appreciated it, even as I was ready to take his head off.

"I'll be there." I hung up without saying good-bye or thank you. That bothered me as I raced for the bridge across the river. A little.

# CHAPTER 19

I reached Karen's farm right behind Joe, though the roads were slick from rain. He'd left his car and started toward the farmhouse by the time I parked. Ignacio stepped out on the porch, pointing his rifle at Joe. Joe stopped. I ran from my car to keep Karen's shepherd from making a tragic mistake.

"Ignacio, don't!"

He shook his head, features stern. "He's come to take Karen to jail."

"Yes," Joe said quietly, standing with his hands out at his sides, openly harmless, rain dripping from his hair and nose and running down his neck. "If you care about her, let this happen. All you'll do is make things worse for Karen if you don't."

Ignacio flicked his attention from Joe to me for a second. "She's not well, Skeet. This is a lie the real killer's put together. I won't let him take her and lock her up to get more depressed and do herself harm."

"Listen to me," I said quietly. My shoes squelched in the mud as I passed Joe where he stood carefully still. "Put the gun down and let Joe arrest Karen. I'll go with her. Make sure she gets an attorney. Get her out on bail. Don't do something a prosecutor can use against her in a trial."

I knew appealing to his own interests wouldn't sway him. Pointing out he could damage her case might. I walked slowly through the rain. He stood on the porch with the rifle. "Where is she?" I asked.

"Lying down. She doesn't know about this." He looked at me intently. "You won't let them keep her in jail? I'm afraid for her state of mind. The despair this could tip her into."

I shook my head. "I'll get her a good lawyer and bail. She'll be back tonight. I promise." I could see him hesitate. "Put the rifle down, Ignacio. Please."

With a sharp nod, he turned and laid the rifle on the porch table. Joe let out a long breath behind me. We climbed the wooden steps to the porch together.

"If you must arrest me, I won't fight you." Ignacio looked straight at Joe.

"I don't think that'll be necessary," Joe said. "You just got carried away trying to protect your boss."

By that time, I was past them both. I raced through the door and up the stairs with no thought to the mud and water I was tracking in.

"Karen," I called. She came into the hall, smoothing her hair, looking half asleep.

"What is it? I was resting my eyes. You know how Ignacio gets. The only way to shut him up is do what he wants. He's so damn stubborn!" She looked ready to laugh but caught herself when she saw my face. "You're soaked! What trouble is it now?" Her voice filled with fatigue.

I reached for her hand, drawing her toward the stairs. "Joe's downstairs—if Ignacio hasn't shot him yet. He's got a warrant for your arrest."

She stopped and stared. "Did Liz press charges on that incident at their house?"

I tugged at her again and got her moving. "It's murder. Mel's. I'll get Marsh Corgill to represent you. Don't say anything until Marsh gets there. Do you hear me? Keep silent. I'll see about bail. We'll have you out by tonight."

"Mel's murder?" she repeated as we descended. "But why? Because of the wool comb? But I didn't . . . You know I couldn't kill someone. Anyone."

At that point, we reached the ground floor where Joe and Ignacio waited.

"Remember," I told her, my voice fierce. "Don't say a word until Marsh gets there. Not one word."

"But I'm innocent—" she started to object.

I overrode her. "Keep your mouth shut until Marsh can protect you. Be smart."

She looked around at us, confused and frightened. I put my arm around her.

"Karen, I've got a warrant for your arrest for the murder of George Melvin," Joe said. "I've come to take you to the police station."

Karen stared at him. She looked over at me. I put my finger to my mouth. She nodded. Ignacio stepped forward. They stared at each other for a second. Then he held out his arm. She placed her hand on it. Silently, they walked out through the kitchen to the yard and Joe's car. Joe and I followed.

"It's a good thing I told you," he said quietly. "I might've had a hard time convincing that shepherd not to shoot me."

I stepped down from the porch into the mud. "His name's Ignacio. I probably should have let him put a bullet in you for stupidity. Falling for this. Karen's been set up. Can't you see?"

As he moved through the rain, Joe glared at me, no sign of his usual amiable smile now. "What do you want me to do? I've got the mayor and every other political power in this end of the state on my neck. You see how the evidence has piled up. You'd let him kill me for doing my job?"

Turning my face away, I sped up, trying to catch up with Karen without slipping and falling in the muck. "Ignacio wouldn't kill you. He's a good shot. He'd just cripple you a little."

We slogged through the mud in angry silence the rest of the way to Joe's car, where Karen and Ignacio stood waiting in the steady downpour. The wind whipped up and blew chill rain into our faces. Joe put Karen in the backseat. As if the reality was just sinking in, she looked up in fear. "Take care of the place until I get back, Nacio."

He nodded as Joe closed the door gently, putting glass and steel between us.

"I'm sending Marsh Corgill over for her," I warned Joe.

"Good. She'll need a first-rate lawyer." With a wistful half smile, he got into the driver's seat.

I ran to my car, trying to keep the rain off my cell phone long enough to dial Marsh's law office. I'd failed to keep Karen out of the trouble I'd seen coming since she woke up in the emergency room after Leonard's death. Maybe Marsh would do a better job for her.

The train that had been a lonely moan in the distance came hooting and rattling through the heart of town just as I came out of Ace Bonds after making Karen's bail. I waited a second under the entry overhang, hoping the rain would slack up so I could get to my car without more drenching. As I watched the wind-whipped clouds and sheets of freezing rain darken the day, Terry Heldrich sped past in Walker's Lexus, screeched to a halt, and splashed into a parking space in front of me.

"I hoped to find you." He leaped out, hat, hair, denim jacket, and close-fitting jeans all clean and dry, making me realize how wet and bedraggled I looked. "Liz and Angie had a nasty fight. Angie's headed for the city in Mel's car. Brian's with her. Liz went after them, swearing like a bloody drill sergeant."

I forgot the rain and wet clothes. "Angie doesn't have a license. She's not old enough to drive. Why would Brian go with her?"

"He was trying to stop her or persuade her to go to your house. She wouldn't listen. She's convinced Liz wants to kill her." He held his hat out over my head like an umbrella in the rain, but I brushed it and him aside, heading through the still-steady rainfall for my Crown Vic. Terry kept pace with me.

"Those kids will kill themselves on the highway in this weather." I looked at the dark sky that had been pouring badly needed rain on us all day and thought of slick roads and flash-flood warnings.

I pulled out my phone and hit Karen's number on speed dial. Ignacio answered. I told him to come pick up Karen. I'd paid her bail but couldn't wait around. Her minister, Starkey Rayber, would stay with her until he arrived. I started the car and hung up before he could ask any questions.

I'd hardly noticed Terry get in the car with me. My focus, even while on the phone with Ignacio, was out on the highway, leaving town with those two scared, reckless kids in that car driving into disaster.

"You're sure she headed for the highway?" I asked Terry as I pulled out.

"She was going to Kansas City." His tone was grim. I looked over at him for a second. Water beaded on his dark hair and skin. Scowling, he stared at the sky, probably also conjuring thoughts of flooded roadways and slick bridges.

Cursing, I turned off toward the highway, siren blaring, lights flashing. Things could go bad so quickly for an inexperienced driver at highway speeds, even in ideal weather. All the awful wrecks I'd seen through my years on the Kansas City police force ran through my mind.

"Why haven't you and Walker gone back to KC now that Mel's dead?" I asked, leaning forward to peer through the rain-blurred windshield.

"Liz feels she needs protection from the killer and asked us to move back in. I think she has her eye on Walker as the next mate." He also struggled to see through the blinding rain.

Earlier in the day, the rain was a steady downfall. Now, it poured in drenching bouts, whipped by wind only increasing in velocity. I switched my wipers to high speed. Visibility was getting worse. I had to slow down, much as I wanted to floor the gas pedal. I passed two cars pulled under an overpass and saluted their good sense, wishing one of them was Mel's silver Lincoln.

It was dark as twilight, hours ahead of time. Off to the right side of the road ahead, someone in a yellow slicker and rain hat waved me down, standing at the spot where the guardrail was out. In the rain-smeared dark I could see the barricade crumpled flat. I'd have to stop pursuit of Angie and Brian—at least long enough to give whatever help was needed. People had gone off into the river, and their lives—if they'd survived the wreck—were in danger. I tried not to think it might be the kids I was chasing.

Flicking off the siren, I pulled over, leaving lights flashing so no one would hit me in the dark. "Trouble. Let's see what they need."

Trying to ignore fears that Angie and Brian drove farther away toward catastrophe every second I delayed, I grabbed my

Maglite and left the car. The figure in the slicker splashed over to us.

"Thank God, it's you!" Helen shook rain out of her eyes and off her face. Even the rain hat wasn't keeping her dry.

"What happened?" I asked.

The passenger door slammed shut. Terry squished over to join us as we walked to the cliff edge that led to the river.

"I was behind two cars. The SUV was chasing the other. Caught up with it here. Smacked it right over the edge. Hit it twice to make it go over. Then sped off."

My stomach dropped. It couldn't have been the kids with Liz behind them. She wouldn't actually try to kill them. Surely. "I don't suppose you got a license number in this muck?"

Helen shook her head. "All I could see was a reddish or brown SUV."

Liz often drove a red Volvo SUV.

We reached the edge. "Be careful," I warned. "The ground's water-soaked. Ready to crumble and slide you down with it."

"Did anyone survive?" Terry asked.

"Two that I could see," said Helen. "One seems injured."

"Hell!" I wished for a hat like Terry and Helen had, so I could hit something with it. "We'll have to get them out. Terry, call 911."

He pulled his phone out, turning slightly and bending to shelter it from the rain as he called.

I turned to Helen. "Show me."

She pointed down and to the right. I peered over the edge, careful not to get so close I caused a mudslide. Down below me, Mel's Lincoln Town Car teetered at an angle on the half-finished levee, lying partly on the driver's side. The front half of it hung in the air over the high, wild river. The back half rested partly on the side of the embankment and partly on the outer half of the un-finished levee. Standing on the levee leaning into the car through the half-open passenger door was my son.

"Brian!" I called. "Be careful. Don't tip it into the river."

He looked up, blood on his face. "Skeet! Angie's hurt bad. I can't pull her out! The steering wheel's in the way. My arm's hurt." His left arm hung at his side.

I looked back to my car where I had nylon rope in the trunk, only to see Terry had opened the trunk, set out flares, and was carrying the rope toward us. I turned back to Brian. "Is Angie conscious? Can she help?"

He shook his head. "She's out. Her head's bleeding." His voice broke, hinting at hysteria.

"Okay. We're here, Bri." I watched him take a deep, shudder-ing breath. "Is she bleeding anywhere else?"

"I can't see. I think she's hurt pretty bad. We've got to get her out." He looked up at me as if I could reach down and lift them to safety with my hands. I would have given anything to be worth that look.

"We will. Calm down, Bri. We've got an ambulance and fire truck on the way."

Terry stopped beside me with the rope over his shoulder. "Who's going down?"

"Best if it's me," I said. "You'll have more upper-body strength to pull us up. I'll send Brian up first."

"Better keep him with you to help get Angie out." He wrapped rope around my waist and tied it with a professional-looking knot.

"Can I help?" Helen asked. "I could go down after Skeet and help get the kids up. If Brian's arm is hurt, he won't be much help in getting the girl out of the car."

"That levee's only going to take so much weight before it gives way." I gave a sharp tug on the rope. The knot held strong. "Terry's probably going to need help to pull us up one after the other."

He shook his head. "I've had to do this before. If you send Brian up first, I can send her down to help after that. I can always tie the rope to the car, and we should have more help out here soon."

Brian gave a yelp below. I moved back to the slippery edge to look down. "What is it?"

"Car started to tip." He looked up in fear. "We have to get Angie out before it goes into the river."

Terry stepped up behind me. "I've got you. Just take it easy going down. I'll keep the rope taut so you shouldn't slide too much. Be most careful when you hit the levee. Land as soft as you can."

I sat down gingerly on the edge and turned around to face the side as I slid myself off, feeling for footholds in the cliffside and gouging them into the slippery mud with my clumsy duck boots when I couldn't find any. I felt Terry pay out rope. I dropped and clawed at the embankment with my hands, as well, to keep from swinging too far out. I suspected he'd have been much better at this. He probably climbed mountains for fun. But I'd never have been able to pull everyone up to safety.

I dropped and jerked as he paid out the line and caught me up over and over. I felt my toe touch the levee top and shouted, "I'm here. Don't pull on it."

Carefully, I placed first one foot, then the other, on the sodden levee surface and turned slowly to find myself about a step away from Brian and the car.

"You made it." Brian might have been crying, but between

the rain and the blood on his face, I couldn't really tell. The powder from the car's airbag deployment had covered his shirt and was smearing in the rain.

"Of course. Now you're going up on this rope." I smiled at him and lightly touched his left arm. "Do you think it's broken?"

He shook his head. "I don't know. It just hurts. I can't really use it. I can't climb with it."

"You don't have to climb. Terry will pull you up. All you have to do is hang on." I clapped and rubbed my hands together to take off most of the mud on them. Then I clumsily untied the excellent knot Terry'd made and hoped I'd do as well. I looped the rope around Brian's chest. "I'll tie it in front. Like this." I struggled to tie as strong and firm a knot as I could in the orange nylon and tugged on it sharply. It held.

"How are you coming?" Terry called down.

"Sending Brian up. Take it slow and easy. He's only got one arm to work with." I turned back to Brian and put his left hand on the rope as it came out of the knot, making him flinch. "Hang on to this. Don't move the arm. Just hold as tight as you can manage. Use your good arm to help you up the cliff."

"Ready?" Terry called.

"Pull him up." I watched the rope grow taut. Brian's face tightened with pain. His feet left the ground.

"Use your feet on the cliff to help you move up with each tug of the rope." I moved up under his hips and gave him a push upward from below. Brian reached out to the earthen wall with his feet. He rose in herky-jerky movements as Terry pulled the rope. I held my breath as he was yanked higher and higher. Helen appeared at the edge to help him over. He disappeared into safety.

Terry would untie him and tie up Helen for her trip down. I turned back to the car that resounded with the sharp patter of rain upon its metal frame. It shuddered occasionally in the wind, making creaking sounds, but its rear end seemed lodged into the muddy cliffside fairly securely. Who knew for how long, though, as this rain kept turning the hillside to mud.

The unfinished top of the levee consisted of a layer of earth over an openwork frame filled with dirt and plant debris. The rain was turning the soil into mud, so the surface was slippery and uneven.

I took careful steps to the open car door. Leaning in and over the front passenger's seat, I could see Angie. Her face had obviously smashed into the driver's side window, which was almost completely broken out. Perhaps at first impact from that car behind them. Her chest wasn't smashed by the steering wheel, which I feared from what Brian said. She slumped to the passenger side of the wheel, as if she'd ricocheted in that direction from the impact with the side window. The deflated airbag on the driver's side partially covered her. The steering wheel crunched down at an unusual angle toward the seat. Her left arm was pinned between the edge of the steering wheel and the back of the seat.

I reached over to free her arm. It was too firmly lodged between seat back and steering wheel. Suddenly the car moved with a loud creak. I let go of her arm and cautiously pulled myself out, trying not to upset its balance any more than I already had. The last thing I wanted was to send that car sliding down into the rushing river with an unconscious Angie inside.

While I was in the car, Helen had begun her trip down. She seemed to have a harder time than I had, swinging and twisting in the gusting rain. I took several careful steps across the levee to be in position to help her when she reached the bottom of her drop.

As she came swinging and kicking toward me, I caught her legs. "Careful. I've got you. Stop kicking."

I felt her legs relax as she heard my voice. I realized she must have been terrified. She'd come down on the rope anyway. Brave woman. She hadn't had training and practice in rescuing people the way Terry and I had. My respect for her rose back to where it had been before she told me of her affair with Jake.

"Got her," I called up to Terry. I guided her feet to stand on the levee. "There you go. You're here now."

"I see why Brian was only half conscious when he got up there. That's a terrible trip. Must have been hell for him with that arm."

Terry's face appeared over the side of the embankment. "Have you had a chance to look at the girl?"

"Face cut up. Unconscious. I could bring her out, but her arm's caught. I don't know if it's injured. I'm afraid I'd injure it trying to get her out. The car's not stable."

As I looked up into his face, he frowned. "Be careful! Don't go climbing around in that car if it's going to tip you and her into the river."

I glared at him. "I'm no fool. It's steadier in the back. I'll try getting to her from the backseat and see if I can get the arm free."

Terry's voice grew louder. "If the bloody car's going to shift—"

"I know what I'm doing, damn it." Whatever happened to "You're an unusual, capable woman, Skeet"?

He leaned farther over the cliff edge. "The ambulance and rescue people should be here soon."

"Hell, they're under our worthless sheriff now. They could take forever. The car could hit the river and drift halfway to St. Louis before they get here."

I turned my back on him and faced Helen, who looked nervous. "I'm going to get in the back of the car and work her arm free. You'll need to carefully pull her out of the front door."

She nodded, water flying from her ridiculous yellow rain hat, looking like a filmmaker's idea of a New England fisherman. Drenched as I was, I envied her the stupid slicker and hat. They were keeping her warm and dry.

Stepping carefully past her to the back door of the car, I tried the handle. It wanted to open, but the door wouldn't move. I tried again, pulling up hard on the door as I pulled out. It swung about halfway open but no farther. It'd be a tight squeeze getting in. I hoped I didn't have to evacuate in a hurry once I got in.

I took a deep breath and let it out. Sucking in my stomach and pressing down my breasts, I wriggled my way into the backseat without the car bobbling and tipping. Just more of the ominous metallic scraping sounds. As I'd thought, it was wedged more securely at the back end.

I slid down the seat to get behind the steering wheel and rose up to lean over the driver's seat, slipping my hand down the seat to compress the cushioning as much as I could as my hand approached Angie's arm. As I pushed the seat back away from her arm, the arm fell back slightly in following motion. This gave it enough slack to come loose from the steering wheel.

"Helen, try to pull her now." Out of the corner of my eye, I saw Helen's head and arms in the opening on the passenger's side.

I squeezed that seat back as flat as I could and held it as Helen gently pulled Angie's body from the car. The arm slipped free of the steering wheel. I let out the breath I hadn't been aware of holding. Angie's body moved slowly toward Helen and the open door.

"She's coming," Helen cried. I didn't know if it was to me or Terry. "I've got her. Be careful. The car may bounce when I lift her all the way out."

I could hear Terry's voice shouting something in the distance.

With the car walls, rain, and wind between us, I couldn't tell what he said. I figured that was probably good.

Helen managed to slide Angie's legs out. Carefully picking up her shoulders from the car, she stepped back as the front of the car shifted with a screeching and grinding noise, flying up into the air several inches and then flopping back down. This caused the back to shift against the muddy cliffside, creaking and grinding more. Not good news.

Angie was clear. I needed to get out. I didn't have to worry about tipping it over since there'd be no one in it. Getting out might be tricky. The car felt as if it could plunge into the river any moment.

I carefully slid toward the door. The car groaned and shifted. I stopped until it settled down, then pushed my legs toward the half-open door. The car shifted again.

This time I didn't wait for it to settle but shoved myself across the seat at that narrow opening, propelling myself from behind with a push of my hands against the car seat. The car tilted precariously as my legs made it out the door.

It kept tilting farther and farther. I frantically wriggled the rest of my body out to drop on the levee. The car rested at a much more acute and precarious angle once I was free, its nose aiming directly toward the river's angry, whitecapped surface.

I caught my breath for a second in relief at having made it safely out. Then I turned to Helen, who was kneeling by Angie's unconscious body.

"How is she?" I struggled to my feet, my back completely coated in mud.

"Pulse is irregular and respiration's shallow. I wish those paramedics would get here." Helen looked up at me in frustration. "Out here in the chill and rain, shock could set in real quickly."

I pulled off my jacket. "Lift her head."

Helen held Angie's head and shoulders up. I leaned down and laid the jacket across the muck of the levee surface with the clean dry inside facing up. She gently settled Angie back onto the jacket and brought the sides around and over her arms.

"That should help some." She began checking the girl's pulse and respiration once again.

I took a step toward the cliffside. "Terry, is there any sign yet of the ambulance?" I called up to him.

His dark head leaned over the edge to look down at me. "You know you could have gone down into the river in that car," he said in a matter-of-fact tone.

I gave a slight shrug. "It's still not gone all the way in. I had enough margin to make it."

He nodded. Behind him, I thought I heard a siren. He whipped his head around and disappeared from my view.

"Is that the damn ambulance?" I cried.

"Please let it be," added Helen as she looked up briefly before returning to her patient.

Terry's head reappeared. "No ambulance, but it's the fire truck."

I could feel some of the tension begin to drain from my body. Help was here at last. They could bring Angie up to the roadway and stabilize her. Surely the ambulance would be here soon to transport her and Brian to the hospital.

Suddenly I heard a rasping and grating noise behind me. I turned to see Helen getting to her feet and Mel's car sliding and banging on down to meet the water. First the nose slid into the river's wild, high current, but soon the entire vehicle had entered the flood. It floated for a short time until the raging waters filled the car's open interior and dragged it down under the surface.

My breath caught in my throat as I imagined it doing exactly the same things earlier when I was still inside. I heard a whistle from behind me. Turning, I saw Terry.

"You have the luck with you," he yelled. "I expected to see that with you inside."

"Sorry to disappoint you." I could hear how breathless my voice sounded.

He chuckled. "You never disappoint me, Skeet."

I heard another siren in the distance. He looked behind him and answered before I could ask. "Your ambulance. Finally. This town's emergency services suck. You really should do something about that."

I huffed and started to retort when I noticed the big smile on his face. I decided not to give him that satisfaction and turned back to Helen and Angie. "We've got help now. It won't be long."

Helen gave me a tremulous smile, turning back to her patient. There was a great core of strength under that seemingly fragile exterior. I began to see what had attracted Jake to her. Even as I recognized her strength, part of me wondered how far it would take her. Could this woman have killed Jake? Leonard? Mel?

Things moved quickly once the firemen got a ladder set. Helen climbed up first so a paramedic would have room to go down and start Angie's care. As soon as the paramedic made it down the ladder and knelt at Angie's side, I climbed up so his partner could join him down on that narrow, muddy ledge.

One of Joe's officers directed traffic around us. The EMTs already had Brian cleaned up with a bandage on his upper forehead, his left arm in a sling, and wrapped in a blanket in the backseat of my car when Terry helped me off the top of the ladder. They thought Brian's shoulder was dislocated and wanted me to drive him to the hospital for treatment. The ambulance needed to be reserved for Angie.

By the time they brought Angie's still form up and transferred her into the ambulance, I'd finally stopped shivering, wrapped in the warmth of my car's heater and another blanket. Terry gathered my rope and flares and stowed them back in the trunk of my Crown Vic. We'd be able to head out soon and follow the ambulance to the hospital.

Since Terry had shoved me into the passenger seat of the car after he wrapped the blanket around me, I needed to get out and walk around to the driver's side. Everything in me protested at the thought of that short exertion in the rain. I'd had a lot of practice at being firm with myself, so I opened the door and levered myself out into the driving rain, which still showed no sign of letting up.

A siren screamed in the distance as I walked up to Helen's car and knocked on her window. She rolled it down enough to hear me.

"Would you rather not drive after all this? You can ride with us in the back with Brian and return with Matt to get your car later when you've had a rest."

"I'd like that but don't want to leave my car here. It would be easy for someone to hit it in the dark." She sounded weary and weak.

I nodded. "Terry could probably drive it back to town if you'd like."

Terry approached on the other side of the car when he heard his name mentioned. I turned to ask him. Helen stepped out of the car.

At that moment, a police car pulled in behind the ambulance and fire truck, shutting down its siren and flashing lights. Helen and I turned to stare at it for a moment. Two men slammed out of the car and raced down toward us. I had a bad feeling that one of them was Joe, even before their faces became visible through the rain-filled dark.

Helen moaned. "I hoped I'd make it home before he heard."

Terry moved around the car to stand next to me as Joe and Reverend Matt sprinted up to us. I'd just as soon have had him stay out of sight. I wasn't ready for a repeat of the scene with Joe and him outside Karen's shop.

It was Matt who blew up. He snatched up Helen and scowled at Terry. "What's going on here?"

I stepped between the two men. "Nothing. Helen bravely helped us get two injured kids out of a wrecked car in danger of going into the river. We managed to get them out in time. The EMTs brought them back up here to treat. Everything's over."

If anything, my words increased his fury. I'd never before been able to reconcile the kind, gentle minister I knew with the warrior who'd earned medals for his battle prowess. Now, as he directed a steely glare at first me, then Helen, I could see this man mowing down crowds of enemy troops in Africa.

"What were you thinking, risking your life like that?" he demanded of her, shaking her slightly. "Do you ever think of me? Of the hell my life would be if you managed to die? Are you so in love with the thought of death you can't even think of your husband?"

Helen's head swung back and forth like a child's rag doll as she went limp in his big hands. "They were children, Matt," she cried. "What did you expect me to do?"

Her words inflamed his anger. He began to shake her in earnest and not gently now. "Always, always, you think of others, of someone else. When are you going to start thinking of me?"

I reached out to stop him and saw Joe do the same, but before either of us could, Terry slapped his hands against Reverend Matt's upper arms. "Stop manhandling your wife. If this is the way you treat her, why would you expect her ever to think of anything but getting away from you?"

Helen didn't cry. She looked as if she had curled up somewhere deep inside herself and was hiding there.

Matt released Helen as if she burned his hands and turned to Terry with his mouth open to shout at him. There were bloody marks on his sleeves. I watched his big hands curl into fists. At the same time I caught Helen who'd gone so limp in his grasp she'd have fallen when he released her if I hadn't.

Joe stepped forward to stop whatever Matt intended to do to Terry. I expected to see the angry minister take a swing at Terry. He seemed prepared for the same thing. At the last moment, though, Matt recovered himself.

He looked at Helen where I held her upright. "I'm sorry. I just . . . I couldn't bear to lose you. You know that." He reached out to put his arm around her. I felt her flinch.

"Would you rather ride back with me?" I asked. Anger flashed through Reverend Matt's eyes at the thought, immediately replaced by a contrite look.

"I'm so sorry, sweetheart. You know I'd never hurt you. I was just terrified at the thought of losing you. I could never survive that, you know." Tears gathered at the corners of his eyes.

Helen straightened herself in my hold and pulled away from my hands and his arm. "I know, Matt," she said with a sigh. She looked drained of emotion. "It's all right. Matt can drive me home."

She took a weary step toward him. He threw his arm around her shoulders once more and guided her to the car with that gentle and careful solicitude I'd seen in Helen's shop. It didn't seem as harmlessly loving to me now. He tenderly tucked her into the passenger seat and closed the door.

As we watched him walk around the front of the car to the driver's side door, Terry muttered, "Something wrong with that one. I don't like it. He smells off."

I turned to him in surprise. "What do you mean, *he smells off*?"

He looked embarrassed, as if thinking aloud and not aware I could hear. He shrugged. "When a soldier's going to lose it— suicidal, crazy—you can tell. Something's gone wrong deep inside. He's given up a part of himself in some important way. I've had to learn to tell. He's a man in deep trouble."

"That's bullshit," said Joe. "You should have stayed out of it. I could have handled it. He's no soldier. You're not, either, now. You're just a civilian who needs to let the police do their job."

"Matt was a ranger once," I told Joe. "In Somalia. Decorated."

Joe glared at me. "Well, he hasn't been for a long time. Neither has this one."

"Do you think he'll hurt her?" I asked Terry, ignoring Joe's angry statement.

Terry shook his head hesitantly. "More like he'd hurt himself or someone or something else. Sick of himself and sick at heart right now, but I don't see him hurting the wife."

Joe snorted in disgust. "Of course he's not going to hurt her. Damn! A man just gets shook because the woman he loves risks her life. I can understand that, even if you can't, Heldrich." He turned to me. "I suppose it was really you taking all the risk, though, wasn't it?" His voice was just as irate as it had been when he chewed out Terry.

I tried to keep exasperation out of my own voice. It wasn't easy. I was chilled through and tired, in no mood for Joe to start getting chauvinistic. "I'm a cop. I'm trained to take risks to save or protect people, just the way you are. You know that. Besides, it was Brian and Angie."

Joe looked taken aback for a second, then his anger seemed to catch a second wind. "Why wasn't mister big-shot soldier-guy here the one down there risking his life?"

I could see Terry bristle and tense to return the attack. I beat him to it. "Because I told him to stay up here and pull us up and down with the rope. It takes a lot of upper-body strength to do that. I admit that's one thing you Neanderthals have over me."

I looked over at Terry's big hands, remembering the bloody stains on Matt's sleeves. Grabbing his left hand, I turned it over to see the palm rubbed raw and streaked with bloody lines from the nylon rope that had taken my weight, then Brian's and Helen's, without letting any of us fall or slip. He pulled his hand from my grasp.

"Why in hell didn't you have the EMTs look at those hands?" I was ready to explode. I hadn't thought about the toll all this was taking on him.

Terry rolled his eyes. "They've had their hands full. I know perfectly well how to tend these. I'll do just that as soon as I'm back in town."

The ambulance siren screamed as it pulled out and U-turned across the median to head back into Brewster. The fire truck shut its flashers off and followed suit.

"Let's get you and Brian back to town then, so you can both get treated." I shoved Terry toward the car without budging him a fraction of an inch.

He looked down at me with raised eyebrows, then smiled sweetly. "Yes, ma'am."

Joe glowered at us both. It was my turn to snort in disgust. I turned my back on them and walked the few steps to my car. As I pulled open the driver's door, Terry opened the door on the opposite side.

Brian had fallen asleep in the back from the pain medicine the EMTs gave him. We slammed our doors. I started the car in silence and drove off, leaving Joe behind, staring after us.

"That man's in love with you." Terry pointed back in Joe's direction.

"I don't want to hear it," I snapped, and drove on in silence.

Love. That was what Sam called the way he tried to control me. It was what Reverend Matt called the way he tried to control Helen.

I thought about what Terry'd said earlier. "Something wrong with that one."

# CHAPTER 20

Brian and I spent the first half of the night at the hospital. After his arm and shoulder were X-rayed and treated, we waited for Angie to come out of surgery. No one could find Liz to notify her of Angie's injuries (though I suspected she knew all too well). Brian and I were all Angie had.

Terry walked out shortly after we arrived. At a time when my attention was on Brian and calling Sam to take care of Charlie. I decided not to worry. He probably had a lot of experience doctoring injuries much worse than his hands.

Joe came by, all apologetic, and offered to take Brian home once he was treated. Brian refused to leave until we knew Angie was all right.

Sitting up half the night in a hospital waiting room with the daytime activity halved and the noise levels blunted offers a perfect time to think. So, I thought. About Karen. About Mel's murder. About Leonard's murder. About Jake's. About Reverend Matt's obsession with Helen. I'd come to realize it wasn't really love he felt for Helen but something darker. I thought about Bob and Kathy, who was so worried about something, Mel's sad marriage, Helen's ill-fated passion for Jake, Liz's affair with Randy and her hots for Walker, the sense of evil I could now perceive around Walker, Terry and his background, and the way Leonard's words had thrown Karen's entire life and personality out of balance.

After a while, I thought I could prove Karen's innocence. I began to catch glimmerings of the real killer.

Liz finally appeared after midnight. She started to explain herself. I pointed to Brian, sleeping on the sofa with stitches in his forehead and his arm in a special cushioned-and-supported brace/sling. I had no desire to hear her excuses. I was doing well not to beat her half to death for what I suspected she'd done to my kid. I could hardly keep my hands off her throat whenever I looked at my boy, remembering that car tilted and sliding into the river. I didn't want to be arrested for assault, so I ignored her and walked out the door to cool off.

Once outside, I noticed her red SUV illegally parked in front of the emergency room door. I decided to check it for damage from hitting the kids' car, but I couldn't find anything. Of course, she'd certainly been gone long enough to have any paint or dent removed in the city. It would take a citywide search to find the place that did it—if she hadn't bribed them to keep it secret—and I had no legal reason to ask the police to make such a search. I reentered the hospital with a nasty taste in my mouth.

Shortly after my return, the surgeon came out to tell us Angie was in the recovery ward. "We needed to remove her badly damaged spleen, set her broken collarbone, and put a number of stitches into her face and head. The spleen was the most serious. We had to stop the bleeding and give blood transfusions. She'll always need to be under a doctor's care now that her spleen is gone. She'll have to take various vaccines on a regular basis and watch her exposure to any infectious diseases."

With every word about the lasting damage done to Angie, my fury with Liz rose. But I had no proof her car had smashed into the kids and forced them off the road. Brian couldn't see who it was in the dark and rain.

"She'll have the best medical care," Liz said in an offhand manner. "She's my stepdaughter. I'll spare no expense to see she has everything she needs."

The surgeon continued in a hurry, as if to get it all out before we collapsed into hysterics. "She'll be in the hospital for a week, recovering from injuries and the surgery. After she's discharged, full recovery may take a month or more. Infection's always a problem to watch for. She'll always be more susceptible with the spleen gone."

Dabbing a tissue at crocodile tears in her eyes, Liz nodded. "She'll have round-the-clock nursing for as long as she needs it."

The doctor frowned slightly. "Also, she has a nasogastric tube inserted down into her stomach that will come out in a day or two. She may not feel up to talking, at first."

Liz would only be allowed to see Angie for a few minutes in recovery, the doctor said, but Liz could stay with her once she was moved to a regular post-op room. Staying in a hospital room overnight was something I couldn't see Liz doing.

"That won't be necessary," she said. "I'm sure Angie's so doped up she won't even know who's there."

Angie would have to wake and recover alone, since Brian and I weren't allowed to see her because we weren't relatives.

"We'll keep her contact with all but hospital staff low the first few days," the surgeon said, "because of the dangers of infection."

At least she wouldn't have to wake to find Liz, terrified that

Liz would harm her. Brian and I wouldn't have to lie awake, fearing what would happen to Angie in the dark hospital room.

On the way out, I asked a nurse to make sure Angie knew we'd been there. Then I took a worn-out, sad Brian home.

"What'll happen to Angie, Skeet?" he asked on the way home. "Liz hates her."

I sighed. Hard to know how to answer.

"I suspect Liz'll be on her best behavior with Angie for a while. We'll keep an eye out all the time, anyway. I'll let Liz know I'm watching everything she does."

My answer didn't satisfy me, but it worked for Brian. I remembered that look of faith he'd given me at the scene of the wreck. I suspected it satisfied him because he thought I would do more than I actually could do to protect Angie. That upset me, but it allowed Brian to go upstairs and sleep as soon as we got home, accompanied by a very concerned collie and cat.

I paced the floor and went over everything in my mind until I was certain. Then, I called Sid.

"Do you know what time it is?" Sid answered the phone.

"I'm sorry, but this is important."

"Hmmpf. What is it?"

"Mel's murder. Could a small, older woman have plunged that wool comb into his carotid artery with enough force to bleed him out?"

"I don't think so. The killer used a lot of force. To pierce the carotid artery, you go through a great deal of muscle. It would take a strong person. One with some training to know just where to shove those spines. This wasn't trial and error. It was done with one sure blow."

"Thanks, Sid. Luck with the fish tomorrow. Ought to be good with all the rain."

He slammed his phone down in my ear.

I could show that Karen was innocent. One thing was going right. I'd call Joe in the morning and get the charges dropped. Now I could sleep.

The next morning was a Saturday. Still exhausted, I woke up early. My mind had gone on all night, rehearsing the different things I'd learned about these murders. Now I had a direction and a person who fit the silhouette of murderer. First, I had to ask some questions and check some facts.

Brian heard me showering and wandered down, white-faced with pain, for breakfast and a pain pill. He wanted to go back to sleep. Later, if I wasn't back, he planned to ask Joe for a ride to the hospital to see Angie.

"Maybe they'll let me in. I could sweet-talk them the way Sam tries with you. I've been listening." His grin made me see for a second what he'd look like as a grown man.

That brief flash ahead caused a stitch in my heart. Brian would grow up, of course. That's exactly what I wanted and worked toward. He couldn't stay this kid before me forever. I realized his adulthood meant the loss of the boy I loved. That loss was coming much sooner than I'd expected.

He laughed at my expression of dismay, thinking it was due to his threat to imitate Sam. He sat down to eat as I headed out the door.

I drove to the Lawson house first. Helen met me at the door, looking much stronger than she had the night before. "Matt's not here," she said, as if no one would have a reason to come see her. "He headed into the office early and left a note for me."

"Actually, I wanted to talk to you again. About Jake."

"Oh. Well, sit down then. What can I tell you?"

"Did you tell Reverend Matt about the affair?"

Helen blushed. "Yes. It sounds cruel. It was vicious of me to do that to Matt. I . . . I really wasn't myself. Jake ended things and wouldn't see me. I still hoped he'd come back. I couldn't believe he was strong enough to lock away all we'd had and leave. But he was. Strong enough. I was the weak one."

I leaned forward, keeping my voice sympathetic. "I can understand. How was it you actually told Matt about the affair?"

Looking uncomfortable, Helen shrugged. "I guess he'd been suspicious for some time. One night while I took a shower before bed, Matt pulled my cell phone out of my purse and . . ." She took a deep breath and looked at the rug on the floor. "He found a lot of messages from Jake. Some of them . . . pretty explicit."

I nodded. "What did he do?"

Helen stood, still avoiding my eyes, and began to pace around the room. "He confronted me with the whole thing. I'd actually been in the shower, bawling my eyes out over Jake, realizing he was probably never coming back and my life might as well be over, so I admitted everything."

She walked over to a hand-painted Mexican pot and lifted its lid, pulling out a pack of cigarettes and a lighter. "Do you mind if I smoke?"

Without waiting for a reply, she lit up and inhaled. "I started smoking because Jake did. After he died, it made me feel closer to him."

I said nothing. She began to pace again.

"Matt wanted details. Details!" Her voice rose in disgust on the last word. She straightened her shoulders and turned to me with defiance on her face. "So I gave him details. Details a lot more explicit than he wanted. It was like I'd been angry with him for years without knowing it. So I poured out everything Jake and

I did. I was horrible. After a while, I saw I was devastating him, but a part of me said, 'He wants details. I'll give him fucking details.' It was like I was trying to emotionally kill him."

She looked straight at me, daring me to judge her. I didn't dodge her gaze. Finally, she turned away to resume her pacing.

"He was so angry I thought he'd kill me. And I welcomed it." She turned to face me again. "I didn't want to live without Jake. I didn't want to feel anything any longer. I used my husband like a gun or knife to try to end my life."

She turned away and smoked in brooding silence. "Matt's too good for that. He left and stayed out all night. I was sick with worry. I'd put him in such a terrible state before he left. I was afraid he'd do something to hurt himself. I should have known better. He showed up the next morning, hungover and apologetic. As if he'd done something wrong because he went to a bar, got drunk, and slept it off in his car. After what I told him." She shook her head.

"What happened then?" I asked.

Helen stubbed out her cigarette in a small bowl with gold designs all over its teal surface. "I tried to kill myself that afternoon. Matt came back early and found me, called 911, and kept this farce going." Her humorless grin made her face resemble a skull.

I walked over to where she made a small figure against the fireplace. "When he left you that night, did he still have your cell phone?"

She looked up at me in surprise. "He'd forgotten it was in his hand and gave it back with an apology—an apology!—the next morning."

I nodded, beginning to see what I'd been fumbling my way toward. "When you told him all the things you and Jake did, did you mention the times Jake let you in the secret door and took you upstairs to his office?"

She blushed and dropped her gaze to the floor. Then she lifted her face and held her head high. "I'm ashamed to say I did. I'm not ashamed of anything Jake and I did. Never! I'm heartily ashamed of telling Matt about those visits and the sex on the desk and floor. Rubbing his face in it. I never should have told him any of the things I did with Jake, no matter what he demanded."

It all fell into place.

"Does he have guns, other than the one you bought in the city and kept in your car?"

She nodded, looking at me in puzzlement. "They're old. From his ranger days. He hates them. All that stuff. Hates what he did in those days." I saw realization hit. "You can't think . . . Oh, God! It's him, isn't it?" Her eyes flew open wide. "He keeps his guns and old army stuff packed away in his study."

I followed as she ran down a narrow hall and into a large room furnished with a desk, bookcases, and a big, battered trunk. She went straight to the trunk and opened its lid. "They're gone."

"What's gone?" I moved to her side and stared into a trunk half full of old uniforms and books.

"His ranger uniform. His guns. All his guns. His ranger stuff. Grenades. Survival stuff. He bought them when he left the army. He couldn't feel safe without them. Not for years. They're always on top. They're gone."

My stomach dropped. "Karen's out of jail. He's been trying to kill her for days."

Helen stared at me in horror. "But why? Why all these deaths?"

"He called Jake that night and made him open that door.

Maybe he threatened to tell Karen. Then he killed him. Leonard knew something. So Leonard had to die. After that, it was like bowling pins. Karen might remember seeing him kill Leonard. Mel, maybe he knew what Leonard knew—or maybe Matt just thought he did. He could frame Karen with that killing to get her out of the picture, as well."

Helen shook her head at everything I said. "No," she whispered hoarsely. "It can't be."

I was already on the phone to Joe. "It's Reverend Matt Lawson, Joe. He's the killer. He's in full ranger gear and armed. Headed out to Karen's farm, I'll bet. I'm on my way out there. Bring all the help you can, please."

I didn't wait for his answer. Just hung up and called Gil to say the same as I rushed out of Helen's house to my car. She called something after me. I didn't hear what it was as I jumped in the car and headed for Karen's farm, praying I wouldn't be too late.

I'd just turned out of town onto the first twisting country road when my phone rang with a call from Karen. "Skeet! Someone's out there. He's shot Nacio in the leg."

"Get Ignacio and yourself upstairs. Barricade the door with any furniture you can."

"Nacio won't leave. He's down there with his rifle. He made me come up here to call. Says his arms and eyes still work, and he'll keep whoever it is out of the house."

"It's Matt Lawson. Ignacio won't be able to keep him out. He needs to be up there with you. I'm on my way. Got lots of cops coming. Tell him he's got to get upstairs and keep you safe until we get there."

She hung up. Because something happened? Had she run downstairs to bring Ignacio up? I couldn't do anything but pay attention to the country road I was taking at speeds anyone would have called suicidal.

Sirens wailed in the distance behind me, reassuring me. Joe and Gil had called out the troops. I hoped we wouldn't arrive too late. Didn't have my own siren on, just the lights. Didn't want to push Matt into doing anything stupider than he already had. I hoped to arrive while he was still outside the house or, at least, the room in which Karen and Ignacio were barricaded. I wanted us to capture him without the situation devolving into a hostage scenario.

Gunshots blasted as I turned onto Karen's long, straight gravel driveway. I couldn't drive any faster. My Crown Vic already bounced alarmingly over the gravel at high speed. As I skidded to a stop in the farmyard, spinning my car sideways to the house in a whirl of muddy gravel and dust, a tall figure in combat fatigues dove into the house through the front door. Another burst of automatic-weapon fire exploded.

He was in the house. Ignacio might be dead by now. I hoped to hell Karen was barricaded above and Joe and the others arrived soon. Matt should see that she was worth more to him as a hostage than dead. I hoped.

I grabbed the shotgun from its holder and leaped from my car to take shelter behind it. Behind me, sirens cut off at the gravel driveway.

"Matt Lawson," I yelled at the house. "We know it's you. You can't get away. You might as well give yourself up. It's over now. It's all over."

"It's never over, Skeet." Matt sounded different, his voice higher, younger, without the deep, reflective timbre it always had. "Not as long as I'm alive. My sergeant taught me that. Never give up."

"What do you plan to do?" I wanted to keep him talking. If he was talking, he wasn't shooting Karen or Ignacio. Help was coming. "If you kill Ignacio and Karen, you'll die. You're not the kind of man who wants to go out in a hail of bullets."

"You think you can scare me with that shit? I've been through hails of bullets that should've killed me. Hell, fucking tornadoes of bullets and rocket fire that killed much better men than me." In all the time I'd known him, I'd never heard Matt curse before. "I'm still here. I'm a hard mother to kill. Neither God nor the devil wants me."

"You can't get out of this. We know you killed Jake. We know you killed Leonard. We know you killed Mel. You need to try for a defense of mental illness."

He roared with laughter. It sounded like he'd no intention of claiming insanity.

"If you kill Karen and Ignacio in cold blood with us out here, there's nothing to keep us from coming in after you."

Police cars pulled in on either side of mine, swinging around as they stopped to put their sides to the house as a shield, as I had. A solid wall of metal stood between us and the house—for all the good it would do.

I called back to the house. "You see, Matt. You can't get out of this."

He didn't answer. I could hear him shouting obscenities inside the house. Maybe Ignacio wasn't dead. Something was causing him trouble. I thought about what Matt had yelled out to me. He hadn't sounded like an educated minister in his forties. He'd sounded like a twenty-something soldier speaking in profanities to other soldiers.

Joe and Gil, stooped to use the cars' protection, joined me behind mine in the center. My phone rang. Karen.

"Skeet, he's yelling at me to come down and take care of Nacio. He says Nacio's dying." Karen's voice was full of tears.

I found myself shaking my head, vigorously. "Don't listen to him. Don't. Stay barricaded upstairs."

"He says Nacio's bleeding to death. I have to go down and help him." I could hear the panic in her voice. Matt knew the way to get her out of her barricade was to use her friendship for Ignacio.

"No!" I screamed at a dead phone. In my mind, I saw her pull the furniture back from her bedroom door and creep to the top of the stairs. From the house, Matt's angry voice shouted more profanity-laden orders. She was running down those stairs to try to help Ignacio. That move could kill them both.

"He's got her as a hostage, too, now?" Joe asked.

I nodded dully.

Joe took out his own phone. "We need the county SWAT team."

I nodded. "And a hostage negotiator. I'll call KCPD for that." We both knew the county had no trained hostage negotiators. I was the closest thing to a hostage negotiator we had, short of KCPD. At least, I'd had some training.

We made our calls, keeping our voices as quiet as possible. While we did, two more police cars pulled up. They were all the reinforcements we'd get until the sheriff let loose some personnel. Joe sent his guys to circle the house and set up an outpost with shelter from gunfire in back, so Matt couldn't take Karen and slip out that way.

Another car bounced at high speed down the gravel drive. Walker Lynch's Lexus with Terry behind the wheel. He pulled up behind our police-car barricade and got out.

Gil whistled quietly. "I sure wouldn't want that coming after me. Guess he thought you'd been taken hostage, Skeet."

Both Joe and I frowned at Gil. He shrugged apologetically. I looked back at Terry as he walked over to us. Carrying an AR-15 rifle, he wore a quick-draw tactical vest over a black shirt and black tactical pants with a mag thigh rig on his right leg, holding extra ammo. His hair was tied back in a ponytail, but he walked with the same deadly grace he always did.

His dark eyes found mine and made promises. Some of them concerned the danger Karen was in. I clung to those, ignoring the rest. I had no time for that crap right now. Somehow I did feel better because he was there. I didn't believe Terry would let Matt kill Karen. Not if he could keep it from happening.

"What the hell are you doing? All dressed up for Halloween? You're a few months early." Joe's voice had moved into that harsher, rumbly range that only Terry elicited.

None of it bothered Terry. "I heard your call on my scanner and thought you could use some experienced help. I've seen first-hand how slow emergency services are in this town. I'm an experienced sniper, among other skills I suspect might come in handy for trying to take him out without losing the hostages."

"You're a civilian, is exactly what you are," Joe snarled. "Go back where you came from and get out of the professionals' way."

Terry laughed. "You may be a professional at giving tickets and breaking up barfights, but when it comes to a situation like this with a combat-hardened ranger, I'm probably the most professional you'll get, short of a few people at Fort Leavenworth, most of whom I trained."

Beside me, I heard Gil snicker softly. Joe's face hardened and his jaw set.

"That's fine, Terry," I said to forestall the outbreak from Joe that I could see coming. "I don't think we'll need your skills. Yet.

At least, I hope not, but I appreciate the offer, as does Joe. I hope you'll stick around."

"Of course." Terry nodded his head.

"Now, wait—" Joe started, but Gil interrupted him.

"Joe, with things as bad as they've been with the county, we could wind up sending to Kansas City and having to wait an hour or more for the KCPD SWAT team to show. If things turn ugly, we may be glad he's here."

"Walking around better armed than we are," Joe muttered.

Terry shrugged. "I've got a bigger budget. Besides, Missouri's a concealed-carry state. I've got a permit for everything I have that needs a permit."

I turned back to the house. Let them fight it out. I was troubled by the silence from the house and punched Karen's phone number on my cell. On the second ring, Matt answered.

"I've got her putting compression on this guy's wound. Hate to see him bleed out. Good man. Stupid but brave."

I signaled for silence to the men around me and put the phone on speaker. "There's no need for him or any of you to die. Just give yourself up, and all this will be over. Wouldn't that be a relief?"

"Hell, no, I'm not giving myself up. But if you don't try any tricks, I might let you—you only, Skeet—take this guy out of here to get patched up before he dies. I'll keep Karen as my hostage. If everyone stays cool and does just what I say, she won't get hurt."

Karen came on the phone suddenly. "Skeet, do it, please. Nacio's dying."

Matt was suddenly back. "What do you say? You got the guts to do this?"

"Why me? If it's only going to be one of us, I'd rather have one of the bigger guys who could carry him. I'll probably have to drag him. That's not good for someone who's seriously wounded."

"No. Only you. You're less likely to turn hotdog and try to prove you got balls by risking his or Karen's life. Only you."

"No, Skeet," Joe said. "He might try to grab you for a hostage."

That gave me an idea I knew Joe would hate. I thought it out for a couple of seconds.

"Listen, Matt. Here's a deal for you. I'll come unarmed. You let both of them go and take me for a hostage. As a cop, I'm worth more, and unarmed I'm no threat." I tried to sound weaker and more female than I usually did.

"Are you out of your bloody mind, woman?"

"Skeet, no! Don't do this!"

"Dammit! What are you thinking?"

I ignored the outbursts in rapid succession from Terry, Gil, and Joe. "What do you say, Matt? Other cops won't want me to die. You know how we are about our own."

"Leave no man behind," Matt said, as if reciting scripture in that higher, strangely young voice, full of nervous energy.

"The bloody ass is insane, Skeet. He thinks he's back in combat. Don't do this." From behind me, Terry sounded furious.

Terry in a rage might have been pretty frightening, except I'd just volunteered to step into the den with a crazed lion, so nothing much else could penetrate the control I'd had to wrap around myself to do that.

"I'll have to think about that. Give me a minute." Matt hung up.

"He'll take it." Gil's voice was morose.

"Fine. Let me go." Terry moved up close to me and captured my gaze. "I can go in unarmed and have him incapacitated or dead in minutes. I don't need weapons. Let's do this and get it all over with."

"Absolutely not, you blowhard!" Joe kept enough control to hold his voice down as he spat his words at Terry. "You're just a civilian. We don't let civilians go into danger."

"Certainly not to protect cops," I pointed out. "This is my job. Besides, guys, Matt's gone crazy, not stupid. He might take an unarmed female cop because she's a woman and he'll feel in control. He'll never take a male cop or someone everyone in town knows was some special-forces mercenary."

"You're right, I know," Gil said. "But I don't like it."

I looked at him gratefully. "At least you've stopped trying to clap the women and children under cover." I forced a little laugh. "I appreciate it, Gilberto."

"He's having battle flashbacks, Skeet." Terry grasped my arms and pulled me back to face him. "The way he was talking. That's a ranger motto. That 'Leave no man behind' shit. You don't know what you're getting yourself into."

"Absolutely not, Skeet." Joe's voice had gone to its deepest timbre.

"Guys, I'm the only person in town he talked to about his battles. He respects me." I looked at them, defying them to deny it.

Joe kept frowning and shaking his head. Gil looked like he was grieving for the death of a family member. Terry stared at me intently.

"I know things about what started all this," I continued. "Things none of you do. Things he doesn't know I know. I think I can talk him into surrendering. If not, if he goes into some flash-back battle rage, I'm better able to defend myself and survive it than Karen is."

Terry nodded slightly, releasing my arms. "I don't like it. But you've made your case."

I tried to grin. "Hell, I don't like it, either, Terry."

"No. No. Is everyone here but me crazy? Skeet, you can't do this." Joe kept clenching and unclenching his fists. I'd never realized how stubborn he could be.

The phone rang again. It was Matt. "You disarm. You take off your jacket. I *will* search you. Don't think I won't. Don't try any stupid fucking stunts."

I wondered if he was reliving one of the battles he'd been in, perhaps Mogadishu. He sounded further and further away from the man I'd known and trusted. There must be some way to bring him back to sanity. If I could, I was sure I could get him to disarm and surrender.

"I won't carry any weapons with me, Reverend Matt." I decided one way to appeal to the reasonable side of him was to use his title every chance I got. To remind him of the man he'd worked so hard to become after he rejected the soldier.

"You come only as far as the steps of the porch. Karen will drag this guy onto the porch. I'll be holding the gun to her fucking head. If anybody tries to shoot me, she dies, too. Then we go back in the house, and you can drag him off. Hope he lives. Good guy."

"What about the trade I proposed?" My mouth was dry. I suddenly wished I had some water. I'd bet Terry had a canteen or two, full of water, in his car, along with other survival equipment.

"I'll take you up on it. Don't get cocky and do anything dumbass, though. I'll search you. Don't think you can beat me at hand-to-hand because that flat out ain't going to happen."

"Reverend Matt, I don't want to fight with you. I want us to find a way out of this without any more fighting or killing. Aren't you tired of killing?"

"Not nearly as tired as I'd get of dying." There was a pause for a second or two. "Come get him. Let's do this. Now." He hung up.

I gave Joe my phone. "Have someone ready to get Ignacio to the hospital. Better call KC's SWAT team. I don't think we're going to see the county's."

"I am going to personally shove my foot right up Sheriff Dick Wold's ass when this is over," Joe grumbled.

I smiled a little at him. Then I turned my back on all three of them and unbuttoned my shirt, slipping my left arm out of its sleeve. I unbuckled the shoulder rig and slid it off my upper body, gun and all, sliding my left arm back into its sleeve. I buttoned the shirt while turning back to the men behind me. I handed my gun and holster to Gil. I didn't look at either of the other two men I was leaving behind.

Taking a deep breath, I approached the house, moving slowly and surely, so Matt wouldn't think I was up to anything but what we'd agreed on. At the porch steps, Karen appeared, pulling and dragging Ignacio's limp body. Matt gripped her from behind, one arm around her waist, holding a big SIG pistol to her head with the other hand. Karen looked terrified.

"He's dying, Skeet," she said frantically.

"He's gut shot," Matt corrected her. "They'll need to get him to a hospital right away. He might live if they do."

Karen held a mass of bloody fabric to Ignacio's stomach. I stared at it for a second before looking at Matt. "She needs to keep compression on that. Go ahead and take me in there. Let her get him off the porch. That way they can come get him faster."

He stared at me for a minute, then gestured to the door behind him with his head. I eased past Karen and Ignacio and then past Matt, who didn't look like himself, at all. His jaw was set with a smear of blood along one side. His eyes, always so warm and accepting, were now cold and calculating.

Once I was inside the doorway, he whirled and pulled the door behind himself, aiming the gun squarely at my forehead. Karen screamed for Joe to come help her with Ignacio.

"Come in. Sit down." Matt gestured toward the kitchen table and chairs with his gun. "We may be here a while."

# CHAPTER 21

I chose a chair with a view of the windows. Matt came up behind me, pulled my wrists behind the chair back, and suddenly wrapped duct tape around them, securing them together. Then he grabbed my hair with the hand that also held the gun, pulling my head up and back so fiercely my eyes watered from the pain, while he ran his other hand over my chest, back, and stomach. He dropped it to my waist and then ran the hand down my hips and legs. All in a cold, businesslike manner.

"Good. You didn't do anything stupid." He let go of my hair and took a chair next to me that also had a view out the windows.

I wanted to always use his ministerial title when talking to him, as if he were still the man he'd created of himself after he rejected the soldier's life. I wanted to remind him of Helen, waiting for him.

"Reverend Matt, Helen told me about the affair with Jake. It was a horrible surprise. Jake was like a father. I had him on a pedestal. It must have been a real shock for you."

He stared at me, face working as if he'd start to yell or cry. "She told you?" He shook himself like a dog coming in from the rain. "I had Helen on more than a pedestal."

"You love her very much, don't you, Reverend Matt?" I sat very still. I'd try to loosen the duct tape on my wrists later when—if—I managed to move him out of his past and into the present, though I knew it made a secure restraint.

He looked at me, confused. "I'll always love Helen." Standing, he began to pace around, checking out each window, continually keeping me within his view. "My bottom line is always Helen. She's everything. I'd do anything for her."

I nodded. "You've tried to take care of her, haven't you, Reverend Matt?"

He stopped and stared wildly for a second. "I don't understand why it is that the more I do for her, the less she loves me."

"Who can understand why we love some people and not others?" I tried to catch his gaze, which flicked back and forth between me and the window through which we could see police gathered behind the line of cars. "You know, Reverend Matt, I left Helen at your house to come out here. She's worried about you."

He grimaced. "She always worries about me. She cares. I thought that would be enough. I thought it would turn into love. Eventually."

From his voice, I could tell I was connecting with the mature man who'd chosen the ministry instead of the wild, young soldier. His voice slowed and deepened.

"I was drowning in blood-guilt when I met her. I killed more people than Hannibal Lecter. But they sent me home to the normal world where none of the people I passed each day knew there was a murdering monster walking around among them."

He began pacing around the room again. "Her glowing goodness drew me to her. Like a drowning man to a lifebuoy. I wasn't sure if God would save me after all I'd done, but I knew Helen would. She became the plumb line of my life. As long as I had her goodness, I was saved from the evil I'd done and become." He stopped pacing and stared directly at me. "So you can understand why I couldn't afford to lose her."

I could see another unmarked car pull up behind the police-car barricade out front but not who got out of it.

"Of course, Reverend Matt. You haven't lost her, you know. Helen's still waiting for you back at the house."

He looked around wildly for a second, as if confused to find himself where he was. Finally, though, he seemed to settle back into the scary self. His face changed again, jaw setting in a hard line. He took a firmer grip on his pistol and glanced over at the semiautomatic rifle that looked like a SCAR 16 or 17S leaning against the wall near the window. Stepping backward to keep his eyes on me, he stood to the side of the window and picked up the rifle, shoving his SIG back into its hip holster but leaving the flap on it open.

"I didn't mean to kill Jake—though the bastard had it coming." He turned sideways so he could glance out the window and watch me at the same time with little swivels of his head. "Unfaithful to his own damn wife and making my wife cheat on me with him." He spat on the floor in a gesture of disgust. I could tell I'd lost the ground I'd gained.

"You took Helen's phone in a rage and called Jake to let you into the courthouse, didn't you, Reverend Matt?" I tried to keep my voice calm. "Did you threaten to tell his wife? Is that how you got him to unlock that door for you?"

"Yeah. He sure didn't want her to learn about his fun and games with Helen." He gave a rough laugh.

I could see Terry leaning back against the Lexus watching the house. "Why did you want to see Jake, Reverend Matt? Did you intend to harm him?"

"No." He looked distraught and shifted closer to me. "I just wanted to tell him to stay away from my wife." His voice rose in anger. "All right, maybe I wanted to slug him a time or two. He deserved it, damn it! The thought of him touching my Helen, undressing her, fucking her."

He shook the rifle at me. "It all makes me want to kill him all over again." He lowered the hand holding the rifle. "But I didn't mean to kill him that night. I just wanted to scare him away from her and get a little of my own back."

I nodded. While he spoke, I'd seen the passenger from the newest car outside. It was Brian in his high-tech sling. Who was stupid enough to bring him out here into the middle of this situation that could turn nasty at any second? I looked up at Matt and couldn't think of anything to say.

"I waited until he took me upstairs," Matt continued. "Old Jake was trying to keep things quiet, and I threatened to make a loud scene or tell his wife if he didn't talk to me. Soon as we got to the top, I started hitting him. Didn't say anything. I didn't want anyone to hear. The first two blows knocked him off his feet. I swear I'd have stopped with the next one if it hadn't lifted him up and knocked him down the stairs."

He looked at me, as if asking me to believe him. I nodded my head and tried to put a reassuring expression on my face, even though I was hearing for the first time the violence done to my beloved father figure. I'd have time to grieve later for Jake if . . . after I got out of this alive.

Matt shook his head in disbelief. "He fell down both flights. I watched him tumble down. Over and over. I couldn't believe it. I just stood there, staring in dumb silence. When he didn't get up, I ran down to him. He didn't seem to be breathing, and his face was turning blue, but he had a real weak heartbeat."

So Jake had survived the fall down the stairs. I wanted to close my eyes, but I didn't know what message that might send to the volatile man in front of me. I stared straight ahead and nodded in dumb pain. I tried to pull my wrists loose from the duct tape, but it just adhered even tighter and held them together.

Matt went on as if my nod had absolved him of guilt. "I knew he'd probably die. I've seen guys in that state before. At best, he'd be a vegetable. They'd arrest me and take me away from Helen. I broke his neck without thinking about it. Just did it. Like I was trained to do. Don't think. Just do. Like I've done so many times before with full approval of the US of A."

I sat and listened to him and shoved down the rage I felt for poor Jake. Who told Matt Lawson he could decide who lived and who died? Then his words reverberated in my head. "Like I was trained to do. Like I've done so many times before with full approval of the US of A."

What did we do for those boys we trained so efficiently to kill when they came back? Pin a medal on them maybe. Shake their hand. Send them back into a world we'd made alien to them in order to use them in battle.

"Reverend Matt, I'm sure a court would understand your situation. You could plead to a much lower charge."

He didn't hear me. He was caught up in that single moment when he'd used his skills for something his country wouldn't countenance.

"I went out that back door he'd let me in, shaking like a new recruit after his first battle. Next day, that son of a bitch Leonard Klamath called me. Said he'd been there when I called Jake. He knew I'd had a hand in Jake's death, and he started blackmailing me."

So Leonard hadn't retired early right after Jake's death because of his grief for Jake but rather because he had another guaranteed income. Now he'd known he was nearing death from cirrhosis and developed a guilty conscience, wanting to tell Karen so he could feel better when he died. Probably that's what he intended that day he'd caught Karen and me at lunch. He was frightened away by my presence, just as Annette thought. No blackmailer wants the police to know what he's done.

"It seemed just—to be blackmailed," Matt continued in the slower, deeper, more mature voice that gave me hope. "I'd sinned so horribly. I'd have to pay that bloodsucker all my life. Fair punishment." He dropped himself into the chair beside mine again.

"But that wasn't the end of it, was it, Reverend Matt?" I looked away from him out the window just as Karen's phone, which had been lying on the table, rang.

"Talk," Matt said into the phone in the cold, young soldier's voice. Then I watched his face soften. "She's okay." His voice switched again to that of the man I knew. "You can talk to her and see."

He held the phone up to the side of my face.

"Skeet?" It was Brian, sounding teary and afraid. "Skeet, are you all right? Has he hurt you?"

"I'm okay, Bri. You should go home. This will all work out. You shouldn't be out here."

"I called Sam," he said. Brian despised Sam so that was a surprise. "I thought maybe he'd hurry up the SWAT team from the city."

"That's okay. Stop worrying about this. It'll all work out."

Matt took the phone away. "Let me talk to Joe, Brian. And do what Skeet says. Go home."

He was silent and listening for a second. "Listen, we've got to find a way for me to get out of here with Skeet. Once I'm free and clear, I'll set her free. I don't want to have to kill her, but I will." He listened for a moment, then his face hardened again, and his voice snapped back to that other voice, young, cold, impatient. "You guys are idiots if you think you can rush me in here. I know you've got that outpost in back. I've booby-trapped the back door and all the windows. Anyone tries to get in—they trigger a massive explosion."

He listened for another moment. "Fuck that, Joe. Not going to happen. Call me when you're ready to bargain. In the meantime, if you want Skeet and your men to stay healthy, keep away from the doors and windows." He clicked off the phone and stood, resuming his restless roaming around the room's perimeter.

"Reverend Matt, you know they're not going to let you drive away from here with me. Think about Helen. She's still waiting at the house. She's probably heard about this now. She'll be worried sick."

"What the fuck can I do?" he yelled at me, then shook his head and came back to sit beside me. "I try to make things right for her, but it never works. Right after Jake died and Leonard started blackmailing me, Helen tried to kill herself. I knew I had to make things come right. So I quit my job and took over this little Brewster church."

He laughed and shook his head. "What a comedown for the big professor! I worked like a dog to get it, to move us, to set up a shop for Helen, anything to make things better for her, to make it all come right with her and me again. But it didn't."

His voice rose to an angry pitch on the last word. "I started to think that she never really loved me, not like she loved that fucking Jake." His voice escalated with each word until Jake's name was almost a curse.

"That must have hurt you a great deal, Reverend Matt." Out the window, I watched the SWAT team arrive, along with Sam.

I needed to keep Matt talking. I was making progress and might be able to talk him into surrendering, but I'd have to do it before the SWAT team decided on the action they'd take. My alarm grew as I saw one of the SWAT guys and Terry greeting each other like old friends, slapping shoulders and smiling.

I turned to Matt. "To try so hard to please Helen and take care of her and then to feel she didn't love you, that must've really hurt, Reverend Matt."

"It was scary," he said in a weary voice. "It made me so stinking angry with her. I didn't want to go there. I couldn't handle being that mad at Helen. So I just poured all that into trying harder. Then Leonard Klamath showed up at your party and started mouthing off. Old drunk!"

I nodded while I tried again to pull free of the duct tape holding my wrists together.

Matt rose and began walking around checking out the windows again. "I couldn't let that crook tell Karen or anyone else. I'd paid him plenty for his silence, damn it! I slipped out the kitchen door when you took him out front."

"How'd you get the gun?" I asked.

He shrugged. "I took Helen's gun from her glove compartment. She still carried it around the way she had in KC. I think she just never bothered to take it out. Later I bought one just like it and replaced it with that so when you did a ballistics test, it would show up clean."

I twisted my hands and tried to pull them apart, but the tape just tightened. "But how'd you know where Leonard would go?"

He shrugged and stared out the window, watching the SWAT guys. "I was ready to follow his car, but he went up the hill on foot, so I followed. He was obviously waiting for someone there in the Caves. I couldn't let that meeting take place, so I shot him. Then suddenly, Karen was there. I hid behind a car. I didn't want to shoot her. She was as much a sufferer from Jake's sin as I was. Besides, I'd already killed her husband. I couldn't shoot her. She found Leonard and started to make a call. I knocked her out and ran away."

"And so you got away with it again," I said. I could hear the bitterness in my voice. I hoped he wasn't paying enough attention to me to hear it, as well.

He stopped peering out of window after window and looked at me, his face appearing heavier and softer edged. "Everything should have been taken care of. I wasn't sleeping well at night, though. Started having nightmares again the way I did for years after I came back to the States. It was like I was back at war, on full battle status. You don't know what it's like. When you're like that, you don't think normally. There's no right or wrong. It's all *neutralize threat*. Each day is either *all threat* or *no more threat*. You know it's kill or be killed."

He looked down at the rifle in his hand, then began moving from window to window again. "I heard Karen had seen the killer but lost her memory. I knew that could be just temporary. If she'd seen me, I had to silence her. I should've killed her in the first place. I went out to her farm, but she had that Mexican with a rifle watching out. I'd have got them both, but you cops showed up, and I had to run for it."

"Why kill Mel?" I asked from simple curiosity.

"I'd been worrying about Mel. If Leonard had known about me, Mel knew also. Helen said he and Leonard were both on the take for Lynch's trafficking. Could be they'd both been with Jake when I called. Maybe they'd been splitting the blackmail money. Every way I looked at it, he was a threat."

"You weren't thinking clearly at all by then, were you?" I wanted to sound sympathetic.

"I wasn't thinking. At all. It was all reflex. Threat response. Threat response. And I started to see threat everywhere. I was surrounded by it."

I felt that it was the man I'd known talking to me now. If I could keep reaching him, I could end this standoff.

Outside, a small crowd gathered behind the police lines. Suddenly I saw Helen Lawson get out of a car and make her way to where Joe, Gil, and Sam stood.

Matt continued talking, as if he needed to finish confessing. "Next, I saw Karen screaming public accusations at Mel. I decided Mel could go, and Karen could be convicted for his death. That would keep her out of my way. If she regained her memory, no one would believe a convicted murderer against the local minister."

"I see. Karen was knocked for a loop and not reacting normally, so people would find it easy to think she'd gone insane." I couldn't decide whether to let him know Helen was out there. It might be the final bit to break him down and make him surrender—or kill me and go out in a blaze of glory.

"Yeah. I broke into her shop early the next morning, just to get that scary-looking comb. She was there and called the cops on me, so I shot at her." He turned to me with a look of protest. "Believe me, if I'd been trying, she'd be dead. I just wanted everyone to think the break-in was all about the killer trying to kill the witness again."

"You went right from jogging in the park to her shop, didn't you?"

He sighed and nodded slowly, almost reluctantly.

"Why move the body? You managed to kill him in her shop with her comb. Why not leave it there?"

"I thought someone might have noticed me in the square. So I put his body where it would be found a few days later. How could

I know you'd find it the next morning?" He held out his hands, rifle and all, as if begging me to understand. I decided it was time to make my move. "I knew the mayor planned to start work there. I thought the body wouldn't be found until they started work. Muddy the water as to when exactly he was killed."

"It almost worked. Would have if you weren't so good at it. The coroner never believed a small, untrained woman could do that in one thrust."

"I was trained by the best."

Terry checked his rifle methodically. The SWAT guy who knew him said something. Terry nodded, walked away from the car, and disappeared from my view. Had they decided to send Terry into position as a sniper?

I had no doubt he was good, especially if the SWAT guys accepted him. But I've been out there behind the barricade in these kinds of situations before. I've seen snipers go after bad guys and take them out. Chances were about fifty-fifty Matt would take me with him when he went. I didn't like those odds.

"Reverend Matt, everything you've told me— If you tell it to a court-appointed psychiatrist, they're going to tell the prosecutors to lower those charges. Surely you realize that. Put the guns down and release me, please. You don't need to die."

"Maybe I do, Skeet. Look at all the things I've done. I never intended to do any of this." Now he was fully the man I knew as Reverend Matt.

"That's why you need to stop all of it now. Surrender your arms. Helen's out there now with the police, waiting for you. You didn't come out here to commit suicide by police barrage. You don't want her to see you die that way."

He turned and stared out the window. I could tell when he saw her because his eyes teared up. "No. That's not what I wanted.

Karen was arrested. Everything was going as planned. I started to hope I could sleep again, though the nightmares only got worse. Then she was out. It was like I'd gotten separated from my unit in Mog with hostiles surrounding me, every hand turned against me."

"Reverend Matt, Helen's waiting out there for you to come out of this house." I put all the persuasive force I could into my voice. "Think of everything you've put her through. Don't add any more to it. This is not the man you've made of yourself. Remember why you went into the clergy."

"Looking for peace. I wanted to help people." He was crying full out now, tears streaming down his face. I had him—if only Terry held off with his shot.

"Cut off this tape, Reverend Matt. Hand me your guns. I'll call out and make them hold their fire." I could see his hands were down at his sides with the rifle barely held. "Pull out your knife and cut this tape."

He walked over to the table, still crying, and set the rifle on the table before pulling a knife out of one of the pouches on his fatigues. He slit through the duct tape. I pulled my hands loose and separate and around in front of me. Tape still clung to them. I ripped it off, tearing the skin with it.

"I'm going to take the guns now, and we'll walk out the door together," I said slowly and carefully as I picked up the rifle—it *was* a SCAR, I noted with the back of my brain—and held my hand out for his pistol. He handed it to me. We walked over to the door. He'd stopped crying.

I yelled as loudly as I could. "Joe, it's me. We're coming out. I've got the guns. He's surrendered. Make sure everyone holds their fire." I repeated myself twice.

I could hear Joe and Gil and Sam yelling at everyone to hold fire. Together, Reverend Matt and I stepped out into the afternoon.

# CHAPTER 22

I came out from a world that had shrunk down to only Matt and me into a whirl of images, noise, and activity. Multiple cop radios buzzed and squawked as a background to orders snapped by the SWAT leader and Joe.

Karen was with Brian, waiting outside the house behind the police line. After the SWAT guys circled us and grabbed and cuffed Matt, Karen and Brian came barreling through the cops to wrap me in their arms, both crying, Brian trying to hold on to me with one arm in the padded sling/cast.

I figured Joe had let them through. I sent him—and Gil who stood next to him—a big smile. Behind them, Sam shook his clasped hands over his head in a boxer's victory gesture. Farther back and to the side, Terry dropped to the ground from a tree as silently as he'd gone up. He smiled and tipped an imaginary hat before strolling over to the Lexus to stow his rifle.

Someone let Helen through the lines. She walked toward us in a daze, wearing an oversized jacket that must have been one of Matt's. She seemed to shrink farther inside it with each step, her face turned into a death mask.

I turned to look behind me, with Brian still clinging to my

waist with his good arm. Matt stood as if turned to stone, his hands cuffed behind his back, an officer holding each arm. He was oblivious to them. His entire attention focused on Helen as she approached him. His eyes were full of pain.

Helen walked right past me, straight toward Matt. No one else seemed to exist for her. At the very last second, she pulled her hand from the jacket pocket with a gun in it aimed at Matt.

I yelled, "No!" Other officers shouted and started to run toward her, but before any of us could reach her, she pulled the trigger twice, screaming, "You killed my Jake! Because I loved him and he loved me! Die! Die!"

The three of us who were closest slammed into her all at the same time, and she went down, the gun flying from her hand. A SWAT officer picked it up.

Lying on the ground under three cops, Helen kept crying, "He killed my lover. He killed my lover." I got to my feet, leaving her to the two other officers who'd also taken her down.

As I stood, I could see Matt had bullet wounds in the chest and gut. Helen was a good shot, just as Gil had suspected. EMTs who'd been standing ready, in case Matt shot me, now rushed over to Matt and started IVs, working to keep him alive and stabilize him enough to transport him to the ER. I turned away, avoiding the sight of Helen who still moaned her reason for shooting as she was pulled to her feet and cuffed. I just wanted to grab Brian and head home.

Next to Brian stood Karen, her eyes huge, her face white. She stared at Helen. I thought of the words Helen still cried, realizing Karen had just learned of Jake's infidelity in this awful, public way, and hurried to her side.

"Are you all right?" I asked. She looked more fragile and aged than I'd ever seen.

She looked up into my face. "Jake. And her." She shook her

head. "Has my whole life been some fairy-tale dream on my part and a lie on his? Is that all it ever really was?"

I put my arm around her shoulder carefully, since she looked as if a sharp touch might shatter her. "He'd left her at the time he was killed." I hoped she'd find comfort in that. "He told her he loved you and would never leave you, that he regretted getting involved with her."

"Or he just got tired of her." Karen's voice sounded profoundly weary. "Who knows how many Helens there've been while I lived my fool's dream of a happy marriage?"

I didn't know what to say. Brian looked stricken. I could imagine how upsetting this had been for him. Maybe the Family Services bitch was right, and I was actually a disaster for him. I gathered him in with the other arm.

"I don't know. But I know we love you. Don't we, Brian?" He nodded his head. "And Ignacio cares enough about you to risk his life." I pulled her closer to both of us. "I think you have to hang on to that. People love you, and you'll make it through this."

"Maybe you shouldn't, Skeet." She looked up at me, her eyes still stricken but dry. "I haven't been a good friend lately. I've caused you all kinds of trouble. Most of all, I made trouble for you and Brian."

Tears came to her eyes. She pulled away. "After years of listening to you about your mother and Charlie, I know you're not big on forgiveness. So I don't expect you'll forgive me for everything I've done. But I hope you'll forgive Brian, and he'll forgive you. It would destroy me to think I'd permanently damaged your relationship."

"No, Karen," Brian cried.

"Maybe I've grown up enough to learn something about forgiveness," I said. "If I have, it's because you've taught me, Karen."

I pulled her and Brian back in for a big hug. She pulled away and wiped her eyes with the heel of her hand. "I'm going to the hospital. Nacio's still in surgery. He'll need me now."

I nodded. It was probably good for her to have someone who really needed her to take care of. She was right. Ignacio would certainly need someone to take care of him during a long recovery.

As she headed toward the cars parked back behind the line of police cars and the crime scene tape that kept the curious away from the heart of the scene, Joe and Gil walked over.

"You did it!" Gil gave me a big hug. "You got him out of there."

I smiled at him, then looked back at the EMTs working on Matt and the cops hauling Helen away. "Yeah. But it didn't play out quite the way I'd hoped."

"Doesn't matter," Joe said, with his old smile that used to make me feel so good inside. "That's out of your control."

I wondered why I didn't feel as calm and just plain happy when he gave me that smile as I had before. I smiled back at him. Even I could tell it wasn't the smile he'd always elicited in the past. A slight cloud moved over his face for a second. Then he gave me a quick hug and another warm, accepting smile before he and Gil headed over to the other cops holding Helen.

That was it. I'd always felt accepted for myself when Joe smiled at me, no matter what. After the arguments we'd had recently, I didn't trust that smile. I knew he didn't completely accept who I was. I slipped that thought into the back of my mind to deal with later—as Sam joined us.

I put a smile back on my face. "Please tell me Charlie hasn't driven off that nice Erika, Sam. I don't think I could handle one more thing without a shower and a good night's sleep."

He gave me his patented I'm-the-best-thing-you've-ever-seen-baby smile. Fortunately, I was too washed out and empty to feel any response. "You don't have to worry. I think she's staying. As for the other one, we'll talk after you have that shower and sleep. I could help with both, I suspect."

I frowned and glanced at Brian. "That's not necessary."

A little shamefaced, he looked at Brian, as the EMTs wheeled Matt to the ambulance behind him. "Just joking," he said quickly. "We'll talk tomorrow or the next day. When you've had a rest. I can handle stuff till you're ready."

"Thanks. I'll call tomorrow. I appreciate the help. You know that."

He waved my thanks away. "Hey, it's family."

I gave him a quick hug and stepped back, not wanting to encourage anything more. Sam was tough to deal with. If I wasn't careful to keep lines drawn all the time, he'd move right back into my life. He and Brian shook hands solemnly. They seemed to have come to some new understanding. I'd see how that played out once there was no emergency going on.

The police car with Helen in custody moved out after some jockeying among the cars parked around us. Several had to leave first to give it room to get out. We left Sam standing there and walked over to my car.

Terry lounged against the driver's side. I was glad Joe couldn't see him from where he stood, directing the site cleanup. Terry straightened as I walked up. Brian went around to the passenger's side. I pulled out my keys and gestured with them toward the car. Terry smiled and moved. The doors unlocked, and Brian got in.

"I said once you were an unusual woman." Terry's focus on me was intense. "That was an understatement."

I shook my head and sighed. "Thanks for offering your services."

I pulled open my door. He moved over to let me open it all the way. As I started to get in, he touched my shoulder lightly to get my attention. It got my whole body's attention. I didn't like that.

"I am tired and overwrought and irritable," I said to him in a low voice that I hoped Brian couldn't hear. "What do you want?"

He looked at me, all amusement wiped off his face. "The chance to know you better."

I looked up into his smoky, dangerous eyes. "Terry, you work for Walker. I think you know how crooked he is. I think you know he's involved in human trafficking. You may believe you can take his money and keep your hands clean, but as long as you work for him, you're dirty in my eyes."

I slid into the car and pulled the door shut. All I wanted was to make it safely home with Brian and go to ground in my house with my kid and my pets and maybe some good-quality hot cocoa with lots of whipped cream while I focused entirely on the lace pattern of Gran's shawl. I didn't want to deal with one more person's emotional needs or demands. I was completely burned out.

"Are you okay?" Brian asked.

I looked over at him with a smile. "Yeah, Bri. Let's go home."

I didn't look behind to see who watched us leave or whether anyone else left right behind us. We drove in exhausted silence through the countryside and the town until we reached our house.

"Oh, for pete's sake! I don't believe this." I parked the car on the street behind the old blue pickup that sat in front of my house.

"Who is that?" Brian asked, as I turned off the car and got out faster than I would've thought I had in me after the day I'd just endured.

Sitting on our front porch, surrounded by suitcases and cardboard boxes, was my tough old grandmother, Amelia Ward Bushyhead Whittaker.

"Gran, what's going on?" I asked.

She held her hands out with an expressive shrug. "You asked for help. I'm here."

I closed my eyes for a second. Life was about to get even more complicated.